THE ONE BEFORE THE ONE

EMMA COOPER

Boldwood

First published in Great Britain in 2025 by Boldwood Books Ltd.

Copyright © Emma Cooper, 2025

Cover Design by Cherie Chapman

Cover Images: Shutterstock

A CIP catalogue record for this book is available from the British Library.

Paperback ISBN 978-1-83656-938-1

Large Print ISBN 978-1-83656-937-4

Hardback ISBN 978-1-83656-936-7

Ebook ISBN 978-1-83656-939-8

Kindle ISBN 978-1-83656-940-4

Audio CD ISBN 978-1-83656-931-2

MP3 CD ISBN 978-1-83656-932-9

Digital audio download ISBN 978-1-83656-934-3

This book is printed on certified sustainable paper. Boldwood Books is dedicated to putting sustainability at the heart of our business. For more information please visit https://www.boldwoodbooks.com/about-us/sustainability/

Boldwood Books Ltd, 23 Bowerdean Street, London, SW6 3TN

www.boldwoodbooks.com

For my agent, Amanda Preston... the woman who changed my life

1

Seven years ago, Kit, the love of my life, left me to go on a hike and never came back.

Today, I'm getting married.

Kind of.

I hurry up the path of number 37 Hilton Close: two bedrooms, white PVC door, neat square garden. I slide the key into the lock and step into the hall, memories of my childhood rushing towards me like an old friend.

'Mum?' I throw my keys into the bowl on the shelf above the radiator, taking off my coat and hanging it on the banister.

'I'm here!' she shouts.

Mum hurries into the hall from the lounge, her dark hair swept up into a chignon, a large purple fascinator balancing precariously. Her face is flushed with excitement and a tiny bit too much bronzer. 'Happy wedding rehearsal day!' She rushes forwards and pulls me into a Coco Mademoiselle-scented hug as I register the low murmurs of conversation coming from the lounge.

'Nice hat,' I say examining the purple lace.

She strikes a pose. 'I know it's a bit extravagant, but I *am* the mother of the bride and where's the fun in being agoraphobic if you can't use it to your own advantage now and again?' She winks.

When James and I had decided to get married, we'd originally suggested having the ceremony here. But when I had told her our plans she was furious. 'Absolutely not!' She had shut down the conversation in an instant, holding my hands and looking at me furiously. 'You will not sacrifice your wedding day for me. I won't have it, Olivia. And besides, all those people, with their dirty feet and men who don't wash their hands after they've been to the lav? I don't think so.'

Mum has always batted her way of life away with an 'it is what it is' but it can't be easy for her – to not go to her daughter's wedding. A walk to the corner shop on a Wednesday is fine, as is taking out the bins on a Monday and mowing the lawn every other Sunday, but a wedding? Going in a car? Being around people she doesn't know? That's like asking her to walk on hot coals. Actually, scratch that, Mum *would* walk on hot coals for me, as long as they were in the hundred square metres of lawn inside her garden fence.

She grins broadly, the same wide mouth and straight teeth as my own. 'Where's James?'

'He's on his way.'

'Fabulous. Now, go up to your room and put on your dress.'

I begin climbing the stairs as someone knocks on the door behind me.

'Hurrah! He's here!' I turn to watch her open the door. She takes a quick step back, letting my husband-to-be through the door. 'James! At last. In you come.' She closes the door behind him swiftly, double locking it. He's wearing a suit, a white rose in his lapel. I don't think I've ever seen him in a suit before, but he looks like he should be in an aftershave advert, all dark hair, brooding eyes, open-necked shirt, California sand in the background, a beach-blonde beauty with tousled curls in his arms as he runs into the surf. Instead, he's inside an ex-council house, about to 'marry' me, Liv Andrews: medium height, medium build, dark hair prone to frizz at just a whiff of humidity, mouth a little too wide, and a nose a little too long.

'Ivy, you look gorgeous,' he says. She shushes him but I can see she's pleased at the compliment. He makes his way towards me.

'Sorry I'm late, couldn't find anywhere to park,' he says as he climbs the stairs, stopping two below me so we're face to face. He kisses me softly, his eyes on mine.

'Will you two stop smooching? There's plenty of time for that after. Olivia, go and put your dress on. The reverend has a dentist appointment at four. James, can you give me a hand in the kitchen? I can't get the little plastic bottoms to stick on the champagne flutes.' I head up to my childhood bedroom, although it's unrecognisable from the room of my teenaged years. Back then, there wasn't the world of online shopping; even getting a weekly shop meant relying on the Smiths from next door. But now, *now*, Mum has a whole new world that she can live in, a world where everything that was so hard to come by back then, can promptly be delivered.

Alexa is Mum's closest friend.

Over the past ten years, the whole house has been redecorated. Whereas for most of my childhood and early teens this room remained wood-chipped and pink, now it's all whites, oatmeal, and sage green; the thick white curtains swollen by the cool April breeze coming in through the open window. Another reminder of my childhood. Windows open as much as possible. It was like she wanted the world around us to come into the house, but only through the crack of a window that she could control. I close the door behind me.

I didn't have an unhappy childhood. Yes, during my formative years, I didn't leave this house, but this house was safe; filled with fun and laughter and smiles. And outside? Well my four-year-old-self suspected that it was a *bad* place, filled with *bad* people and *bad* things. But inside this house? I was safe. I had everything I wanted.

Mum would pretend that we would be going to the cinema, put chairs in the hallway, hold a saucepan as a steering wheel, make brrrrrrm noises until we parked the 'car'. We would make tickets to hand to the imaginary desk. We'd close the curtains, arrange the sofas so they were directly in front of the TV. We'd have Coke in plastic cups, a straw to drink from and popcorn filled in cardboard candy-striped boxes that we'd coloured in ourselves.

On sunny days, I could play in the garden. We would have water gun fights with empty bottles of washing-up liquid. I would wake up and she would be standing there with gardening gloves, seeds, or chalks and paint. On rainy days we would splash in the puddles, make mud pies. It was only the days that were overcast, the kind of days that are grey and oppressive that were *bad*. The kind of day when my father had been hit by a car while fetching the newspaper, killing him instantly. I was two years old. But, you see, I didn't have an unhappy childhood, entirely the opposite: I was loved; I was safe.

I yank the window closed. Lying on my bed is my dress. This is the dress I have always wanted: an ivory vintage, 1950s A-line tea dress. A neat belt cinches around the waist and a delicate lace tulle creates the illusion of a sleeve that will sit just beneath my elbow. I finger the material, a smile rising; it's perfect.

My phone buzzes in my jean pocket.

> Need any help? I'm drowning in small talk.

I snort. It's his idea of hell. I can already guess the guests in the lounge: Mr and Mrs Smith, Reverend Vickers (I *know, the irony*) and Patsy from number seven. People she knew before Dad died.

> I may have problems with the buttons.

I reply, adding a winky face.

I sit on the bed, my heel kicking against something. I bend down and pull out an old cardboard box before lifting it onto the bed. Inside are my old schoolbooks from when I was at primary school. I smile as I open them, but there is a tug of memory, of not fitting in, of feeling like an outsider.

It wasn't until I was seven, when the visits from social workers became more frequent, that Mum found the courage to let me go to school.

At first, I didn't think that it was weird that Mrs Smith would walk me to school with her children. I didn't think it was strange that my teachers would come to our house, bringing my books for parents' evening, when everyone else's parents came to the school. But soon I did. Soon I started to suspect that the way I had been brought up wasn't the same as my friends. They would talk about going on holiday with family and friends; they would talk about trips to the park. But how did you stay safe, I had wondered, how did you escape the bad guys? The monsters on the bus? How didn't you drown in the swimming pool? Why didn't your plane crash?

Mum needed help back then. She knows it now; I know it now, but then? Why would she seek out *help*? Our life was happy. We were happy, despite what teachers and social workers thought. That's Mum's biggest regret: that she didn't get the help she so clearly needed. As she tells it now, in her mind, she was doing everything right. She had to keep me safe, and for her, that meant keeping me inside as much as she could. Until the day when I'd asked her why I wasn't allowed friends. Was I a 'bad girl'?

That was the switch for her; that was the moment where she realised that something had to change, that she had to let me go.

So she did. She did everything she could from the confines of her home to make sure I had every chance at a normal life.

And oh how I hungered for it, but everything was so big, so bright. The sounds overwhelmed me, and I would find myself with my hands over my ears, arms wrapped around my body, red fear thrumming beneath my skin. It took me a few years to adjust. But with the support of the school, I started swimming lessons, I learnt to ride a bike, I had a friend whose house I would go to for dinner.

It's no surprise that I became a teacher. The head teacher of my junior school, Mrs Lee, changed my life. It's only when I look back as an adult that I can see just how much she did to help me and Mum.

When I think back to those days, I wonder if with each fear I conquered, I became a little high on life, high on new experiences. They say that your school days are the best of your life, and for me, they were, despite feeling that I was different to everyone else, despite the fear that still stung beneath my skin. But the high I would feel when I overcame those fears was addictive.

It continued through secondary school: the first try of a cigarette, the first time I kissed a boy, the first time I got drunk and was late home; with each first time, the heat beneath my skin would cool.

But it still kept me close to home. When all of my friends moved to different cities for uni, I made a short forty-minute commute instead.

Five years later, with a first-class degree and a couple of years' teacher training under my belt, I met Kit.

It was August. Two weeks of the lethargy only a good old British heatwave can provide had left me desperate for the relief of the River Wye, for the shelter beneath the thick trees surrounding it. I'd roped Ava into agreeing to a day at Waterways Adventure Park. It wasn't far from us, and I had plans: canoeing, kayaking, indoor rock climbing with glorious air conditioning – the whole shebang.

When I began to live my life further from the clutches of Mum's condition, I had been so awestruck by the world outside my house. The clutches of small villages, churches, forests – thick, dense and rich – painted in so many greens it would be impossible to capture them all on one palette. I had spent my entire childhood with only one tiny corner of our neighbourhood but the country surrounding our PVC windows was vast, vibrant, exciting. I still love it here.

We'd rock-climbed, zip-lined, and when the day was at its hottest, we kayaked along the river, the water deep and brown. It was humid. Thick clouds had gathered and the rain that we'd been hoping for began to fall in fat heavy droplets as thunder rolled behind the hills. The trees became heavy, moss-green leaves making them lean towards the water.

It all happened so fast, and at the same time in slow motion: the flash of lightning, the overhanging branch that had cracked into the water in front of us, the panic as we tried to manoeuvre, the perfect arc of the revolution as I fell out – gradual but at the same time, immediate – the impact, Ava's voice screaming my name, the smack of the water, the clunk against my head, the sense of weightlessness as the river tried to pull me under despite my life jacket. But then I heard a voice: *it's OK, I've got you.*

He'd swum me back to shore and when I came to, he was leaning over me. A droplet of water fell from his hair and landed on my lips. Long eyelashes, a line of freckles like a check mark on his cheek.

'Hey there.' He had smiled: light brown hair, his sea-glass-green eyes searching my face. 'You've had an accident, but you're going to be OK.'

Twenty years old and already convinced I'd met the love of my life. I had no idea that five years later I would lose him.

But that was then. And a whole lifetime has now passed.

The door opens.

'So these buttons?'

I smile up at James as he joins me on the bed, reaching for one of the books, grimacing at all the red-penned crosses beside wrong answers.

'Maths was never Mum's thing, so I was quite behind when I started school. But look at my English!' I point to a page covered with teacher comments like: *Amazing Olivia, wow! Well done!*

He puts his arm around me and pulls me in closely.

'I can't believe tomorrow's our wedding day,' I say quietly.

'Having second thoughts?' He makes light of my observation.

'No,' I say, tapping the dip in his broken nose, extracting myself, replacing the books and box under the bed.

'Good, because' – he looks at his watch – 'in approximately twenty minutes you will be a fully rehearsed Mrs Palmer.' His eyebrows furrow. 'Um, just a thought, but if the rev performs it' – he scratches behind his ear – 'doesn't that mean we're *actually* getting married?'

'No, I don't think so. He retired last year.'

'But he's still ordained, isn't he?'

'No idea, but we're getting married tomorrow anyway so what does it matter?' I plant a quick kiss on his lips, feeling the familiar scar in the cleft of his upper lip that he'd got in a fight.

'True.'

We both turn our heads to the sound of Mum's voice bellowing my name.

'Right then, you'd better get down there and wait for me at the end of the aisle.'

He unfolds his frame, hesitating as he opens the door. 'I love you.'

'My Olivia,' Mum says, tears in her eyes as I descend the stairs. 'Have I told you today how beautiful you are?' she asks, holding my hands at the foot of the stairs, repeating the words she said every day of my childhood. *No, not today.* I can almost hear my infantile voice, feel her arms around me as she would hitch me on her hip and cover me with kisses. *I haven't?* she would say with a gasp and I would wiggle as she tickled me and told me I was the most beautiful girl in the whole wide world.

'Well here I am, telling you, you're the most beautiful girl in the whole wide world. Inside and out. Ready?' she asks as I take her arm.

'Ready.'

Mum walks me into the lounge, and we stand by the door as the wedding march begins playing through her Echo Dot. Standing at the window is Reverend Vickers and my fiancé.

She squeezes my hand and I feel a rush of love for her.

'Lead on, Macduff.'

We walk slowly, and I keep my head down for fear of laughing. I know if I meet his eyes, I will lose it. This means so much to

Mum, but I feel kind of ridiculous walking towards the bay window where behind it an Asda delivery van driver is honking his horn and the reverend is standing next to Mum's TV where a scene from *Four Weddings* is paused.

She passes over my hand and I dare to look up. I expect him to be looking awkward, but instead, there is love in his eyes.

'You look beautiful.'

'You don't look so bad yourself.'

The reverend jumps straight in, his voice so loud that we both jump, stifling the urge to laugh.

'We are gathered here today' – he looks down his nose at the lounge is if it's packed to the gills – 'to celebrate the special love between Olivia... or Liv as she's known' – he smiles at an imaginary crowd – 'and James Palmer.'

I meet James's eyes, as the rest of the words flow over me and I am lost in the unspoken conversation passing between us, the beginning of our story, the day we first kissed, the day we decided to get married, the day Kit went missing. The days when Kit never came home.

Our eyes didn't meet over a crowded room. We didn't have a meet-cute. Our love story began when we were looking for his brother.

Here is where I tell you that I'm not ashamed of falling in love with my first love's brother. Really, I'm not. I don't feel the need to justify it, to make excuses; it is what it is.

Our relationship grew from our love for Kit, true, but that doesn't diminish the feelings I have for him or the feelings he has for me.

It just didn't start the same way as most love stories.

Losing Kit upended my life, but James? James stabilised it, steadied me, like finding a familiar foot hole on the side of a cliff.

The reverend has almost finished talking about two souls becoming one, interrupted by the occasional sniffle from Mum.

'Do you, Olivia Andrews, take James Palmer to be your lawfully wedded husband?'

'I do.'

'And do you, James Palmer, take Olivia Andrews to be your lawfully wedded wife?'

He looks into my eyes. They are the opposite of Kit's in every way: dark, intense, serious. James opens his mouth to speak. 'I do,' he replies.

Mum claps and we all turn to her with smiles and laughter.

'With the power vested in me, I now pronounce you husband and wife. You may— Oh, well righteo.'

James's mouth is on mine, powerful, strong, yet tender. And as I let myself sink into him, as I hear the claps and cheers around us, I wonder if I've just imagined it.

If I just imagined the slight hesitation before he said I do.

2

'Shit-piss-bollocks!'

In the space of five minutes, I've stubbed my toe, broken the handle on my suitcase and now this.

'You OK?' James calls from the bathroom, where he is having the world's longest wee. You'd think we'd been travelling for hours rather than the twenty-minute drive from our house to the hotel. The door is wide open, a sign that we are *way* too comfortable in each other's presence. If I'm honest, I suppose there is still a part of me that thinks Mum will somehow find it in her to make it to the wedding. Living in Hereford, and being so close to the Welsh border, means we could have had our pick of castles, but we settled on this manor house close to home instead. It's beautiful in its own right and could easily be part of the set for the next Austen adaptation.

'I'm fine,' I answer rubbing my arm and flopping onto the hotel king-sized bed. 'Just smacked my funny bone.' I examine the bone in question where I'm sure I can see the beginnings of a purple bruise already expanding like ink on blotting paper. Great. That'll look gorgeous on the wedding photos. 'Why is it even called a funny bone?' He flushes the loo and turns on the tap, meeting my reflection in the bathroom mirror.

I point the elbow in his direction as he towels his hands and joins me on the bed.

'Because it's called the humerus.' He smiles, kissing the end of my elbow and lying nose to nose. 'Better?' he asks.

'Much.' My finger runs along his top lip, tracing the small scar. He takes my hand in his, bringing it to his lips. 'Can you believe that this time *tomorrow* I will be Mrs Palmer.' I run my nose alongside his. I love kissing him: the way he tastes, the way our mouths fit, the rhythm of it. He smiles into my mouth, his words spoken with his breath and mine.

'You know you don't have to take my name. I could always take yours.'

'James Andrews?' I question, as his hand slides beneath my vest top, his thumb running over my ribs. 'It sounds like it needs another barrel – James Andrews Smythe. Hmmm it does have a ring to it.' The humour of the conversation is transitioning, the haze in his eyes making the browns of his eyes almost black.

'Nope. Liv Palmer it is. It feels like it was always—' He steals the rest of my sentence with his mouth, the remainder of the conversation lost in a tangle of limbs.

* * *

We're late to the dinner. Our faces flushed, our hands in each other's as we approach the dinner table where the wedding party have assembled. From the raised voices and animated conversation, I can tell there have already been a few rounds bought.

'Finally!' Ava pushes back her chair and stands, blonde hair neatly plaited around the front. She looks as close to her Scandinavian roots as possible tonight. All Viking shield maiden. I lean in to kiss her on the cheek.

'Hi! Sorry we're late, stuck in traffic,' I say, but I don't know why I'm trying to make justifications – Ava will be able to see through my flimsy excuse for being twenty minutes late. 'You're so full of shite,' she says pulling me into a hug, her voice close to my ear. 'Feeling satiated are we?'

'Very,' I reply. She laughs. This is the thing when you've been friends with someone since childhood; no matter how 'grown up' you become, you still somehow can't help but regress to your teenage selves. She's still the girl who offered me half of her Kit-Kat on my first day of school as I stood on the outskirts of the playground, worrying about falling on the hard concrete ground. We're still the girls who practised kissing on the mirror and gave each other marks out of ten for technique. But we are also the women who support each other. Ava was the one to hold me up when Kit disappeared.

It was Good Friday the last time I saw him. We'd spent the morning in bed, and then I'd put a washing load on, gone for a run. He was going hiking, he'd said. Pembrokeshire, coastal walks, cliffs… one of his favourites. I had work to catch up on, and wanted to finish my planning. He'd packed his gear, kissed me long and hard at the top of the stairs, and then closed the door behind him. I didn't know that it would be the last time I'd see Kit.

Ava was the one who – rather than try to force me to eat when I couldn't – made me take vitamins and drink water, who sat with me for hours in silence when she knew I couldn't speak. And she was the one who told me I was allowed to love two men, to fall in love with his brother. When everyone else was looking on in judgement of James, she was the one who defended him. When people whispered about how wrong it was for us to be together, Ava was there with a quick retort, volleying back opinions and telling them to mind their own sodding business.

'I'm so jealous,' she says, looking over to James's friends. 'It's been an age since I got laid. Who's the *Bridgerton* duke lookalike who keeps throwing me shag-me eyes.'

I follow her gaze.

'Simon? He's one of James's boxers.'

She takes a dainty sip of her prosecco.

'Stay clear. He's a player. And he has a girlfriend.'

'Shame.' She straightens the collar on my silk shirt before I'm pulled into more hugs from my other bridesmaids.

My eyes trail James as he begins shaking hands, making his way around the room. Space always seems to part around him. He's the same height as Kit was, but broader, more solid: commanding. The air around Kit would skitter, bolt, magnify, pulling everyone into his orbit.

There are times when I would fall back into the past: the edge of an elbow at the same angle to the table we'd once drunk coffee at; the back of a man's head with the same flick of brown curls around the collar; a row of trees similar to ones that we had climbed, drunk and high on each other... and I'd think, I've found him. He must be here somewhere – look, everything is still the same.

And then I'd realise that that line of thinking was stupid, ridiculous, cruel. Because yes, everything was the same, but I wasn't, because he was gone.

I turn my attention to Libby, James and Kit's cousin, who is already flushed and is talking a few notches higher than the rest of the group. I was always grateful that she stayed in touch. She was one of the few family members who didn't turn her back on us. Her wife, Paige, is already heading back to the bar.

'How are you feeling about the big day?' Libby asks, taking a huge sip of her glass of white.

'Good.' I catch James's eye, across the room. He tilts his head, his eyes lingering on mine for a touch longer than needed. 'Excited.'

'Do you wish you could go back and do it all again?' Libby asks.

'Sorry?' I say, eyebrows furrowing.

'I said I wish I could go back and do it all again.' She smiles over at Paige. 'It was the best day of my life.'

'Oh, right. Yes, it was a beautiful day.'

Memories of Kit's hand on the bottom of my back, of catching the bouquet, his eyes glinting as he made the toast as Libby's best man. Had James been there? I have a vague memory of him arguing with his date. Nisha? Natalie? Tall, big hair, feisty. I recall seeing them arguing in the distance while Kit and I headed towards the marquee: a series of hand gestures and exasperation from James, a determined turn of the back as she stomped across the grass. He must have left not long after that as he definitely didn't join me and Kit drunkenly dancing to 'Sex on Fire' and 'Mr Brightside'. I feel the tug of a smile at a hazy image of me on Kit's shoulders as we arched our arms in YMCA poses.

Later, we'd taken a canoe out onto the lake, Kit's suit jacket over my shoulders, his tie discarded, his top button undone, a bottle of brandy under his arm, a platter of leftover buffet food against my chest. We'd watched the June sun starting to rise before the beginnings of a two-day hangover kicked us back to the hotel room.

I blink as I watch James's attention being drawn away from me, handshakes and back slaps thrown in his direction as he works the room. He has this gift of making everyone feel special and heard, and he has absolutely no idea.

I take a small sip of my drink as I watch him, Libby following my gaze.

'I'm glad you got together.' She gives me a small nudge. 'You're good for him. As far as I'm concerned, the rest of the family can go fuck themselves.'

I snort at that as she gives me a wet kiss on the cheek and joins Paige at the bar.

At least Mum not being here makes it easier that James's parents aren't either. They haven't spoken to him since he told them about us. He says it doesn't matter that they're not here, that they've never really been interested in him, that he's always known Kit was the golden son.

We all take our seats around the long table at the end of the restaurant. This manor house used to be occupied by the army during the Second World War. There's a large open fireplace taking the edge off the late April chill in the air and wall-to-wall books either side.

James's hand finds mine, his finger drawing circles on my wrist as starters are ordered and more drinks poured.

Conversation flows around us, our friends introducing themselves to one another, regaling stories from work and home.

'So... how did you two meet?' Lara, Simon's new girlfriend, asks. The conversation quietens. Glances are cast between Paige and Libby. Ava looks down at her plate and pushes some salsa around. I smile, a well-rehearsed reply ready to fall from my mouth.

I have learnt from experience that saying I was in love with his brother first isn't the easiest of conversation points for others to navigate. I mean, how would you react to that reply? *I was in love with his brother first.* See what I mean? You might laugh thinking I'm joking, or have a look of shock as you realise I'm telling the truth; then you would be left feeling awkward and trying to find the right response. So I avoid telling the whole truth, by sticking as closely to the real truth, as I can.

'We met at Waterways,' I say with my overly large smile. I used to cover up my mouth when I smiled, but Kit would spend hours running his fingers around the edge, kissing it, telling me he couldn't stop thinking about it. That was the thing with Kit: he made me whole again.

And then he broke me.

'I fell into the river.' I smile up. 'James took me to A&E.'

I don't tell them how blurry the image of James is during that trip to the hospital. How all of my focus had been on his brother sitting next to me in the back of a jeep while James drove. James had been the one to call for help, one hand on the radio, voice deep and urgent in the background while I looked into Kit's eyes, water falling onto my cheeks as he leant over me.

'What a hero!' Himad lifts his pint in James's direction. Himad works on reception at Fighting Fit and has one of those smiles that just brightens your day. He's the first face people see when they come into the gym, and the last when they leave. I swear half of our new clients are down to his smile alone.

'I'm going to the bar,' James interrupts. 'Anyone want a top-up?' I shake my head, giving him a small smile that reads: *sorry*. He kisses the top of my head: *nothing to apologise for*.

'Steady on boss, you don't want it to "interfere with your game",' the boys say in unison.

James rolls his eyes at their jibe, and weaves through the tables towards the bar. Ava stands and takes James's seat. 'Everything all right?' she asks, stealing a piece of toast and smearing on some pâté from my plate.

I'm still thinking about that day. Both brothers worked at Waterways in the summer months back then. James for rent money to pay for his bedsit; Kit for fun and to get out from under his parents' feet. I used to help out in the summer holidays for a while, until Kit's business took off and James switched to bar work in the evenings to free up his days for training at the boxing club. He started boxing after he was cautioned for fighting in a bar. An officer had suggested he 'channel his anger in a healthier way'. James never told them that he'd been sticking up for Kit.

The year I met them, he dropped the job at Waterways and started training in earnest. He was on track to win the Middleweight National Amateur Championships the year we lost Kit. I tried to encourage him to go back to it, but he always says he missed his window and is better at training others. It was like the fight in him disappeared along with his brother.

'Yep.' I give Ava a reassuring smile. 'I just hope everything goes smoothly, you know. I'm worried I'm going to fall flat on my face.'

'It will and so what if you do? You'll get up and carry on walking, won't you?' She crunches on my toast; eyes searching mine. 'All you have to do is walk into a room, say I do, get pissed, dance and then shag your husband senseless. Easy.' I laugh, leaning against her with my shoulder. This was one of the tactics she would use when I couldn't get out of bed. When I would wake up with that flame of fear in my chest. It would be there every morning after he disappeared. I would hold my breath some mornings, because I knew. I knew that the minute I exhaled, the minute I allowed myself to add oxygen to my thoughts, to my fears, to the day looming ahead, that flickering flame would ignite. And for the rest of the day, it would feel like my insides were on fire.

But then Ava would be there: *all you have to do is push off the covers, put your feet on the floor, and walk into the lounge. Then you turn on the TV, lift a cup of tea to your mouth and drink. Easy.*

And that's what you do, isn't it? When you've lost someone?

You learn to ignore the fire burning your insides; you learn to control the flames. You walk, you eat, you drink, you put the bins out, you go to work, you search for clues, you replay conversations, you call his brother. He comes over.

We travelled again and again to the cliffs, the caves, the hills: the place he disappeared. We ignored the fact that his car was still in the car park, that his backpack had been found a few days later further down the coast. Instead, we stayed up all night searching newspapers for signs of a missing person, a climber with head injuries. When spring gave way to summer, and stepping out of the house became harder for me, we drank cold beer in the garden, we ate cold pizza, we kept our phones on us at all times. When the void over the front door threatened to swallow me, James would take my hand so I could step over it. He would drive us when I couldn't find the strength to sit behind a wheel. He sat with me in hospital waiting rooms on Bonfire Night when a climber with amnesia had been found. We spent Christmas together; we found solace in our companionship. I found strength when I was with him, and when Good Friday came back around, we waited. We waited. We waited. Even though the police told us that he was missing presumed dead. We waited.

Then, after three years had passed, we fell in love.

'And you know,' Ava continues. 'There are worse things that could go wrong... You could do a Ross from *Friends* and say the wrong name.' She shrugs her shoulders. Our friendship allows her to say the things that most wouldn't. 'Too much?'

'Just a touch, and thanks a lot, that's made me feel a *whole* lot better.' She dusts off the crumbs from her hands and stands back up, placing a hand on my shoulder. I look up at her; her face is serious for a moment.

'You're doing the right thing you know, marrying him.' She nods over to the bar where James is looking at me.

'I know.'

He smiles; even from here I can see the intensity of his gaze. I smile back. We may not have had the meet-cute Kit and I had, we might not have had the most conventional start, but it's moments like this, where the sound falls away so the voices and scrapes of cutlery are dimmed; moments where the edges around us blur, where it is just me and him. Looking for answers. And instead, finding each other.

3

The next few hours pass quickly, James and I go easy on the drinks and say goodnight, leaving the rest of the group in full swing. We're halfway up the stairs to our room when I realise I've forgotten my bag.

'I'll get it.' James goes to turn.

'No it's OK – you go up.' I lift myself onto my tiptoes and kiss him before heading back down the stairs.

I return to the restaurant and grab my bag undetected. Ava and Simon are locked face to face in a heated debate, his new girlfriend nowhere to be seen. I look around for Libby and Paige, but they must have gone up too. I shoulder my bag and detour to the loo. I have the bladder capacity of a three-year-old.

I step into the ladies'; the room is empty and I take a cubicle.

'God I'm pissed.' Libby's voice. I turn my head; there must be a window open. I can smell the tang of cigarette smoke. I'd hazard a guess that Paige is having a sneaky smoke around the back of the building.

'I can't believe Aunty Lynn and Uncle Alan aren't here. I thought that they would have at least made an effort for his wedding day, you know?' Libby is very drunk, her words running into each other. I hold the breath in my lungs.

'They still won't speak to them?' Paige replies in a stage whisper.

'Nope. Said it was a betrayal to Kit's memory or something like that. Fuck 'em.'

Actually what Lynn said was that James was no longer their son, that he should be ashamed of himself, and that I was rotten. *To your core.* His mum had pointed her finger into my breastbone as she said it.

'But they don't know if Kit's actually dead though. They never found a body, did they?' Paige brings the conversation back.

'Oh, come on, you think he could be alive?' I can imagine Libby shaking her head, shivering and taking a long pull on one of Paige's cigarettes. 'No way. They found his car and that couple saw him heading towards the cliff. No money withdrawn after he disappeared. No word or sightings... they just haven't found the body.' I swallow hard. An image of Kit falling, of his beautiful smile, his body that I knew as well as my own being pounded by rocks. A thin coating of sweat forms on my skin, an aftershock of the nightmares that used to plague me every night.

'It makes you wonder though, doesn't it?' Libby reflects, her voice tight on the intake of smoke.

I tilt my head to the right, my pulse quickening, my blood racing through my veins.

'What?'

Libby exhales. 'Well... if Kit hadn't have died... would she still be marrying him?' I close my eyes and try to ignore the words. 'James must be thinking the same thing, don't you think? How could he not? He's nothing like Kit. He's always been the quiet and broody one, even when we were kids.'

I want to cover my ears, but I don't; I let the conversation continue around me.

'So what are you saying, that he's a rebound?'

'No, of course not. They've been together ages.'

Three years. Three years and four months before we kissed, but I already knew I was in love with James, before that.

It was a Sunday. Raining outside.

I'd reached for a glass of water from my bedside when I glanced at the clock, wondering if I would see James that day. It was the first time I hadn't woken feeling like my skin was covered with the mosquito bites of Kit's loss, where my first thought hadn't been if today would be the day: the day Kit came home. I had dropped the glass, the water sinking into my childhood bedroom carpet.

I'd rung Ava, sobbing, asking her to come over. She had thought it was news about Kit, that a body had been found. I'd finally got the words out, words fighting against guilt and self-hate: *I think I'm in love with James.* She had held my face in her hands, wiped the tears away with her thumbs and kissed my forehead. 'Oh, my wonderful friend. Of course you are.'

The guilt has never left me. I don't think it ever will.

'But...' Libby's voice continues to pour into the room. 'I'd bet my bottom dollar that if Kit hadn't gone poof, they wouldn't have got together. She's completely different with James to how she was with Kit.'

'People change though, babe; we're older now. I spent my twenties bumming around Europe, stoned, and dropping out of uni. Now look at me – as bloody corporate as they come,' Paige states, an edge of pride to her voice. Paige is a divorce lawyer.

'Oh shush. You know as well as I do that she changed once she was with James. And I reckon she'd be teaching in, oh I don't know, Borneo or somewhere. If Kit were here, they'd have got married during a skydive, or on a beach in Bali, not twenty minutes down the road from her secondary school.'

'Babe, they've been together for years and it's not like they haven't taken their time. And, for what it's worth, I think she really loves him. You can see it.' I smile at that, even though tears are forming behind my eyelids. 'But...' Libby continues. 'Well, I suppose, if we're really getting into it...' She pauses, hesitance that is being softened by alcohol. 'James did always...'

'What?'

'It doesn't matter.' I hear the twist of gravel, Libby crushing her cigarette butt. 'I've had too much to drink.'

'Oh, go on, what?'

I can hear a handbag zip closing. I pull up my legs and hug my knees.

'Well, it's just that James always fixed Kit's mess, didn't he? Always picked up the pieces. Remember that New Year's Eve party when Kit got mouthy with that guy and James ended up paying the cheque for the whole table?'

I frown. I don't remember that.

'So, you think he's, what? With her out of... duty?' Paige asks.

Duty?

'Maybe. You wouldn't put them together, would you. If circumstances were different. What if he's just doing what he always did? Sorting out Kit's mess. You know how it was when Kit disappeared. She was a mess and James... well James was always *there*. You know she wouldn't even leave the house without him for a while?' They're quiet for a moment and I hold my breath. 'And...'

'And?'

'Look, I love James – he's the brother I never had – but let's be honest, James did always live in Kit's shadow... He always wanted what Kit had.'

'You think he was jealous of Kit?'

I can practically hear Libby shrug. 'Everyone was jealous of Kit.'

Libby's words are swirling around my thoughts. Is he marrying me for the wrong reason? I shake my head. No.

'Oh Christ. I shouldn't have had sambuca. Ignore me; I'm talking bollocks.'

'You OK? You've gone a bit green. Let's get you back inside.'

Their voices are quietening, the crunch of gravel extinguishing their words.

I return to our room, Libby's words echoing through my mind.

James is in the shower.

I unbutton my shirt, letting it fall to the floor, step out of my trousers, discard my underwear as I walk towards the bathroom and step into the shower.

I wrap my hand around his waist, and kiss his back, my other hand sliding along the black tattoo that runs from his back to his ribcage: a phoenix rising from the flames.

He turns, combs his dark hair back with his fingers. I look up at him. Steam surrounding us.

'Tell me you love me,' I say. He stares into my eyes, dark eyebrows above dark eyelashes, water falling from them, his gaze intense, unwavering, *passionate*.

'I love you.' He doesn't break eye contact as he lifts my body. My legs wrap around his waist; his body solid, firm, safe.

He kisses me. My teeth pull at his bottom lip.

'Tell me again.'

His eyes search mine. 'I love you.'

He adjusts my body, until he's inside me. I pull the back of his hair, my legs tightening around him. 'Again.'

'I love you.'

And as I begin to lose myself in his touch, in the strength of him. I let the water wash away the words: rebound, guilt, jealousy, *duty*.

4

The hotel door closes and I wake with a start, reaching over for James, but the bed is cool and on his pillow is a note.

Gone for a run.
Back in an hour.
I love you.
x

We never leave each other without letting the other know where we're going. It wasn't something that we discussed, but we both recognised the need for clarity, for an expected return. I groan. How can he have gone for a run already? I reach for my phone: 7.13. Tuesday 4th April. Our wedding day. I know Tuesday might sound like a strange day for a wedding, but not when you're a teacher, it's the end-of-term break and the majority of my guests are off work. Plus, it was half the price. Bonus.

I stretch and smile, my finger running along the swell of my bottom lip, still slightly tender from last night.

4th April.

How will we start this day next year, and the years after that? I close my eyes and imagine them, time skipping forwards: breakfast in bed, themed gifts – paper, cotton, and whatever the third wedding anniversary theme is. I imagine children bounding into the room, holding hand-made cards. I picture James getting older, greying at the temples... our future anniversaries that will bring back memories of this day, the day I'm about to live.

We'd better make it count.

I get up, pull on his green sweatshirt, burying my nose into the shoulder. I'd love to be able to describe his smell, talk about sandalwood or mint or rosemary, but then I'd be describing the smell of his aftershave, the hint of his deodorant. This smell is all him and smells like home, not our place, a two-bedroomed semi in need of some repair, but of just... him.

I turn the kettle on, a teabag already waiting in the cup. I smile. It's in these little details, isn't it? These details that let us know we're loved. It's not red roses and surprise tickets, jewellery in blue boxes or poetry; it's in the simple things that show me I'm on his mind. I make the tea, warming my hands on the white mug, and pull back the curtain.

The manor house looks out over fields, a patchwork of countryside. The watery sun is beating back the mist while the haze lingers like the smell of an old lover. I half imagine Mr Darcy emerging through the haze, white shirt open and wearing a sultry expression. I try to scan for signs of James, of his grey hoody, head down, dark hair falling into his eyes, ear pods in, sweat forming around the rim of his neck, along his spine, his steady determined run, but the mist is obscuring the ribbon of road, the morning exhaling its last breath like a final drag on the first cigarette of the day.

I drink my tea, scroll through my phone, until I start pacing.

He's been gone for over an hour. I try his number, but it just rings out. I send him a message:

> Hey, getting a bit worried. You OK?

I bite my nails, looking back across the landscape. There is a man in the distance crossing the road. I feel that familiar jolt of recognition; that falling into the past feeling that I had so many times in the aftermath of Kit's death: a similar gait, the set of shoulders. Kit. I blink. The man has gone. The mist is just starting to lift but there is no sign of James.

I feel the familiar panic starting to rise. I lie down on the bed, close my eyes, forcing my breathing to settle, to feel present, to feel in control.

My phone buzzes and I scramble up the bed, swiping the screen.

> Sorry. Got lost. Back soon. X

I let out a long plume of air, lie back and clutch my phone to my chest. See? Nothing to worry about, I try to tell myself, but that's the thing with anxiety. No matter how much you tell it there is nothing to worry about, it doesn't stop the symptoms; it doesn't automatically relax your stomach muscles; it doesn't stop your heart from racing around your body.

There's a knock on the door and I hurry to open it, expecting James, but Ava is standing there, hair in rollers, a matriarchal expression on her face.

'What are you doing?' She looks me up and down, a hand on her hip. 'Have you even had a shower?'

'Not yet. James is on his way back after his run and then we're going to get breakfast.'

'What?' she asks, her eyes widening. 'You've stayed in the same room?'

'Well yes, what did you think was going to happen?'

'I thought that he was going to sleep in Himad's room?'

'Why would he do that?'

'Because it's in the timetable!'

'What timetable?'

'The one I sent to you both weeks ago?'

She gives an anxious glance towards the stairs as though a James-shaped bomb is about to go off. 'Never mind.' She pinches the bridge of her nose. 'It's a good job I'm here. Please tell me you haven't seen him yet?' She peers over my shoulder as if to check he's not hiding behind me.

'Well, no, I was asleep before he left for his run.'

She scratches a piece of scalp between her rollers. 'Good. I'm maid of honour and as such it is my duty to make sure that you do not see the groom before you get married.'

'I don't remember agreeing to that. I don't believe in bad—'

'Shhhhhuuush!' Ava screeches. 'Have you not heard of jinxing things? Jesus, you're practically inviting Murphy and his law into the hotel.'

I raise my eyebrows at her and shake my head. I'm about to refuse, but she is pleading with me – could it be that she actually believes that it will be bad luck? That if we split up, she will somehow be responsible? I think about Ava, and her horoscope reading, her crystals and tarot cards. It's not such a broad stretch to think that she really does think it'll be the kiss of death to our relationship if we spend the morning together.

'Fine,' I say resolved. 'Can I at least grab my things?'

'No, you may not.' She takes my hand and pulls me over the threshold. 'Here's the key. I'll grab your things and you are to go straight to my room, no detouring, do not pass go, do not collect £200.'

'I need to leave him a message. He'll wonder where I am.'

'You can text him! Now please will you go?' There are tears in her eyes, actual tears, and I feel my chest swell with love for my friend and her misplaced faith in the powers that be.

'OK, OK... I'm going.' Ava practically sags with relief as I step into the corridor and she hurries into my room.

* * *

'Keep still!' Ava says through a mouthful of hair grips.

'I am keeping still!' I reply, scratching the back of my ear. Around her room is the contents of a beauty salon. My wedding dress – still pristine from yesterday – is hanging on the back of the wardrobe. 'Do you think I've got too much hair to keep up all day?' I ask her reflection in the mirror. Her own hair still bulging with Velcro rollers.

'Not once I've worked my magic.'

My fringe has been swept to the side, the remainder of my dark heavy hair brushed into a victory roll spotted with ivory-coloured lace flowers.

There's another knock on the door, and Libby and Paige chatter their way into the room. Both in claret-red shoulderless silk dresses, their backs exposed in a waterfall drop.

'I'm almost finished.' Ava adds a final slide into my hair and stands back to admire her handiwork. 'You'll do,' she says with a grin.

Libby's voice from last night keeps nipping at the edges of my thoughts: *Would she be marrying him if Kit hadn't disappeared? He always picked up the pieces; always wanted what Kit had; duty.*

A pop of champagne makes me jump. Libby pours it into

flutes while Paige runs her hands along the fabric of my dress. I shake the words away. It doesn't matter what might have been; all that matters is now. This is my life. Kit's gone. I love James. He loves me. I saw the look in his eyes last night as he said the words. There was no double meaning, no hesitation when he said it. It was pure, unadulterated. True.

'This is gorgeous,' Paige says over her shoulder.

I grin, pushing back the chair. I join Paige, accepting a glass from Libby on the way. 'It's beautiful, isn't it?' I say, my voice wistful.

'Oh, I almost forgot!' Ava sweeps across the room and pulls open a drawer. 'Something blue!' She catapults a blue garter across the room. I laugh and pick it up.

'Thank you.' I prop my leg onto the bed and roll it up my thigh. 'What do you think?'

'Sexy as hell,' Libby says downing her glass.

'Go easy, eh?' Ava frowns. 'We don't want you falling down before the reception.'

'Hair of the dog,' Libby says with a wink. 'I'll just have two glasses and I'll be as right as rain. So have you got something old?'

I drop my leg from the bed. 'Yep.' I twist the diamond studs in my ears. Ava's eyes widen briefly but she quickly rearranges her expression. I know she recognises them; she was there when Kit gave them to me. They were a birthday gift. It feels right to be wearing them, to have part of him here.

James and I know where our love for each other came from. There is no point trying to hide the past, to be ashamed of it. I like to think that if he were here, he would approve of me marrying James; that he would be wishing us luck, that he would forgive me, forgive him. Kit was never one to hold grudges. He lived too much in the now; he never regretted a thing.

I have a flash of memory – actually it's more of a memory of a dream, an image. I used to have them often. It's been a long time since I've tortured myself with the way Kit may have died, but for a fleeting moment, I see him again, still in the same clothes as the day he left, falling, falling, falling... high dark rocks around him, thoughts running through his mind: *I shouldn't have left; I should have stayed at home; I don't want to die like this.* Did he even have time to regret leaving me that day?

'Right then.' Ava's voice brings me back. She lifts the dress from the wardrobe and passes it to me. 'Let's get this show on the road, shall we?'

There is much oohing and aahing as I come out of the bathroom. Fingers on the dress, straightening the short veil clipped to the back of my head. I stand in front of the mirror. There is something dreamlike when you see yourself in your wedding dress, like you're seeing a different version of yourself, a paradoxical image, in the present but somehow in the future as well; a future version of the woman you were when you got up that morning, a future woman who will stare at you for the rest of your life through the picture frame on your wall, from a side table at your mother's house, encapsulated in an album, brought out on special occasions.

How will I feel about this woman, in this dress: thirty-two years old, young, her whole life with her husband ahead of her. Will I be jealous of her, as time etches its way across my features, as it erodes the images, the smells, the people around me? That's how I used to feel when I would look at photos of me and Kit. I would sometimes hate her, the woman in the photo who had her arms around him, I would hate the smug look on her face as she kissed him while taking a selfie on the French Alps, skis held aloft. I would want to scratch out her eyes, that stupid girl who didn't know how lucky she was in that moment to have him next to her, to be able to wake up with him beside her, not wake with the vomiting reality that plunged into her chest every morning for a year after he disappeared.

I can't look back on photos of this woman and have any doubts that she was making the right decision; I can't look back on photos of her and hate her, the woman facing me in the mirror. The version of the person I am today needs to know how lucky she is. She needs to not take one moment of this day for granted.

'You OK?' Paige puts a hand on my arm.

'Shit,' I say, trying to catch the tears that have formed. Ava is there with a cotton wool pad beneath my eyes as I laugh. 'Sorry.'

'It's fine. I'll touch it up in a minute. It's an emotional day; a few tears are to be expected.' She blots beneath my eyes and rubs my arms.

'You look beautiful, Liv, really something.' She smiles at me and turns me back to face the mirror, Libby and Paige to one side, Ava beside me. Ava's phone buzzes. 'They're all downstairs. Right then, are you ready?'

I nod, smiling, getting up and smoothing my hands along the fabric of my dress, adjusting the veil as they all flutter and buzz around me. For the first time in a long time I feel an unfamiliar pang for Mum. To have her here with me. It used to come with the sting of resentment, of disappointment when she couldn't be there at my graduation, when she couldn't come to see my first flat with Kit. But today, I just feel sadness – she would have loved this, the excitement, the drama.

'I'll see you down there, OK?' I say to Ava. 'I want to call Mum, just so she can see me before I say I do.' Ava hesitates then nods, safe in the knowledge that James will be downstairs where she can keep an eye on him.

'But be quick!'

'I will, promise.' I air-kiss her on the cheek, and then there is quiet. I swipe the screen on my phone. James's last message, a quick reply back:

K. See you soon x.

Shit. My phone is almost out of charge. I grab the key to my room and hurry along the corridor.

I step into our room, the bed still unmade, his suit cover hanging empty. I smile, then rush over to my bag to search for my charger but it's not there.

I pace around the room, lifting the duvet cover, opening and closing drawers. I stand with my hand on my hip, glancing at the clock. I've got ten minutes before I walk down the aisle. I chew my bottom lip, lifting my clothes from last night. I pick up James's hoody from the back of the chair, still damp from his run.

A blue velvet rectangular box falls to the floor with a soft thud.

I stare at it.

I should put it back.

I know I should.

But I don't.

I step back and sit on the bed, my thumbs prising open the box, my breath sucked into my chest, my hands beginning to shake.

In my hand is a necklace just like the one I wanted years ago. It's a heart-shaped locket, silver, pearl insets at small intervals along the chain. It was in a small antique shop in Devon. We'd been on the beach all day, Kit teaching me to surf. My shoulder had been aching, my nose red with the bite of sunburn when Kit and I had wandered into the shop, salt in our hair, a cold can of Coke in my hand. It was out of our price range, but I'd tried it on anyway, his fingers against my neck as he closed the clasp. He'd met my eyes in the reflection in the mottled mirror on top of a French writing bureau. 'One day, I'll be able to buy you things like this. Promise,' he said, resting his chin on my shoulder. I'd leant my head against his as we stared into the mirror.

And he did. He bought me the necklace for my birthday. He had it the day he went missing. Said he was going to get it engraved. I'd pictured that necklace lying on the seabed, sinking into the silt, like a relic from the *Titanic*.

How can James have it?

I turn it over; it's engraved:

Just jump, K xxx

My hand covers my mouth.

The two words we would say to each other whenever we were getting cold feet before a jump, before a dinner with his parents, before my job interview. Just jump.

OK, Liv, think this through. Kit could have given it to James to keep before he left that morning.

I place the necklace around my neck. It feels exactly the same – the same weight, the smooth back resting at my clavicle. I reach for the box, a black card falling out from inside. I turn it over. It's the receipt and warranty. And it is dated a week ago.

This can't be real.

My fingers hold the locket, my nail snagging on the clasp. I click the locket open, a small note fluttering to the floor.

I bend down, my dress whispering, my heart thudding as I unfold the paper. Kit's handwriting, the same slant to the right. The paper is white, fresh, the ink clear and defined.

I'm sorry, Liv. I had no choice. K xxx

I jerk my head towards the window, to the image of the man I saw this morning. The same build, the same stride.

Kit's alive?

He can't be. I re-read the receipt. The engraving was definitely from a week ago.

The thought is like melted plastic. Everything that was fixed has lost its form, lost its shape, the colours fading.

If Kit is alive, does James *know*? It's in his pocket.

I hurry across the room, my hand yanking open the door, my feet stepping over the threshold.

But I don't step into the corridor of the hotel.

Instead, I find myself somewhere else entirely.

5

SIX DAYS BEFORE HE LEFT ME

This isn't possible.

The door behind me doesn't belong to room 307.

The door behind me doesn't even belong to the Grange Hotel.

The door behind me belongs to Flat 2, 14 Winchester Road.

This is our flat. Kit's and mine.

What the actual *hell* is going on?

Smells and sounds I recognise assault my senses from every angle, all merging together, soup-like. I can't differentiate them.

I understand that I'm standing still, but the sensation feels like I'm spinning, as though my arms are outstretched, my feet stepping around and around on a playground.

And I'm in the private stairwell that leads to our second-floor maisonette.

I look up the stairs: grey carpet, white walls, film poster of *Highlander* – one of Kit's favourites – hanging on the wall, chipped banister, fake potted plant beside me. We'd tried keeping a yucca alive the year before but neither of us ever remembered to water it.

My eyes continue gliding upwards; Kit's jacket is hanging on the top of the banister. It's his brown leather aviator jacket. The one I bought him for his birthday along with a pair of aviator sunglasses, a nod to his love of *Top Gun*.

When the sequel came out, my heart ached that he wasn't here to see it... I think of the necklace, the warranty... Could he have been around all of this time? Did he go and see *Maverick* and think of me?

My thoughts are thick. The feeling of movement slows, but my surroundings are cylindrical, like I'm looking through a fisheye lens, like everything is wide view.

My right hand grasps at my throat, around to where the locket should be sitting, but the necklace is gone, my skin at the nape of my neck bare beneath my fingers. My hand rides further up, to the short stubble of the back of my pixie cut. I hold out my hand, my engagement ring isn't there: gone is the French manicure; my nails are painted turquoise. Kit painted them the week before he went missing. We'd been watching *World's Toughest Jobs*. There was a woman working as a window cleaner on high-rise buildings in Canada. We had been discussing if we could do it.

After he disappeared, I remember not taking the polish off, and with each passing week, there would be less and less paint on the nails. I'd sobbed the day the last piece of colour flaked away in Mum's washing-up bowl.

I notice that I'm gripping something in my other hand: a bottle of brown sauce.

What. Is. Happening? A wave of nausea rises through my chest, and I swallow hard as I try to concentrate on what I can see, what I can hear; I need to ground myself. I need to focus.

The cacophony of sound is starting to separate: a news report on the TV in the lounge, a radio playing, the parp of a horn outside, the slam of a door in the flat beside ours. Their names pop into my head: Jenna and Phil... We used to call them the power pair, all business suits and sharp creases.

I can smell bacon; the fabric softener on my clothes: honeysuckle and sandalwood; the Dove deodorant I favoured; the plug-in air freshener at the top of the stairs, something vaguely vanilla... and just... *here*. Our flat.

The flat Kit and I lived in.

How is this possible?

The motion slows and I look down. I'm not in my wedding dress. I'm wearing a pair of blue skinny jeans, faded along the thighs and ripped at the knees. My white long-sleeved T-shirt is tucked in, my feet in a pair of white trainers.

I'm standing with my back against the front door.

Kit's voice permeates through the sounds and smells.

Kit.

My throat dries as his voice tumbles down the stairs. He's singing 'Seven Years' by Lukas Graham. He always sang when he cooked.

Bacon.

I close my eyes, white light dancing behind my eyelids.

I know when this is. This is the Saturday before he left. I went out to get brown sauce from the corner shop.

I tip my head back, my eyes scanning the landing above. I climb the stairs slowly, following the sound of his voice; he's badly out of tune as he always was. The smell of bacon is stronger as I reach the top of the stairs, the sauce still clutched in one hand, the other reaching out, resting on his jacket, on the smooth leather. My throat is tight. I'd always wondered if Kit had somehow modelled himself on Maverick. He didn't look like Tom Cruise – Kit was tall, broad, light brown hair always a little in need of a trim – but he had that same spark in his green eyes, the same easy charm, the grin that could disarm, the confidence that he could try anything and still come out winning.

I carry on towards the kitchen. The pan is hissing. His voice continues. He's singing about becoming thirty years old and his stories being told. I place my hand on the door, adding the smallest amount of pressure, my heart racing, my whole body shaking.

He's here. Right in front of the cooker, his back facing me: khaki shorts, a white T-shirt, light brown hair messy, spatula in hand as he conducts the music echoing around the room from the radio on the windowsill next to the fake potted herbs.

I cross the room quickly, my arms wrapping around his narrow waist, his stomach muscles solid. I bury my nose into the fabric of his T-shirt, the same fabric softener, but beneath that... is Kit. I'm digging my forehead between his shoulder blades; afraid to look up, to let go, to see his face, to lose him all over again.

'Hey,' he says, his voice rumbling through his sternum. 'That was quick. Did you get the sauce?'

I can't speak. I can't pull away from where my face is buried in his spine. My hands are wrapped around him so tightly; he's starting to move from my grasp.

'Liv?' He turns; there's the sound of the spatula hitting the counter; his body moving around; my head being somehow dragged around his side, my cheek now against his chest. 'Baby, what's wrong? What happened?' I want to touch every part of him, to feel everything that I have tried to remember over the past seven years. I can feel his heart beating through his skin and I want to climb inside, to reach into his chest and hold it in my palm, to feel it thumping, working, alive... I would drink his blood if I could. He's kissing the top of my head, his hand finding my chin, lifting my face upwards.

It takes me a moment to open my eyes, to look up, but I do.

'Kit?'

He's got two-day stubble. His nose is longer than James's, lifts at the end slightly; there's a smattering of freckles across it, but those are his eyes. Those eyes that I first saw as he looked down at me on the bank of the River Wye, sea glass, long lashes, mischief behind them that I have thought of so often.

'What happened?' he asks, concern crossing his features. 'Are you hurt?'

How can I tell him? How can I tell him, *he* happened? That *he* is the one who hurt me; *he* is the one who left me, who destroyed all of *this*.

'I... You...' I can't speak. My words are glue and mud. 'Kit?' My legs begin to give.

'Wooah.' He drops down and lifts me in his arms. 'You're fine; I've got you. I've got you.'

He carries me to the lounge and places me down gently on the sofa. I watch as he reaches for the controller just as the news presenter says, 'Good morning if you're just joining us. The time is ten forty on Saturday the 19th of March. Today's headlines—' But Kit has turned off the TV and is crouching beside me, a hand on my forehead. This time next week he will be gone. I'll spend Easter Sunday standing next to police lines, people pressing cups of lukewarm coffee into my numb hands. James will be amongst the search party, the wind and rains buffeting around him, as he takes careful steps forward over bracken and hills, looking for signs of his brother's body.

'Let me get you a drink of water.' He rushes from my side. I try to tell him not to go, but the words are sandpaper in my throat. My eyes dart around the room, taking in the surroundings. Everything is the same as I remember it: the coffee table with a bowl of pebbles in the centre, each one found by us in various places all over the world; the bookcases, jammed with paperbacks of all genres – classics, crime, romance; fairy lights hanging around the edges; our initials carved into one of the shelves after a drunken night.

On the table by the window are my books, planning notes for the start of next term beside them, highlighters and Post-its scattered all over the surface, Kit's laptop open. Mine had been handed over to the tech guy in the shop up the road. A faulty motherboard needed cooking or something like that. I remember how, when I got the call to pick it back up, it felt like another lifetime ago that I had taken it in to be fixed. It was only ten days and my life was not just turned upside down, but hollowed out.

Kit returns, his eyebrows furrowed in concern. For a second he looks like James. I'd never noticed that before. I'd always thought them to look so different, but they have the same wave of movement there. Their eyebrows aren't straight when they frown; they lift and dip: corrugated.

James.

I feel a surge of emotion.

'James?' Kit puts his hand behind my neck and brings the glass of water to my lips. 'What about him?'

I must have spoken that out loud. Is James here? In this... wherever I am? He must be. But so is Kit.

I take a sip and then remove the glass from his hands, placing it on the coffee table.

I'm watching his every move, listening to his breath, noticing the stray hair on the shoulder of his T-shirt, the kink of a curl just below his ear, the fine lines around his eyes, the dimple in his chin, the small mole on his neck.

The sofa creaks with his weight, as he crosses his legs like one of my kids on the classroom carpet. He reaches for my hand: warm, dry, *real*. 'What's happened, Liv? Tell me, because you're scaring the shit out of me.' His thumb runs over mine, his eyes, *those* eyes, scanning my face.

In the year after he left, I always felt like I could still see him, sense him in the shadows, not an outline, more of a smudge, an impression. Now I question, if, just like the image through the window this morning, I *had* seen him. That is the image of Kit that I have lived with for the past seven years, but now... just look at him. Three dimensional, four dimensional even, as the feelings of love, obsession, guilt, swell and subside inside my skin like the waves I had imagined had swallowed his body. That was the most obvious of explanations: that he'd fallen, that he'd drowned. I had preferred that, rather than picturing him deep in a crevice, starving, becoming emaciated in the dark.

'Nothing,' I say shaking my head. 'Just felt faint, that's all.'

I don't know what else to say. I want to tell him the truth, but I don't know how to begin to describe what's happening. I could tell him, but that might change the future and this wouldn't just be the butterfly effect; this would be a whole-stampede-of-elephants effect.

Because how can I begin to tell him everything that has happened? How do I say: well, you see the thing is, Kit, seven years ago, or in six days' time, you will pack a bag, tell me you're going for a hike and then you will disappear from the face of the earth. I thought you were dead; *we* thought you were dead, so did the police. It's official now, by the way; you're presumed dead now, did you know? We had a funeral. Oh and by the way, I'm about to marry your brother – you don't mind do you? Cool.

'You sure? Because you look... spaced out.'

'I'm fine.' I try to keep my voice steady, crossing my legs, mimicking his posture. I take his hand, turn it over in my palm, memorising every line; he has a cut around the base of his thumb. I'd forgotten that. He'd cut it picking up a pasta sauce jar that I had knocked over. He brings his palm to my face, cupping my cheek. I close my eyes, letting the warmth of his touch hold the weight of the past seven years in his palm. I open my eyes as he brings his forehead against mine. He's so close, I can see the green and blue pigment around his pupil, like the inside of a marble.

'I love you,' I say those words, words where the consonants are sharp and determined, but the vowels are broken around the edges. These words that I didn't say the day he'd left. I never said it back. I was busy hanging the washing over the radiators, distracted. It was hammering down with rain, a storm that soon swept him away in gale-force winds – at least that's what I've always thought. If only the weather forecast had been more accurate, he wouldn't have gone; the winds were set to die down by the afternoon, he'd said. The rain was supposed to have moved on by the time he got there. But the storm didn't abate until the next day.

'Hey, *hey...*' He pulls me against him, wrapping his arms around me. I can feel his ribs, the strength in his arms. My face is wet against the curve of his neck, always tanned from his love of the outdoors. I breathe him in, my body shaking and sobbing.

I don't know what is happening. I don't know if I've time-travelled, if I've had an aneurysm, if I'm asleep or if I've been pulled into some weird alternative universe... maybe I'm doing a Gwyneth and this is a sliding-doors type thing – I've got the same short-hair look going on – but one thing I do know is that I'm grateful for this. I'm grateful that even if this moment is an illusion, that I get to hold him, that I get to tell him I love him.

Kit pulls away, a gentle kiss; but my whole body tightens slightly.

James. I love *James*. But I think of the necklace in James's pocket. The warranty. Did he know Kit was alive? Did he always know? If he hid that from me, I can't trust him. Our entire relationship is built on us looking for Kit. On our grief for him, on our search, on our acceptance.

Downstairs, the door slams. Kit turns his head towards the door. 'You ready?' James's voice shouts up the stairs: the man I'm marrying, here in the past with the man that I lost.

The man that I still love.

Kit rolls his eyes, oblivious to the thoughts wrapping themselves around my brain. He smiles at me, kissing the top of my nose.

'We're in here,' he says. I look up and there he is. James fills the door frame. He isn't as tall as he looks, but there is something in the way he holds himself, chin slightly lifted as though he's ready to take an insult that makes him seem taller. He's younger, has a bruise along his cheekbone, and when he sees me, his face closes. Shuts down.

You see the thing is, when Kit was alive, James... well, let's just say, we didn't get along.

6

SIX DAYS BEFORE HE LEFT ME

'We need to get going or we'll hit traffic,' James says to Kit, ignoring me.

I remember this moment – I wasn't lying on the sofa though. My eyes are guided towards the table, replaying the scene as it was at the time, another version of me, hair tucked behind my ears, black-rimmed glasses, white top, books spread out before me. I picture her, this other me: a half-eaten bacon sandwich next to her; highlighter in hand; another version of Kit, trying to distract her, kissing her neck, so he could swipe the rest of her breakfast.

James had come in the same way, uttered the same words, making it clear that this was his time with his brother, not mine.

When Kit and I were first together, I used to try to get James on side, to include him if we were going somewhere, but he made it obvious that he didn't want me around. But hearing his voice, seeing the way he is avoiding my eyes, cuts deeper than it did back then. Back then, I would have just rolled my eyes and inwardly seethed. But today – *Is it today?* – today, it hurts because right now, all I want to do is step towards him, let him hold me and tell me everything is going to be OK, that he will fix this and I will feel safe.

But this isn't *my* James. If my James even exists any more.

This is Kit's brother... Kit's brother who sometimes made me feel like I was an outsider. He was never cruel, always politely abrupt, never said anything that made me feel as though I wasn't good enough for his brother... It was more like I was invading their relationship, like he was jealous of the time I was taking away from him and Kit.

'Liv's not well,' Kit says, putting a hand to my forehead again, as he looks up at his brother. 'I'm staying here.'

'What's up?' James asks, eyes flitting to my supine position.

'She almost passed out.'

'I'm fine,' I say sitting up straighter. 'Honest. Low blood sugar, that's all. I'll be right as rain once I've eaten.'

Kit shakes his head. 'I'm not leaving you,' he says kissing my forehead as I hear a not-so-subtle sigh from James.

'Right. Well, I can't get a refund, so...' James rummages in his pocket and unwraps a stick of chewing gum, avoiding my eyes.

I search my memory. Where were they going? Ah, the boxing club. James didn't own it back then, but he trained there and he would hire the ring and spar with Kit. Kit did it for fun. He was fast on his feet, agile, but he never loved boxing the way James did.

'I can't leave her, bud.'

'James will lose his session if you don't go. How about... I come with you?' I look over at him, the man I'm about to marry. Whose whole body seems to have just sagged. He quickly rearranges his expression, shrugging his shoulders. 'James?' I prompt. Again, he avoids my eyes.

'Don't go overboard with your enthusiasm, will you?' I say. The words are out of my mouth before I can stop them. Life with

James has always been built on honesty. Ever since Kit left, we've always laid our cards on the table. Nothing was hidden; everything kept plain and simple, or so I'd always thought. His eyes widen slightly at my response, as though he's one of the good kids in school who has just been caught cheating.

Kit scoffs. 'Ignore him,' he says. 'Did the honourable Lady Penelope knock back your advances again?'

James gives him the bird.

Kit bursts out laughing, turning to me. 'That'll be a yes. How long has it been since Elizabeth and the EpiPen? Three months? Four?'

Elizabeth, Elizabeth, Elizabeth... I shuffle through my memory until I find her. Ah yes. James had a three-week fling with her. I remember he made her dinner with anchovies in the pasta sauce, and her face blew up like a puffer fish. He'd told me not long after the first time we slept together. From then on one of the first things he asked a prospective date was if they had any allergies. They carried on dating for a while after, if I recall. But it had fizzled out. I forget why.

I'd been lying on his chest as he told me about her face, the way it had swollen so quickly, her eyes shutting. He thought she would die right there at his kitchen table. 'Looking back, it's no wonder I went through a dry spell. I must have come across as a right weirdo asking them if they wanted to go for a drink then quickly following it up with: "Do you have any allergies?"' I'd propped myself up on my elbow, looking down at him, his body naked beneath the sheets.

'Why did you never have any long-term relationships?' I asked softly.

'I'm just not built that way. I mean, I wasn't. Back then.'

'Liv?' Kit asks. I bring my attention back to him, heat creeping across my cheeks, as I appear to have just been staring at James by the way he is focusing all his attention on the car keys in his hands.

'Yep? Sorry, I was in a world of my own. Do I need a jumper, do you think?' I glance towards Kit's laptop. Will there be answers on there? 'I'll take the laptop,' I say. 'Get some work done while you two' – I put my hands into fists and throw a few jabs – 'pow, pow, pow.' I add sound effects to my punches. James frowns, an eye-roll in eyebrow form, then rummages in his backpack. 'Um, I mean while you do your thing,' I add, my voice trailing off.

'It can get pretty chilly in there,' Kit says.

'Right, I'll grab a jumper. Back in a tick.' I hesitate briefly before landing a quick kiss on Kit's mouth. I try to sidestep James's frame in the doorway, trying not to breathe in his familiar smell. He lands a hand on my arm as I pass. I look down at it then to his face.

'Low blood sugar, right?' he says, passing me a breakfast bar. The packet is battered, the bar in question probably in pieces.

'Thanks,' I reply.

He gives me a quick nod, already moving away from me.

* * *

In the bedroom, I close the door, leaning against it with my heart banging insistently against my chest.

Jesus. Is this really happening? Am I really standing here in our flat, seven years ago? My hand reaches up to my collarbone, rubbing along the length of it, a nervous habit. My fingers linger along my clavicle; I can feel the weight of the necklace as though it's still there.

Why did James have it? *How* did James have it?

I place the breakfast bar on my vanity unit, the remains of my old make-up there. I reach for the bottle of perfume, lifting the nozzle to my nose, memories tumbling over themselves for attention. I replace it and glance around the room. The bed is made, light green duvet tucked and folded tightly into place – Kit's doing, not mine; my discarded clothes are on the bedroom floor. I've always been messy; so is James, always too distracted by something else to be able to spare the time to tackle the mundane. But Kit? Kit was always tidy, organised, *methodical*. Just the same as with his work. Neat lines of numbers, neat lines of coding: neat lines. It's the same as the way he climbed. An adrenaline junkie? Yes. But a calculated one. He liked statistics; he liked the idea of being the one in a million. It was analysing the risks and beating them. That's what he loved: beating the odds. That's why his job suits him. Kit was – *is*? – an IT consultant. He offers web design, IT support and cyber security services. Different companies commission him for various aspects. He goes in and cracks their security, then tells them how to fix it. It's like a game to him: cracking the codes.

I walk around to Kit's side of the bed, my hand smoothing over his pillow. I lean in, burying my face into it; it's still rich with the scent of him. The pain of those first few weeks is swollen in the back of my throat as I breathe him in. How many times had I done this after he left? How long was it until, defeated, I had taken off the bedclothes, forced them into the washing machine and sobbed as they spun around, his smell drowning in a sea of Persil.

I close my eyes; see the image of James last night. *I love you.*

I was so sure this morning in the hotel, so sure that he was right. But what if he's been lying to me? If he's been keeping Kit's whereabouts from me, then our whole life together so far has been based on a lie. And if Kit's alive then where the hell has he been for the past seven years?

The thoughts tumble around my mind, the old mixed with the new, with the now, with the then.

'Liv? You ready?' Kit shouts from somewhere behind the door.

'Just a sec!' I reply.

To Kit.

This is going to take some getting used to.

Opposite me is a full-length mirror. I sit up then take slow steps towards it. Woah.

The girl in the mirror is at least three sizes smaller than the woman who is about to get married. I'm a size eight here, I think. I turn to the side, and would you just look at my arse! It's all perky and firm, as are my thighs beneath my jeans. I jab them with my index finger, not even a hint of a custard-cream-induced wobble. I lift up my T-shirt; my stomach is flat, no sign of the gentle weight I gained once James took over the cooking and when staffroom cakes and biscuits started creeping into my daily eating routine. I was much fitter back then, I mean, back *now*.

I lean into the mirror, flashing a grin. Hmmm. Hardly any laughter lines yet. The whites of my eyes are brighter, my skin clearer, my body holding more vivacity. It's hard to describe but I just *feel* younger. I pull open the wardrobe door, my fingers running along our clothes, all of which will be pulled from their hangers in just over a weeks' time. Ava had turned up when the whole flat looked like it'd been ransacked. I'd fallen asleep amidst his clothes.

But that hasn't happened yet.

And that means... I can stop Kit from leaving.

The thought lands like that heart-stopping moment when you're just about to fall asleep.

Because if I stop Kit leaving, what will happen to me and James?

7

SIX DAYS BEFORE HE LEFT ME

I step back onto the landing. Kit has packed his laptop in my old work bag. He flashes me a questioning smile as he hands me the bag. 'Are you sure you're feeling better?'

James is sitting on the top stair, his finger swiping across his phone as Kit asks. He looks up at me briefly before returning his focus to the screen. His hair is longer than I'm used to, more curls. I bring my attention back to Kit. 'I'm fine, honest. Maybe I've got a bit of flu or something coming.' I take the bag from him. Kit was always thoughtful, always making sure I had everything I needed. It's not like that with James. At the thought I immediately feel guilty. Everything with James is different, not worse, just different.

My relationship with James is more about partnership. If he's late up I'll make him lunch for work. If he's home before me, he'll run the hoover round and get the tea on. With Kit, it was more that... I don't know, I suppose I noticed the things he did more. There was always some flamboyancy in his actions. So, take my bag for example, as he passes it me, he's packed it with my work things, but he taps the front pocket with a cheeky grin where there is a hastily wrapped package in tin foil poking out. A bacon sandwich, I'm guessing. James would do the same kind of thing, but for this scenario, I'd find it later, when I wasn't expecting it. I suppose Kit always needed a response from me, whereas James is never looking for recognition or praise. I'm not saying one way is right or wrong. There is a boyish charm that goes with Kit's need for praise, just as there is something sexy about James's self-lessness.

James stands and pockets his phone as Kit bends over, tapping his lower back. 'Hop on m'lady!' I let out a snort. James heads down the stairs, clearly impatient with us. Without warning, I get that old rush, the rush I would feel when I would wind James up. There was something sadistically satisfying in getting a rise out of him. 'I'll be your trusty steed,' Kit continues, his smile and enthusiasm as infectious as they always were. James yanks open the door and strides through without a second glance. I'm going to have to get used to his dismissiveness while I'm here.

How *long* will I be here? How long will it be before I wake up from this... whatever *this* is? Is the week before he goes stretching out before me? Or am I here for an hour? A quick flash of my old life? What if I have to relive it all, bear the pain of Kit going missing again? The thoughts cartwheel around my head. I'm trying to find impossible answers to an impossible scenario.

In my stomach I feel the familiar heat, that tiny flickering light of fear; the familiar urge to hold my breath.

'Kit? Can we... can we talk? Just for a minute?'

'Sure,' he replies, his face melting in concern. 'Later though? You know how he gets. Now jump on. Chop chop.' Kit grins over his shoulder at me, light replenished as he taps his lower back again.

I hesitate. 'Can you just promise me something?' His expression folds – a reaction to the tone of my voice. 'Can you... not go...'

I'm about to ask him to not go hiking, to stay home with me, so that I don't lose him, but the words stick in my throat. I can't get past them, a James-sized lump stopping me. Because if I thought Kit died next week then I would stop him. I would give up any kind of future with James to save his life. But if he's not dead? If he hasn't been lying in a coma for seven years or lost his memory, then maybe I don't know him. I never did.

I'm here to find out the truth. I must be. And until I find out some answers, I will act as though I belong here, that I'm *her* – the woman who grinned up from the photos with Kit beside her.

'Can you not go too fast?' I finish my sentence.

'Pffft! Too fast? When have you ever known me to go too fast?' He winks and nods towards the stairs.

My body knows how to do this without thinking. I jump just the right amount to land on his back, my arms sliding around his neck easily, my legs hitched around his hips at exactly the right height. For a moment, I feel the horizon shift again, as an image of last night in the shower with James flashes through my mind.

'Hold tight, m'lady!' Kit turns his head, kissing my cheek. 'Your carriage awaits!'

I let out a yelp as he jogs down the stairs with me bobbing up and down on his back. He makes ridiculous neighing noises as he gallops me across the car park. James is opening the boot of Bertha the car and yanks open the driver door, sliding into the seat. Kit lets out a whinny and crouches down, placing me firmly on the floor, before taking my bag and heading towards the boot.

I open the passenger door and climb in, pulling the seat belt and plugging it in. James is staring at me, a confused expression on his face.

'What?' I say.

'Nothing,' he replies, turning the key.

'Bertha smells nice,' I say, trying to lighten the mood, reaching for the air freshener dangling from the mirror. He turns towards me sharply.

Then it hits me. I always sat in the back, Kit up front, and I didn't discover that James called his car Bertha until after Kit had disappeared.

I backtrack. 'Sorry, I don't know why I... I'll get in the back?'

He shrugs. 'Makes no difference to me.'

Kit opens the door. 'What's this?' He grins.

'Nothing, I'll' – I unbuckle the seat belt – 'get in the back.'

'Just...' James interrupts, shoulders lifting and falling with an exasperated breath. 'We're already late. Kit, get in the back, all right?'

Kit salutes and climbs in.

James doesn't speak to me for the whole fifteen minutes we're in the car.

I perch on the edge of the chair. In front of me is a makeshift desk made of an upturned crate, Kit's laptop open. I was here two days ago. Two days and seven years in the future. I'd popped in on my way to Ava's. Just a quick visit, a chat and a coffee while he worked on his accounts in the office. James spends most of his days here. It was me who convinced him to take over this place. Above the door outside of the building is an old sign – *Park Lane Boxing Club* – but two days ago, in another life, the sign was navy blue, the words 'Fighting Fit' in white writing.

We'd taken on the lease two years ago and we'd spent the summer holidays unloading the contents into a skip outside, both of us excited and yet exhausted at the end of the first week after the contract was signed. We had the ring repaired, new ropes installed. The brick walls painted grey, the floor scrubbed and varnished. We'd sourced second-hand gym equipment, cleaned it, repaired it, hung framed posters of the greats, bought a water cooler, a coffee machine, had speakers attached to the walls; we'd put our heart and souls into this place.

I look around at the stains on the walls, the tattered ropes, the barely-still-attached-to-the-walls speed balls, the punch bags with split seams.

There are only a few people using the equipment.

'You sure you're ready for me this time?' Kit taunts as he wraps his hands in tape, tearing a piece off with his teeth, his eyes alight with mischief, the right side of his mouth quirking up in a smirk. My head turns quickly to the new-old sound of his voice, the hairs on my arms raised; I wonder if the neurons in my brain are having an electrical surge as they try to process what the hell is going on. I try to settle my thoughts.

I don't know how or why I've been given this second chance, but I have it.

My focus is drawn back to him.

Where did you go, Kit? Did you leave me? Did you leave *us*?

In response to Kit's taunts, James's expression remains calm, but I can see the way he's rotating his head a few times, can see the energy pulsing through him. James finds it hard to keep still. He's always on the move, a leg bouncing when we're watching TV, pacing while he takes a phone call. He hides it as best he can when he's in social situations, this energy that he can never seem to contain.

As Kit bends down to tie his laces, James twangs an elastic band, catching Kit above his ear. It's then that I see him, the man I love, the man I'm about to marry. It's in the smirk, the 'what?' shrug of his shoulders, the light behind those serious brooding eyes, the love there.

I had never doubted James's love for Kit, but I can understand how James could be jealous of his brother. Kit was always the centre of attention with his jokes and easy charm, in the way he was always such an open book. And yet if he's alive, he's more closed than any of us gave him credit for.

James stands, pulls his arm across his body in a stretch and catches my eye. The smirk vanishes and his body immediately tenses. I realise I'm smiling at him. His head shifts to the side as though he's appraising my actions, then he turns his back and steps up into the ring. Kit joins him and they bounce around a bit, throwing a few safe jabs.

I drag the laptop towards me, taking a deep breath, pulling Kit's password from the depths of my memory and releasing it onto the keyboard. I hold my breath, glancing back at him, making sure he's distracted. He laughs and moonwalks away from James. I lean towards the home screen, a photo of us smiling up at the camera. Our hair is wet and smoothed back, and we're sitting on a sun lounger in Greece. That was six months ago, seven years and six months ago. We'd just been snorkelling and we're holding blue cocktails with pink umbrellas in them.

I glance up as Kit laughs. He's skipping from one foot to the other. James mirrors his movements, but he's becoming more impatient as he waits for Kit to throw a punch.

My eyes are drawn back to the screen.

OK, Kit Palmer. What secrets are you hiding?

8

ONE DAY AFTER I LEFT HER

I never meant for this to happen.

I'm not that guy.

The guy who just goes. But then again, maybe we never really know what we're capable of. I didn't think my brother was capable of burning everything we had to the ground. But he did.

My fingers pull up the collar of my jacket, yank the edges of my cap down. Maybe once I'm settled, I'll go full-on hermit, grow my own veg, grow a beard... Liv was never keen, but I figure that doesn't matter now.

I take a quick look through the train window, the Scottish hills rolling their shoulders, straightening up – geriatric giants, watching my progress. *You don't belong here.* I tear my attention away from the vastness of the country I don't belong in.

Across the aisle are a group of kids, all wearing Easter bonnets. They clutch baskets, ready to be filled with chocolate eggs. Liv loves Easter eggs. She has to have them cold from the fridge. They need to snap, she says. I stop myself wandering through the past and tip my head towards the open paperback in my hands. Nothing to see here, kids, I'm just a guy in a hat, reading a thriller novel: a stranger.

All I have to do is stay off grid for a while. Get my shit together and then, I guess, I'll somehow find a way out of this mess.

I keep my eyes on the pages of the novel. The train begins moving again. It's been fifty minutes already. A felled tree on the line. Water on the tracks from the storm, which was supposed to clear. But fifty minutes feels like nothing when you've travelled halfway across the United Kingdom in twelve hours. This is the last leg before I hike to my new home. New home for now, at least. I return my attention to my novel as the train begins to move. The villain's secret has just been discovered.

I hope it's not an omen.

For a second, my eyes are drawn to the majesty of the mountains in the distance, the sheer epic-ness of the Scottish countryside. Countryside doesn't quite fit here though. Countryside to me means gentle hills, fields, perhaps a trickling stream. But this is countryside on steroids. My eyes narrow as I look to the scale of my surroundings, my inner Sean Connery declaring: 'There can be only one!' *Highlander*. It's one of Dad's favourite films. He used to take us hiking. Right back when we were six and nine years old. Just us boys, he'd say; our backpacks filled with drink bottles and a packed lunch, a different destination most weekends, new mountains to climb. We'd pretend we were training beside rivers and streams, build campfires and toast marshmallows, enact sword fights. My brother always won. Even then.

The hikes trailed off when we got older. We always made sure we'd still have a few trips with Dad. He missed us when we left home, I think. Arthritis in his knees has made his own hiking trips less frequent and Mum, well... Mum can be a lot.

An image of my parents snags at the edge of my thoughts. I

hope they're coping. Now that they know the truth. Christ, I hope Liv's all right. Hours into the journey and each time I think of her, it's as though my insides are being scooped out, like a pumpkin on Halloween. I remind myself I had no choice; I did this for her.

I disembark after an hour. It's like a scene from *The Railway Children* here, without the actual children. Obviously. And the retro clothing. But the timelessness of the place makes me think that they could film it here. Anyway, what I mean is that right now, all I need is a gas mask and an evacuation card and I'd fit right in. Hold on. Is that what happens in *The Railway Children* or am I mixing it up with that Mr Tom one that Liv made me watch?

No clue.

Anyway, my point is, it could be the eighteen hundreds, the nineteen thirties, 2045 and I would bet this place would still look the same: quaint, bottle-green paintwork around the eaves, no Costa or Starbucks.

No security cameras.

I tread along the platform, zipping up my jacket as far as it will go and dig my hands into my pockets. My feet echo through the silence as I cross the bridge. I pause, getting my bearings. To the right, a short distance away, is a cluster of houses. Other than that, there is no one around but the mountains, and the hills, and the rocks, and the violet sky.

At the bottom of the steps, I take a right, heading into the toilets. There is one cubicle. A strong smell of urine. No paper towels, and the dryer looks like it may have needed a rotating handle to charge it up. Nevertheless, I go about my business then open my rucksack, because fuck me, it's freezing.

I shrug off my jacket, unzip my hoody and add a long-sleeved thermal vest, a jumper and a fleece. In one of the pockets is a folded-up piece of paper. I open it. Liv's handwriting stares up at me: *milk – full fat, cling film, Jammy Dodgers (not for dunking, you weirdo)*. Each word feels like a gut punch. Each swoop and dent of her writing prods against my skin. I fold the memory of returning home away. Unpacking the shopping as Liv sang loudly to 'Relight My Fire'. Her hands were busy chopping salad. I can practically feel her warm cheek against mine as I leant over her shoulder to steal a piece of cucumber. My hands are holding the paper tightly. It almost tears in two. I'm biting the inside of my cheek so hard I taste a tang of blood. I tuck the list into my pocket, then replace the cap with a thermal hat. Pull on my gloves. Tighten the straps on my rucksack.

Outside, there is a narrow road ahead of me. A small shop with a *Post Office* sign in the window and a road leading towards a few houses, not quite enough to make up a village. I unfold the map, double-check my route and tuck it back into my pocket. The wind is raw. The power from the storm that has followed me across the country has ebbed away, but it still has a bite. The mountains in the distance are snow-capped; the air smells of ice and snow and earth and wind.

It feels weird to be on my own. To not have her next to me. Weird is a bit of a crap word to describe how I feel. It's kind of like that moment when your front door slams and you realise you've left your key and mobile inside. That's how it feels every time I remember what I've done. For a second, I imagine the moment she found out. She would have covered her mouth with her hand, rubbed the back of her dark hair. Her eyes would have been wide with shock, with worry, with confusion, with unadulterated anger, because there is no way to lighten this. She will be furious with me. I can feel the guilt of what I've done to her banging at the edge of my consciousness, not a light gentle tap, more like a fist on a metal shutter.

I cross the road. Follow it away from the station. Leaving the small shop with Easter-yellow bunting, chocolate bunnies and

Easter bonnets, piled high in the window behind. I adjust my strap again. I have to do this. I have no other choice. Not if she's going to be able to live the life she deserves.

She will try to find me. I know she will. My brother will try to find me, too. No matter what has passed between us. But before they do... before I can return to my life, to Liv, I need to find out why he did it.

And there is only one man who has the answers.

9

SIX DAYS BEFORE HE LEFT ME

In between glances towards the boys sparring, there is a swell of guilt, as I begin to dig around in his social media. The woman I was would never have done this, snooped around his private messages, but I force the feeling aside. I have to find out what happened to him.

I begin shuffling through Kit's Instagram feed, all so easily accessible; photos I've looked at before taking on a different filter. Now I can see it through the eyes of a woman who knows more than she did then. Words and phrases flutter in front of me in bold, in different colours, singed at the edges, sparks of fire in the spaces between words.

What are you hiding, Kit?

I scour through the images. The most recent photos are of us, our weekend trips out: getting up early, driving to a beach, going on a hike or a bike ride.

God, we were sickening.

I click on an image of us taken last week. We'd taken the sleeper train to Scotland, walked for hours that day. Kit had a business meeting with a potential client on the Saturday morning, but the rest of the weekend was ours. We'd gone to Loch Killin, in the Highlands. The day was swollen with rain, but we'd made the most of it, pulling on our wetsuits and wading into the freezing water. The photo is of us after our swim, a small fire built as we huddled around it in thick blankets, a hip flask of whisky in my hand, Kit pouring coffee from our camping kettle, the sun setting behind us. A couple walking their husky had taken the photo. The orange glow of the fire was reflected in our eyes.

Did he know then what he was about to do? I look over at him. His eyes meet mine and, for a brief moment, I wonder if he can read everything I'm thinking, but then he flashes me his smile before returning his attention to James, who sidesteps a wild jab.

I lean towards the photo. I had always thought there was nothing about the days before he left that would have indicated that something so huge to even contemplate was about to happen. But maybe it was a massive signal. A sepia-coloured, too-perfect-to-be-true day, which could have had flashing neon signs above our heads reading: *he's about to leave you!*

I open my A4 notebook. In it are notes for my lessons. Highlighted is a paragraph about triangles that I needed to read up on before I taught it. Maths, forever the thorn in my side, even now after teaching for years. I click my pen, firing another glance at Kit before writing down the names of every single person who has commented. It takes a while, Kit had a strong following on there, built up by his adventure posts and by his computing ability. Dream day job meets dream weekend life.

I analyse the comments, adding them against names I don't recognise, questioning if they're really who they say they are.

When James and I had waded through these after he disappeared, the playing field was different. The game had rules we knew: Kit had gone on a hike; he'd gone to a place he went often;

we suspected he was hurt, badly; we tried to deny that he was dead. And so we, the players in this never-ending metaphor, were different, too. We both had different goals. We were trying to find any kind of clue that Kit had got lost, that he may be trying to contact us if his phone was damaged. We waited for updates. We hoped for a picture of him battered and bruised but with a tired smile saying: 'It was a rough one, but I'm fine. Can't wait to get home.'

My eyes continue flicking up towards them. Kit is laughing at something James has said. James takes the moment's pause to land a jab to his stomach. James's eyes are alight, as he avoids Kit's blows. Kit's punches are calculated. There is a game plan, which makes him a good sparring partner. I remember James telling me this when we were painting over the nicotine brown colour that is currently still washed over the bricks.

'That's what made him so good to train with, trying to find a tell, a tick, that would let me predict his next move. I never found one.'

Turns out neither of us did.

I bring my focus back to the screen, my attention so very different from before. Now I'm looking for clues about what happened. What is going on with Kit, right now, that would make him leave us?

My hand hovers over the mouse pad, clicking on his Facebook account. It's not as active as his Instagram, but I soon find myself clicking on the Messenger symbol. Most messages are from me, or James, a few from Jack and Callum, one group chat about his old school friend, Ryan's stag trip in Ibiza next spring that he never went to. Messages I read after he went missing. My finger scrolls quickly until I see a message I don't recognise. It came this morning. I do a quick calculation; it would have been while I was at the shop. It's a woman: Rebecca Bevitt. The name sounds familiar but the reason is hidden from me, just out of grasp. Her profile picture is of a golden retriever. The message reads:

I need more time.

I scroll up to Kit's original message:

You in?

My heart is beating so loudly in my ears that I can barely hear the sounds of the room. I quickly click on her profile. There is nothing there – no posts, no images other than her profile picture.

I look back at the boys. Kit must feel the way I'm staring at him. He takes his focus away from James. Noticing this, James takes advantage and lands a sly upper cut.

'Shit!' Kit says, making a time-out signal with his hands. I exit the app as Kit pulls his mouth guard out and ducks under the ropes. I quickly scribble her name down before closing my notebook. I grab a water bottle and walk over, passing it to him. 'Lucky shot,' he explains with a grin.

'I'll get some ice,' I say.

'No need.' He leans in, kissing me. His lips are warm; I can taste the salt from his sweat. The familiarity of it pulsates along my bottom lip. My finger touches it, so normal, so abnormal. 'It was just a cheap shot.' He raises his voice as if to prove his point to James. 'It'll hardly mark.'

I feel my face reacting to this, a frown almost. Had he always put James down this much? Had I just not noticed? Or was it banter as I'd always presumed?

James shakes his head in response, one hand making notes, the other holding his bottle to his mouth. I recognise the ease of his ability to multitask – often with one hand stirring a tomato sauce, the other ticking off things from a to-do list. James loves a list. He glances up at me as though my stare is prodding him on the shoulder and looks away just as fast, as though I've just flashed him my boobs – which I do on occasion, especially if he's on a Zoom call and I'm out of camera shot. The tips of his ears redden and his words would get all jumbled up.

I pull my gaze away and quickly return my attention to Kit.

Who is Rebecca Bevitt? And what does she need more time for? The words are fizzing on my tongue.

'Who's Rebecca Bevitt?' I ask. My voice is solid, somehow calcified with the pressure of his answer, the answer that may shatter and turn everything I know about Kit to dust. He smiles, but it's like seeing the expression in reverse. The edges are tight, his eyes looking up to the grimy window, examining the water bottle.

'She's a client,' he says easily, adjusting the cuff of his glove. 'She wants me to design a website for her company. Why?'

I think fast. 'A message popped up on your laptop. What's her company?' I ask as he begins to take off his gloves with his teeth. I reach over and unfasten the Velcro for him, yanking them off.

'Huh?' he asks, picking up the water bottle, lifting it back to his lips.

'Her company? What is it she does?'

He crushes the plastic. 'Upcycling I think.'

My attention is drawn to James, like I'm bluetoothed to him. I want to tell him about Rebecca Bevitt, ask him if he thinks Kit is lying, listen to his theories. This is what we did after Kit went – we looked for clues; we told each other every little lead that would help us get closer to finding him. But James is outside of the ring, his back to us, the black phoenix curving towards his ribcage; he's still taking down notes on their fight. Back then, *now*, it used to irritate me, this need to show that he took boxing more seriously than Kit, but the truth was, he did. I don't think either of us gave James the recognition he deserved for the hours he put in, for his determination. All of that was wasted when Kit left, his need to fight physically replaced by his need to fight to find his brother.

'It might swell,' I say pulling away as he tries to wrap his arms around me.

Rebecca. You in? I need more time.

'I'll be back in five.'

'Where are you going?' He grabs my hand, pulling me back.

'To get ice?' I say, extracting myself.

His lip twitches like he's on the verge of laughing. 'Where from?'

'Huh?'

'Ice? Where are you getting ice from?'

Oh yeah. I've forgotten this place didn't have a freezer, just a larder fridge that stank of onion and feet.

'Tesco Express down the road.'

'Can you grab me a can of Coke while you're there?'

'Sure. James?' He looks up, startled. 'Need anything from the shop?' I ask, giving him my most relaxed smile. Nothing to see here. I don't know your orgasm face. I've never told you I love you. You have never made me feel like I'm home. Nope. Not at all. I'm just your brother's girlfriend off to the shops for a can of Coke.

'No, I'm good... thanks.'

'Sure I can't tempt you with a packet of Revels?'

Last week we'd shared a family packet and he'd identified twenty out of thirty-seven Revels in the packet before biting down. I'd had a meagre score of eleven. *I didn't have any Maltesers; you rigged the game. Mine were all coffee and toffee.* We played again the next day. He'd filled my bag with all Maltesers so I'd win. But it wasn't the winning, it was the thought that went into the prank. He says, *said*, making me laugh was worth any amount of chocolate sorting. We'd kissed then, both tasting like chocolate.

James repeats, 'I'm good.'

'Okey dokes. I'll be… well, I'll be off then.' James ignores me.

By the time I get back, the boys have finished. I pass Kit some ice wrapped up in a jiffy cloth and throw James a bag of Revels, which he catches with a look of confusion. I return to my things as nonchalantly as I can, my fingers reaching for the laptop.

Kit doesn't look my way. James is throwing him Revels, which Kit is trying to catch with an open mouth, while still holding the ice against his eye. I click open FB messenger, but the message from Rebecca won't open. Kit isn't paying me any attention. The Revel throwing has stopped and he's talking over his shoulder to James as they pack up. My turquoise nail slides across the mouse pad, clicking on her profile, but the message thread has gone.

10

ONE DAY AFTER I LEFT HER

I glance to the sky. The place is about an hour and a half's walk away and the delay has put me behind time. I need to get moving if I'm going to get there before it goes dark. And believe me, you don't know dark unless you've seen it here. It's properly different to dark back home. In the Highlands, it feels like light has never existed at all.

I cross the small road. Follow the dirt track that leads further away from the small village. The incline is as steep as hell.

An hour later and I turn on my head torch. My fingers are fumbling inside my gloves as I shake out the map again. I hold it tight, propping it against the disused hut beside me. It's broken and consists of corrugated steel with sharp edges. A discarded bike is just visible inside. Christ. Is that sleet or ice being shot into my eyeballs? I wipe my eyes, trying to clear the view. I look back at the map and to the pathway, which appears to split into two here. One heads higher up the edge of the hill, the other leading down towards a forest. My fingers twitch, wanting to swipe across Google Maps. I don't have my phone. I doubt there would be any signal anyway.

Liv would be lost. She has – by her own confession – absolutely no sense of direction. I once had to find her in a maze designed for kids. She'd been sitting there next to a little girl with tears in her eyes, an anxious mum arriving at the same time as me. 'See?' Liv had looked up at me. 'I told you there would be a hero to rescue us and look, we've got two!'

I check my position again. There is a crag to my left, splitting the vast wilderness apart. The sky is darkening, spreading. Like a bruise.

I fold the map away. Two more miles and I should see it. I push on, head down, taking the path leading me further into the hills, boots rhythmic, the sound only punctuated by my breath.

The terrain becomes less craggy. I stop for a moment, drinking from my water bottle as the farmhouse comes into view. Thank fuck for that. It's downhill from where I'm standing. There is a smaller building higher up, set back behind it.

The first time I had seen it, I had thought that from this far away the farm had looked like toys that had been carefully placed by a child: the fences, and the sheep, and the tractor – hell, even the shed looked purposefully placed. The house, though, looked as though it had fallen from the child's pocket and landed further away. The whole building was crooked. Like it had been trodden on. My new home for the time being. Crooked. I let out a sound, one note through my nose, and shake my head, twisting the top back on the bottle.

The sleet has turned into snow and the glow from the farmhouse windows is a welcome sight. I imagine a sheepdog lying beside the fireplace. A pot of stew bubbling away on the Aga. My stomach tightens at the thought. The last thing I ate was something that claimed to be an egg mayonnaise sandwich but that was God knows how many hours ago.

I push on through the final stages of the hike until I reach the small rusting gate, the wind smashing against my body. I close it behind me. Follow the path to the door. I take a deep breath, steady my nerves, and rap firmly on the blue wood. The door is pulled roughly open. A monstrously large brown wolfhound barks at me, practically foaming at the mouth. A well-seasoned man with holes in his jumper, thick grey hair splintered with black, squints at me.

'Aye?' he asks, looking me up and down. His voice is barely a voice at all. More of a wheeze and a growl mixed up in one. 'Lost are you?'

I take in this man. I'm not sure what I was expecting. Recognition, perhaps?

'No,' I say, clearing my throat, pushing back the emotion hot on the heels of exhaustion. 'Not lost.' My own voice is scratchy and I realise that I've not spoken to anyone since I left. 'I'm renting Black Water Cottage?'

'Oh.' He pauses looking me up and down. 'Och, you'll be wanting the key then I expect. Down, Caesar, you bloody great arsehole.' The dog is pulled to attention and released, almost knocking me over with its giant brown tail. The man starts to shuffle backwards. 'Well? You coming in or you want to stand out in the cold?'

I shuffle through the door, closing it behind. Around me are things. Lots and lots of things: boots, bottles, rugs, apothecary bottles, jars, dried flowers, mounted stags, stuffed owls, stuffed hawks, shells, candles, bookcases, tables, chairs, lamps, all thrown together in a strange yet oddly comforting way. There seems to be no reason to the way things are displayed. There is a toilet brush next to the stone fireplace. A cushion on the floor next to me beside the welcome mat.

No photos I notice.

'Cheers. It's brisk out there.'

He practically scoffs at that. I guess this is one of the milder evenings by his standards. 'A writer, are you?' he asks, the dog circling my legs, his weight almost knocking me off my feet.

'A writer?' I ask. Confused.

'That's why you'll be wanting the cottage?' he prompts, like I'm hard of hearing. He has no idea who I am.

Good.

That suits me just fine.

'Oh.' I consider this. It's as good an alibi as any. 'Yes. How did you guess?'

'Most who come and stay think they'll be inspired by the great outdoors. Especially after that *Outlander* series. Time-travelling Scots? What a load of...' He hesitates. 'You're not writing about time travel and all that malarkey are you?'

It takes me a moment to interpret his accent.

'No. No. Horror.' He raises his bushy eyebrows at me. 'Zombies,' I add for good measure.

'Aye, well, you'll have plenty of quiet round here for your zombies. The southern softies don't use it till the summer, an' even then they do nothing but complain. Where you from?' He narrows his eyes. I take off my hat. The heat hitting my skin fiercely after the cold outside.

I don't want to give him any sign of the truth. There is a half-eaten Yorkie bar on the sofa.

'York,' I lie. The man's eyes follow my line of sight. If he guesses my ruse he disregards it.

'Right then, York,' he says, a slight tilt to his voice as his says it – almost is if there is a subtitle running beneath the words: *I know you aren't telling the truth but your business is your own.* 'I'm Mac.'

I know.

'This here is Caesar.'

He passes me a large key, like something more suited to

locking dungeons. 'There's more wood in the back. But you've got some in there ready for tonight. Best get the fire going as soon as you get in. It might be spring where you come from but it isnae spring here yet.'

I hesitate at the door, words forming and fading. He looks at me, waiting for me to move.

'Thanks.' He nods, and I walk through the door.

'York, you say?' he asks.

'Funny accent to have coming from York,' he fires through narrowed yet amused eyes. I'm about to say I've only just moved there but the door had already closed behind me, the orange glow and warmth swallowed back inside. I exit the path, slamming the gate. The hills are barely visible now, dark purple shadows looking on while the wind surges. The cottage looks to be about another five minutes up another steep incline.

I approach, taking in my new home. The black slate roof is dipping in the middle. There is one chimney, and a gate, and two small windows upstairs. One downstairs.

I can barely feel my fingers as I slip the key in and turn. Nothing happens at first and it takes some force. I put my weight behind it until it budges. Resentfully, it lets me in.

I flick the switch beside the door and the light above flickers on, with it, a hum. The room I'm standing in is small. The wind blowing out the navy curtains. There is an open fireplace at one end, a bookshelf on the opposite wall and a sofa – the colour of which is... undecided. Grey? Purple possibly? The floor is carpeted, but as I walk through the room, I can feel the uneven slabs that lie beneath.

I shove open the door. It drags along the carpet to the kitchen. My first thought is Liv would love this. And she would. Right now I'd do anything to be back with her. Her body leaning back against mine, just doing something normal like watching the news, or ordering in.

The light in here is also flickering, and for a moment I worry that for all of my efforts, I'm going to end up dying here. Alone. Cause of death? Dodgy-as-fuck electrics.

The ceiling is low, the cupboards are plain, but there is a decent sized table and chairs at one end, facing a stable door. I'd bet it's quite a view from there in the daylight. There is an Aga like Granny Palmer used to have. She was blind in one eye and used to wear a patch. We would often pretend she was a pirate. 'Hand me your gold, you blaggard!' I'd say to my brother. The thought of him sobers me and a shiver brings my thoughts back to the task at hand. I have a vague memory of helping her light it, but I'd better google that one before I make an attempt.

Christ, it's freezing in here.

I head back into the lounge. Get on my knees and twist some of the newspaper beside the fire into branch-like shapes. I add a few sticks of kindling from the basket on the hearth. My fingers are shaking as I try to light the fire. It takes me more than ten minutes until the blue flame begins to flicker. I wait for it to take hold then add a few lumps of coal.

I walk back through the kitchen, opening the door on the same wall as the Aga, and climb the stairs. Every step creaks with my weight, but despite the groans and complaints, the staircase feels sturdy beneath my boots. There are two rooms at the top of the stairs. To my left a small bedroom, consisting of a wardrobe, a bed, and a chest of drawers. To the right, a bathroom with an avocado green bath, toilet and sink. Liv would not be a fan of the bathroom. For a second it feels like she is here, that she is about to lean her head on my shoulder: *Well it's not the claw-footed bath of my dreams but I do like avocado.* Her imaginary voice makes me feel light for a second but then the heaviness of my actions replaces that feeling. I pull myself together, turn off the lights and return to the lounge.

The fire has taken hold now, so I add more coal and a log. Opening my backpack, I take out two tins of Big Soup. *Why don't they just call it stew?* Liv would say. I drain the last of my water, so cold it puts my teeth on edge.

I dig out the second-hand iPad I picked up on the way here, and turn it on, hoping there is some kind of Wi-Fi here.

The wheel of connectivity spins, and spins, and spins. My eyes are already heavy. After five tries, I give up. I have plenty of coal and logs. I'll sleep in here tonight; then tomorrow, I'll get supplies.

11

SIX DAYS BEFORE HE LEFT ME

Kit's hand skates up and down my arm while we watch TV, and my eyes begin to grow heavy.

The evening is passing by quickly. We eat pizza and I try to search for Rebecca Bevitt on my phone but nothing comes up. We watch the latest episode of *The Night Manager*. I tell him he looks like Tom Hiddleston. He laughs and says maybe when he's older. Tears prick my eyes, a reflex to the years where I accepted his death, accepted that he would never age and would remain forever young in our minds. I picture the man in the distance on the morning of my wedding. That man didn't have the brown curls that are currently resting on my chest. I try to picture an older version of Kit but I can't. Instead, I try to recall this evening from the depths of my memory but it's still just out of my grasp, as is the name Rebecca Bevitt. I can feel the answers to Kit's disappearance rubbing at my skin, like a blister after a long walk.

More disconcerting is how normal Kit is being. He still swipes the last piece of pizza and splits it in half with me; he still adds a running commentary during an eighties film that follows *The Night Manager*, because neither of us can be bothered to change the channel. He adds his own voices as funny anecdotes: 'Of course I could just tell you the truth, but then there'd be no plot to this film.'

I reply, 'And then how would I be able to simper at your smouldering eyes?'

I'm trying to concentrate on the film, but my thoughts are spiralling. This all feels so normal but what I'm going through is anything but. Will I still be here tomorrow? Maybe I will wake up and relive the day over and over again like Bill Murray. I glance at Kit. Can I stop him leaving?

'Bed?' Kit asks, catching me yawning for the seventh time. I want to say no. I want to say I'm too scared. Because if I fall asleep, I might be back in the Grange Hotel, without the answers I need. Without Kit, questioning if James has lied to me.

Kit gets up, walks over to the window and peeks out. He spins around, a glint in his eyes.

'What?'

'It's snowing.' His eyes are alight. I feel that familiar but distant recollection of how it feels to be with Kit. Everything has potential; everything has the chance to be something magnificent.

Now I remember. It snowed tonight. Winter's last rebellion against the coming spring. By the time we got up the next morning it had all turned to slush. I join him at the window. There are four inches at least covering the ground. It's coming down in great feathers of white, drifting past the orange glow of the street lights.

'Let's go,' Kit says, a wide grin across his face.

I have a flicker of memory, this night coming back, soft and slightly out of focus. I had said I was too tired; I had been asleep on the sofa when he'd noticed it snowing. But that was last time. I don't know how many last times with Kit I will have.

Half an hour later and we're running down the bank on to the field at the back of our estate. In the summer, this field is filled with families and picnics, with teens playing football with goals made of discarded T-shirts. But tonight, there is only us. His hand in mine, our laughter echoing in the muted silence that snow brings.

Kit dashes ahead, no hat, his hair already curling and glistening under the full moon.

He releases my hand and cartwheels. I stand back, taking this moment in, watching the way he moves, the whoops coming from his mouth, so effortless despite the snow.

'Come on, Liv!' he shouts, doing another cartwheel. I try to bottle this memory of him, to capture that energy that he always had around him, the pure joy in making the most out of every opportunity.

I laugh, a bubble escaping me and tumbling towards him. I follow him, letting my nimble body cartwheel in the snow, my gloves sinking into the ground, the world turning over and over in whites, greys and blues. I lose my balance after the second turn and land softly next to Kit, snow angel-ing beside him.

He gets up, stands over me, snow on his eyelashes, in his hair. He opens his mouth, letting the flakes fall into it before looking down at me with a hand outstretched.

'Come on,' he says, nodding towards the bank. It's not high, certainly by Kit's standards, but Kit always wanted to go higher, always strove for more than solid ground. I feel that familiar rush, the fear cool and still beneath my skin: try everything, taste everything, *just jump.*

He grabs my hands and pulls me up. My face is cold, my skin tight, but I'm grinning, happy, thoughts of Rebecca Bevitt, of searching the hills of Pembrokeshire, of police tape all fading as if they too are muted by the snow.

He holds my hand tightly in his, glove to glove, as we head up the hill. Once at the top Kit turns me around in his arms, his lips on mine, and just for now, just for this moment, I push thoughts of James away, letting myself be consumed by my love for Kit. When I open my eyes, he's looking at me with so much love that I hold my breath.

Why do you leave me, Kit?

He lets go of my hand and peers down over the edge of the hill. In the summer, this peak is a haven for BMX riders – small jumps over the bump, wheels careering down the grass.

I can read his mind; it's in the raise of his eyebrows, the challenge. Kit grins, takes four, five, six large steps back and then runs past me with a rush of air and energy, jumping off the end. He scissor-splits in the air, landing on the snow neatly. He marks his landing site with a line in the snow and runs back up, his cheeks red, eyes sparking.

I feel myself responding, that need to impress him, to show him I'm not afraid.

This was always the way with me and Kit; why I fell in love with him. I'd spent my life being afraid that something bad was going to happen, spent my life being afraid of the dangers of the world, of sinister men hiding in the shadows. Kit showed me how to be fearless.

I take more steps back than Kit, rub my hands together in challenge. He bends over, hands on his knees encouraging me. 'You ready?'

'I was born ready, baby,' I say, clapping my hands. He laughs, straightens as I ground my weight, sinking pressure down from my thighs into my knees. I run past him. It's only a small jump, nothing in the vicinity of the jumps we make when we ski, or when we cliff jump. This is child's play to us.

I land softly, just past Kit's mark.

I look up to him, performing a little bow. He doesn't wait for me to return. I see him stepping back, see him propel himself further with more vigour, determined to beat my mark. He over-shoots though, lands with a skid and falls onto his bum, then immediately checks his landing point, throwing his hands up. 'I am victorious!' he shouts flopping backwards, his arms still raised in victory.

I bend over and gather snow into my arms, running over to him.

'And to the victor go the spoils!' I dump the snow over him. He's taken by surprise and begins coughing through the laughter. I straddle him, his arms circling my neck and pulling me closer. His nose is red, and his face is wet, but he's high on the rush of jumping, of being taken by surprise.

I'm about to kiss him when in one swift move he rolls me onto my back. My hat has fallen off, the bite of the snow at the nape of my neck, sinking into the back of my scalp, but I'm not cold. The heat from Kit's body keeps me warm.

'I love you,' he says. He's breathless, his hand reaching towards the zip of my jacket. His eyes are glinting when I feel the hit of snow that he's just shoved under my vest. I give a yelp and we wrestle about, until he's back on top of me, my hands held above my head, our mouths meeting hungrily despite the cold.

We bundle ourselves through the door, both of us giggling as though we're drunk. I hush him and point to next door where the power pair are no doubt asleep in their duvet with sharp creases and designer water bottles beside their beds.

We shake off our coats. It's as though the last seven years didn't happen. I join Kit in the kitchen as he spoons instant hot chocolate into mugs adding a large pinch of chilli powder.

I sit down at the small table, drinking in his movements, the sight of him, letting the loss of him simmer beneath the surface of my skin. I look up at the clock, my pulse quickening. What will happen when it turns midnight? Will I suddenly be transported to the Grange Hotel, to my life with James, to my life where the man I'm about to marry may have betrayed me, lied to me for all of our relationship?

Kit opens the fridge door and squirts aerosol cream into his mouth.

'That's disgusting, you know,' I say.

'What?' he asks, mouth still full, cream oozing down the sides. 'Open,' he commands giving the can a shake and walking towards me in a challenge.

'No,' I say but he's tilting my head back with his free hand. He swallows the cream. 'Open,' he repeats. I go to say no again but he blasts my mouth full of cream as I go to speak.

'See?' he says grinning. I swallow and shake my head at him. He hums as he squirts the cream onto the top of the mugs and reaches for his phone. The moment stills. The answers I'm looking for expand into the room, a heaviness descending as I watch him. His face is full of concentration. He taps, glances over his shoulder at me with a smile and swipes the screen closed.

Rebecca Bevitt. *You in*?

The freedom and happiness I was feeling evaporates with the snow on our clothes.

He joins me and blows over the rim of his drink.

'Kit,' I say, my eyes glancing to the clock: 11.45. 'Is there something going on that you're not telling me?'

He glances up from his drink, his eyes sharp. 'No, why?'

I reach across the table and take his hand in mine. 'You can tell me, Kit. Are you in some kind of trouble?'

A cloud passes across his features. It's there for a split second before vanishing beneath an easy smile and a confused expression.

'Why would you think that?' He tilts his head as though I'm talking utter nonsense.

I take a deep breath. 'Are you going to leave me, Kit?'

I analyse every movement, every muscle, the way he looks hurt at the question, the sound of his voice as he asks me why I would ever think that, the way he rushes to my side, the way he kneels down and takes my hand in his, the sincerity in his voice.

'I will never leave you – how could you think that? You know how much I love you. What's this about?' he asks, still kneeling, still holding my hand.

'Who is Rebecca Bevitt?'

His eyebrows crease. 'I told you, a client.'

'You're lying to me, Kit. I know something is going on. Please, just tell me.'

He holds my hand tightly, looks down as his thumb runs across my knuckles. I wait. I look at the clock: 11.56.

'There is nothing going on. Rebecca is a client. That's all.'

'What if I told you I know you're going to leave me, that in a week's time you will go and never come back?'

'I'd say you've lost your marbles. I will *never* leave you.'

Tears swell, pain in my chest, heat and fire simmering beneath my ribcage.

He's telling me the truth. Right now, the week before he does leave me, he isn't planning to. Which means something is about to happen to him that forces him to leave. I have to stop him.

'Can you promise me something? Can you promise me that if something happens, if you're in trouble...' He opens his mouth to interrupt to tell me that I have nothing to worry about but I rush on as the minute hand clicks towards midnight. 'Promise that you'll ask for my help. No matter what it is, no matter however much you think you need to hide something from me, promise that you'll come to me for help.'

He shakes his head, a ready smile already slipping across his mouth. I take his face, hold it fiercely in my hands.

'Promise me, Kit.'

He takes a beat then nods. 'I promise.'

I nod. I can help him.

Midnight comes.

I'm still here.

I can fix this.

We finish our drinks, we brush our teeth, we wash our faces. Kit checks all the locks twice. I climb into bed. He turns off the lights, and gets into bed facing me.

'Hey,' I say softly.

'Hey,' he replies, his hands on my waist, travelling upwards. My body is trapped between, tensing up and then relaxing into his touch.

'Do you mind if we... don't?' His hand stills. 'I'm just tired, that's all,' I say.

'Sure.' He pulls me onto his chest, arms wrapped around me, his breathing slowing until I can feel he's asleep. It feels as though I'm both inside and outside of my body, both here and away at the same time.

I fight against the pull of sleep, focusing on him, his smell, his touch. I stay there as long as I can because I don't know what will happen if I fall asleep. I don't know if I'm about to lose him again or if I'm going to find him.

James's face flashes behind my closed eyes, my heart tripping.

I imagine walking along our street, each light behind closed doors turning off as I pass by until I'm standing outside our house. I look up to our lounge window, blue light from the TV pulsing brightly and dimming with the beats of the storyline. I open the front door, walk into the lounge. He's wearing his glasses. He looks up, a smile. *You're home,* he says and I lie down with my head in his lap, his fingers running through my hair. Can he sense it? Can he sense that I'm here in this timeline? Can he feel the loss of me?

As my eyes begin to grow heavy, the absence of him aches like a phantom limb.

12

FIVE DAYS BEFORE HE LEFT ME

I'm disorientated when I wake. Everything feels wrong and right at the same time. Birds are singing outside. The bed feels different. My thoughts are twisting and dancing: my wedding dress, the necklace, James, Kit, snow.

I will never leave you.

My eyes flash open; the room swims into focus.

Kit.

He's alive; he's here. I'm still here. I can save him.

I reach for my phone. Today's date: Sunday 20th March.

So this is it. I'm actually going to spend another day in the past. I have another day to find out the truth.

I'm on my side; he's facing me. I devour the feeling of him next to me, the warmth of his body, the smell of him, the freckles on his right cheek that, if I were to join them up, would make a tick. I used to say it was like my own personal check mark. Here he is. He's the right answer; he's the one for me. I shuffle forward. Kit's fast asleep and yet his arm reaches for me, hooking over my waist. It fits perfectly in the narrow curve, his finger resting gently on my hip bone. I'm naked beneath the sheets. I must have taken off my clothes in the night. We never used to wear pyjamas; we had an insatiable need to be skin to skin.

My eyes follow the line of his shoulders, freckled, tanned, toned, the shape of the top of his arm just visible above the duvet; the light hairs along them, so much lighter than James's.

James.

Did he lie? I want to push thoughts of him away but they persist, pushing against an invisible barrier, because even though the necklace being in his pocket points towards him knowing Kit is alive, the thought feels wrong. It goes against everything I know about the man I'm about to marry. James has always been so solid, so straight, so safe. But maybe I'm just resisting the truth and James has known this whole time. I *want* to resist the truth, I realise.

I trace the curve of Kit's eyebrow, run my finger gently down the length of his nose. His cheekbones are sharp, his face much more defined and angular than his brother's.

Kit's waking, his mouth curving into a smile, body shifting towards me. It would be so easy to let my body react, for my leg to wrap around him, to feel the weight of him on top of me. But this isn't my life. My real life is me and James. Kit leans forward, eyes opening, glassy and clear; long eyelashes, paler than James's; familiar crinkles at the edges.

A rush of love, of longing. Could I let myself have him? How many times have I thought about his touch? How many times have I wished to have him back for just one day? But that was before I fell in love with James.

'Hey,' he says, his voice husky, softened by sleep.

'Hey.' He runs his hand up over my ribs slowly, a well-practised move, his thumb running over the curve of my breast. My breath catches in my throat.

It would be so easy.

But I can't betray James.

I place my hand on top of his; stopping it going any further. I can't sleep with Kit, but I can get to know him again. I can help him; I can save him.

'Let's go somewhere.'

I move his hand away, bringing it to my mouth, kissing his knuckles. He yawns and pulls our hands to his chest. 'Where do you want to go?'

The answer comes easily. 'Pembrokeshire, the coastal hike you like?'

If I take him there today, maybe he'll go somewhere else on Friday? And if he still goes, and I can see which way he walks, maybe it will mean I can find him, stop him leaving. I lean forwards.

'I was planning to go on Friday.'

My heart is knocking hard against my ribs. So he *is* planning to go, but is he planning to come back?

'Let's go today instead?'

'Today?'

'Yeah. I feel like a good walk. Grab some fish and chips?'

A slow smile passes his face. 'You really want to go?'

'Yeah, I mean, why not?'

'Well I've got work to do for one thing.' His words catch on a yawn.

'It's Sunday; you shouldn't be working.'

'But—'

'I'll drive. You can work on your laptop.'

There must be something in my voice that lets him know how important this is to me.

'I mean... I suppose we could. Sure.'

I sag with relief and lean over him, kissing his head, his cheeks, his nose, his mouth, before pulling back and grinning. He smiles, throwing back the duvet. I watch his body moving away from me. He steps into his boxers, grabs his phone, his fingers already tapping away.

Is he messaging her?

He throws a smile at me over his shoulder. 'I'll make us some breakfast then we'll head off?'

There is nothing suspicious, nothing that would lead me to otherwise believe that he's doing anything other than commenting on social media, perhaps quickly replying to an email.

I reach for my pyjamas from the floor and open the curtains. I look out of the window. Spring has come to put winter back in its place. The sun is high, admonishing the snow with a wag of a finger: you shouldn't be here; it's not your time.

I'm going to change the future. I'm going to see where he walks. I'll watch everything he does and get the answers I need. I'm going to save him.

Then I'll need to choose.

But I push that thought to the back of my mind.

* * *

I sing along to the radio as we travel. It's so easy to fall back into the familiar. As much as Kit loved the thrill of being outside, he took his work seriously. He was never far away from his phone, his laptop. It comes with the territory of being self-employed. I've checked his phone this morning. I hate that I'm snooping around but if I'm going to save him or stop him, then I have to be thorough.

There are no more messages from Rebecca. No more answers or questions.

'And in other news,' the DJ on the radio begins, 'the rumours of Man City midfielder Jack Byrne joining Blackburn Rovers on loan for the season are sounding more and more of a certainty.'

'Huh,' Kit says, turning up the sound. 'Interesting. The whole dynamic of their defence will be different. They'll be in for a good season.'

Kit has always loved sports. As a young child and into his teens, Kit was always on various teams: football, rugby, cricket. When he left for university, he was on a football scholarship, but after a leg injury and operation, he deferred. He doesn't talk about it much, but James told me it was as if the bottom of his world fell out.

He returns his attention to the laptop as I grip the wheel, rolling down the window a touch as we get closer to the coast, the familiar smell of the sea flowing in. I slip the car into a lower gear as we head upwards. Lush green hills surround us, cliffs reaching upwards. The sea soon comes into view: blue, green, vibrant.

The skyline is the same as I remember, only this time the sun is shining. This time, he's here with me. I'm in the car that next week will be abandoned. The roads are so familiar. How many times did James and I return here? Ten? Twenty? I try to reconcile these memories of James, with a man who might have known Kit is alive. The idea pulls at me. I know he had the necklace, but does that really mean he knew Kit was alive? My thoughts twist and turn with the roads.

We drive past a lay-by that we'd had to pull into a few weeks after he disappeared. I'd been driving, but the tears wouldn't stop. James had told me to pull over. I hadn't realised I was crying. He'd gotten out of the car and swapped sides with me. I'd sat in the passenger seat, numb. I remember he'd leant over and pulled the seat belt over me, locking it into place. I barely remember the journey home. I have a vague memory of James walking me back to Mum's, a cup of tea being pressed into my hands; how broken he had looked as he closed the door behind him. The memory is so dark, like the whole day was shrouded. My memories of that time are always devoid of colour, of emotion, just a sense of emptiness, of being hollow. I didn't drive for three years after that.

The lay-by flashes by, the sun dazzling. Kit's voice is singing along to 'Have a Nice Day' by the Stereophonics on the radio. I look up at him, surrounded by sunlight. This is not a man who is about to fake his own death. This is a man high on life, filled with optimism.

I turn my head. The red backpack is sitting on the back seat. The backpack that I last saw damaged by the sea, ripped, torn, his belongings still inside. I push the thought away, my foot pressing onto the brake, shifting gears and slowing down. I indicate right, ready to turn into the car park where this car was left stranded.

He glances up, his eyes glazed from staring at the screen. 'Don't park here.' I turn to him, questioning. 'There's a better one down the road, free. This one gets busy and charges.'

So why did you use this one, Kit?

'Oh, I thought we used this one the last time we came?' I ask, all nonchalance.

'Did we? Huh.' He shrugs his shoulders, closes down his laptop and begins scrolling through his phone.

I click off the indicator and continue down the road, the apparition of this car sitting in the middle of the car park fading away.

'This one,' he says, his focus back on the phone, his eyes narrowed in concentration. I pull into a small car park filled with potholes and two skips in the corner, but it faces the sea.

We get out, and Kit opens the back door, pulling out his back-pack and hitching it on his back as I walk to the edge and look out over the horizon. The cliff face falls beneath us. The sea is calm, the sun catching a ride on the waves, green hills surrounding the coastline.

In the weeks and months that follow, I will be back here. The sea will be hungry, angry, tossing and throwing my emotions around like a game of catch. But today, it is my friend; today it hasn't grabbed Kit's body and pulled it beneath. It hasn't crashed him against the rocks; it isn't hindering the life rescue boats with high waves and strong currents.

He drops my backpack to the ground, standing behind me, arms wrapped around my body, his chin on my shoulder. His hair is fluttering in the wind, tickling the side of my neck.

'I've always loved this view,' he says.

'It's beautiful.'

He laughs and I realise he's looking at me. I roll my eyes, but I can't help the heat rising inside – the way a compliment from Kit always made me feel. Like I'm the only person in the world that he can see.

Why did you go?

'Let's get moving.' He lifts my backpack onto my shoulders, adjusts the straps and takes my hand. 'I thought we'd take the St David's walk? It's about three hours all in?'

'Sure, is that...' I clear my throat. 'Is that where you planned to go on Friday?' I hold my breath.

'Yeah. It's a nice length and there's a good descent down to the caves if you fancy it?'

Of course there would be abseiling; of course there would be caves. This is life with Kit. A hike is never just a hike.

'Lead on, Macduff.'

I say the words, but they come with a puncture wound. The air feels like its escaping my lungs. I said that to Mum just a few days ago as I was about to marry James.

I feel the push and pull between my love of Kit and being with him and the loss of not being with James.

'You OK?' he asks as we start walking. I'm lost in my thoughts, as I follow him, the path narrowing. He's humming, happy, his footing secure and determined. My eyes are drawn to his back-pack, and I think of the pockets that had been torn, the contents saturated: his waterproof trousers, his wallet, his water bottle. All of the things he would need to survive. Even his round tin of travel sweets was in there. The tin had been dented, the contents still inside, the boiled sweets powdered with icing sugar. Kit never went anywhere without them. He'd told me that his mum used to buy them from the petrol station when they were young, told him they'd stop his travel sickness. It was a lie, of course, but Kit always bought the same ones. I'd asked James about them. He said Kit didn't get travel sick, but they were Kit's special sweets. James could make do with a bag of humbugs. He's told me this with indifference, as if this fact alone described his mother's feelings for them both.

The path widens, and Kit takes my hand in his again. His thoughts are somewhere else. The path we are following is popular. We pass dog walkers; we pass joggers. I have walked this route before – not with Kit but with James in the weeks that passed after he left.

'Not that way,' Kit says. I stop in my tracks. He winks and takes my hand. Ahead of us is a tall cliff face, a dead end.

'That's a dead end,' I say looking at the cliff face rising up above us. At the top the greenery is folding over the edge like icing dripping off a cake.

'Oh ye of little faith,' he says grinning. He leads me towards the cliff face, crouches down and lies on his stomach. There is a small break between the rocks, a triangle of light about the size of a toddler. He takes off his backpack and shoves it through the small gap.

'You've got to be kidding!'

He lies on his stomach, and begins shuffling forwards.

'I can't fit through there!'

'Of course you can!' he throws over his shoulder, his eyes alight, adrenaline already making him spark. 'You're half my size. It'll be worth it, I promise. Do you trust me?'

Do I? After everything I know about him now? No, no I don't, but the 2016 version of me trusts him with my life.

'Yes,' I say, the lie swallowed by the wind picking up around us.

13

TWO DAYS AFTER I LEFT HER

I wake. Disorientated. Cold.

It takes me a moment to reconfigure my thoughts.

It takes me a moment to realise that Liv isn't beside me, wrapped around my back, comma-like. To realise that my life, and everything that I had almost taken for granted, no longer exists. Or rather... I no longer exist in it.

It takes me a moment.

It's dark. Stray branches are dragging their gnarled fingers against the window pane. There is a strange tapping sound that I can't quite identify because my body is shivering so much.

I look around for my jacket. It's on the floor; I must have kicked it off last night. It's cold. Cold in a solid way, with no give or flexibility, just hard, stone-like. I pull on my jacket even though right now it's like wrapping myself in frozen bubble wrap. I crouch at the corpse of the fire I'd built last night. Grey ash, grey light, grey mood.

My fingers are shaking too hard to be able to manipulate the matches. I give up and head towards the kitchen. The place is ridiculously quiet. My footsteps the only sound penetrating the silence. My steps sound awkward. Like an overeager laugh from an outsider trying to join in with the popular crowd on the playground. The kitchen light flickers into action. The stovetop kettle is staring at me, challenging. *Come on then, new kid, let's see what you've got.*

I blow into my hands, my own breath echoing the grey light. *OK, you win.* I have no idea how to light the Aga but... I flick on the plug behind the microwave, a reassuring beep and red numbers displaying 00.00. I might not be Aga ready, but I can heat up water in a microwave, thank you very much.

I cup the coffee in my hands and return to the lounge. My fingers are halfway between ice cold and stinging heat as they begin to thaw.

I try not to think about what she's doing right now. Try to block it out. But Liv's face, angry at my betrayal, twists into my chest. We rarely argue, not really. I mean, sure, we bicker – who doesn't? But it's very rare that we argue in the doors-slamming, all picture and no sound type of argument. Liv looks beautiful when she's angry. You know how some people kind of wither when they lose their temper? How they seem to narrow and fold, pinched and tight-faced? Liv is the opposite. She unfolds. Blooms even. It's the freedom of it, I think, the freedom of giving herself wholly to the emotion she is experiencing in that moment. Her eyes widen, and her cheeks flush, and her lips seem to sink into a deeper shade. The same way as when she's turned on. She has every right to be angry. I hope she hates my guts right now. I hate my guts right now.

An hour later, with the fire coaxed back to life, the room is warm enough for me to feel my fingers. I turn to the other reason I am here.

Connor McDonald. Mac.

I have the right place. Now I need to earn his trust if I'm ever going to find out the truth.

I get up from the sofa and walk to the window, watching the dawn approach over the hills.

A squirrel is sprinting along the edge of the silver birch that had been clawing at the window last night. It pauses on its back feet. Small hands perched in front of grey fur as though already clasping an acorn before scaling a tree in front. It hops from branch to branch, disappearing from view.

I go back to the sofa, and try to log onto the Wi-Fi again. I just want to see if she's OK.

There's a knock on the door.

My gut flips. They can't have found me. Not yet. I've left no trace, given no hint of where I was going. Even so, I only pull the curtain back a crack. My whole body tenses. It's Mac.

I pull back the chain, unlocking it. 'Morning,' I say.

'Aye. It is,' Mac replies. He thrusts a plate covered in foil forwards. The unmistakable smell of a fry-up.

'That's… Thank you.' I take the plate, surprised by this generosity. From what I've heard, Connor McDonald is a nasty piece of work. Not the type of man to rock up with a cooked breakfast in his hands.

Mac looks away from me, focusing over my shoulder. 'Figured you'd not been able to light the stove yet?'

'No.' I clear my throat, taking a moment to recentre. 'Not yet.'

'Aye, well, it can be a bit temperamental. Best I show you.'

'That would be great,' I reply, pushing the door further open so he can step into the room.

'Been scribin' already?' He nods to where my closed notebook is sitting on the sofa, a list of everything I know about this man hidden inside. I hold the plate close to my chest while closing the door behind us, drawing the bolt across and turning the key.

His eyebrows draw in.

'There might be bears,' I say in explanation.

Bears? For fuck's sake.

'Bears?' His mouth beneath his beard must be twitching, as the grey whiskers move upwards. 'Well, I didn't see any on my way up, but you never know with bears. There might be one hiding behind that tree, wearing a brown mac and staking out the place through his binoculars. Bears.' He shakes his head, a small chuckle erupting from beneath the coils of beard.

I try not to react to his sarcasm and my own absurdity while clutching the plate against my ribcage. The whiskers twitch again before he turns his back. I follow him into the kitchen, still clenching the plate as I observe this man in front of me. He seems to sense my eyes on him and he turns, nodding towards the plate.

'You gonna eat that or dance with it all morn?'

I land the plate on the table and sit down, peeling off the tin foil. In front of me is an eat-all-you-can-buffet of an English (Scottish?) breakfast. Mac opens a drawer, passing me a knife and fork. I take them and begin slicing into a sausage, clear juices running freely. It's spicy, succulent. All that is missing is brown sauce. I have a flash of Liv, her whacking the bottom of a bottle. She always maintained that it didn't taste the same unless it was out of a glass bottle rather than a squeezy plastic one.

'You need to turn the tank on first, let the oil in,' Mac says, bringing me back. He's crouching down and turning a switch on a grey box to the side of the Aga that I hadn't even noticed.

'Right,' I reply through a mouthful of mushroom as I watch the man I've been warned about. He continues his instructions. I watch him. This man. The man who took a wrecking ball to my life.

'Has this' – I slice into a piece of black pudding – 'always been home?' I ask, hesitantly.

'Aye,' he responds, standing back up and wiping his hands on a cloth hanging from his pocket.

Liar.

'Now that'll keep you warm. Any problems, give me a knock.'

'Thank you, I—' I'm about to reply but he's already striding across the room. The cottage shudders with the slam of the door.

14

FIVE DAYS BEFORE HE LEFT ME

Kit grins at me, then continues his progress through the small nook until all I can see are the soles of his boots. Panic sets in as he disappears. What if, rather than slowing down time, rather than having this gift of this week with him, I've just accelerated everything? What if there's a sheer drop at the other side?

'Kit!' I shout, getting on my knees and combat crawling my way towards him. 'Kit!' I shout again. Shit. I still have my backpack on. I shrug it off and force it through the hole. The bag is pulled forwards, and Kit's face – grinning, excited – peers through.

'Come on! You've got to see this.'

I creep forwards. The space is tight. I can feel the pressure of the rocks weighing down on my body as I shuffle through, my elbows sore, my knees prodding against rocks and pebbles.

I blink as I emerge to see Kit staring out over the sea. The ledge is small, a horseshoe of grass the size of two parking spaces. His hands are outstretched as if welcoming the sky. He smiles at me, then back to the view. I join him, my heart still somewhere in my throat, the veins in my neck pulsing. He puts his arm around me and nods downwards. Below is a small cove, a private beach only accessible by a descent down these rocks or by sea; above us, sheer cliff face. This space is hidden.

We didn't find it.

We didn't search this small outlet, this secret cove.

I look down at the rocks that jut out a few metres in the sea. The cove would have been hard to reach by lifeboat, especially in the weather conditions that followed the week after he disappeared. Did he come here that day? I shake my head; the couple that provided witness statements said they'd seen him attaching a rig, but it wasn't here, it was five miles further up the coast.

Kit looks to the sky, out to the ocean. He's assessing the weather, the tides, the wind strength.

'If we drop now, we should have time. We've got a couple of hours until the tide turns.'

'Have time for what?' I ask, but I recognise the glint in his eyes.

'It's a surprise.' He winks.

I look back out to sea. It's not high tide yet and still the waves lick the rocks below. My eyes travel downwards.

He bends down and begins unravelling his rope.

'Have you done this drop before?' I ask, my voice high.

'Once or twice,' he replies, his focus on the ropes, on his hooks, harnesses.

'You've never said.'

'I haven't? Huh. I thought I'd mentioned it.'

Had he? Maybe he had, but wouldn't I have remembered? Then again, back then – now – Kit was always finding special places, hidden gems. That's what he would say: *I found this hidden gem.*

Kit smiles, hands working the ropes, hair tousled. 'You all right?'

'Yeah,' I say, trying to settle the thoughts battering around me.

We step into our harnesses. Kit sets up the rig, throws down the ropes.

He goes ahead, checking over the side of the cliff then gives the ropes a tug to double-check. I watch the tops of his fingers digging into the rocks, feet finding secure footing. I follow his movements, the harness tight around my chest, the ropes rough but firm in my hands. He's careful, checking his hold on the rock before dropping his feet to the next foothold.

My body is strong enough to keep up with him, but even so, I feel the familiar burn in my thighs.

We begin our descent. I haven't done this since he left, but my body knows what to do. Kit moves quickly, while I take my time, letting my mind focus, recalling all the things I know.

My body wants to continue, but the version of me trapped inside the body of a woman I no longer am stops still. I hear the whoosh of Kit's rope, the sound of his walking boots against the rock, the seagulls, the crash of the waves below. A rash of fear rises up from the soles of my feet to the top of my scalp. This is too fraught, too edged with danger, with risk, with all the things that could go wrong. My feet are firm against the rock face. Kit descends quickly. He bounces out and back in with ease, a look of concentration on his face. He hits the ground, looking up at me with a grin, but I'm frozen to the spot.

'You good?' he shouts up as he unhooks his harness.

'Yeah, just... give me a minute.'

My legs have turned to jelly; they're shaking beneath my clothing. The ropes in my hand feel like they're on fire and, at any moment, I'm going to have to let go.

'Just jump!' he shouts, hand covering his eyes as he looks up at me.

'I... I can't!'

I can't move. My head is spinning.

'Hold on!'

'Funny!' I manage to squeak out. All my memories of Kit's death are crawling over me, the thousand ways he could have died, the images of his body broken, battered by the cliffs as he free-falls, his face withering at the bottom of a crevasse, his mouth gulping down seawater. The images twist and turn.

'It's OK.' Kit is next to me. 'I've got you.' He bounces over so he's next to me. I can feel him unhooking his harness.

'Don't!' I yelp.

'I'm going to clip you to me and we'll do it together, OK? You're fine. You'll be eating fish and chips before you know it.'

We're face to face now, my hand holding tightly to his neck as we begin to descend, Kit talking me through, telling me when to move, as he manipulates the rope.

We land with a gentle thud. Kit unbuckles us and he pulls me into his arms. I've scratched his neck, three lines like he's been Freddy Kruegered.

'I've scratched your neck.' His fingers run over the grooves in his skin. 'It's not the first time you've scratched me and I certainly hope it's not the last.' He's making light, but I can feel his heart pounding against my cheek as he pulls me close.

We're safe; I'm safe: he's still here.

But for how long?

15

FIVE DAYS BEFORE HE LEFT ME

Once I've calmed and the red fear has diluted, Kit leads me across rock pools and pebbles towards what looks like another dead end. He's holding my hand, a smile on his face as I look to the cliff faces towering high above us.

'Ready for my magic trick?' he asks.

I frown, but I can't help but feel that little zing of excitement that being with Kit always held. He takes my other hand, walking backwards. 'Abracadabra,' he says, his voice all exaggerated magic and mayhem.

Just behind him, hidden from view of the sea and the alcove above, is a small entrance to a cave. The opening is about half the size of a normal household door, jagged rocks stacked around it like dominos. Water is only lapping at the entrance, just a caress, the tide nudging rather than consuming the dark slate.

I step forwards into the chamber.

'Wow.'

Inside, sound is distorted, not quite an echo, more an insinuation of sound. Light filters through from the entrance, bouncing off the peaks of the waves and onto the pale grey walls, a continuation of the rhythm of the sea shimmering on the rock's surface. Stalactites fall from the roof.

'Beautiful, right?' Kit says.

My heart is pounding in my chest; the taste of something sour in my throat pushes against the surrounding beauty as a thought careers through me: this is the perfect place to hide. There is no way to get to it by sea, only by the route we've just taken.

I wonder if he could have planned all of this. Parked at a car park so he would be seen, hiked a well-known path so far away from here that we were looking in the wrong place.

The thought feels so ludicrous, that Kit, *my* Kit would concoct such a plan. I look around me. There is so much that could have gone wrong if Kit came here that day. He could have fallen. The tide could have come in too quickly and he could have drowned. There are so many possibilities, and yet... I think about the note, the man in the mist the morning of my wedding, the receipt, and somewhere deep in my bones, I know this place has *something* to do with the night he goes missing.

But if he's planning to hide here, then why show me now? There is only one answer I can think of... he's not planning it at all, at least, not yet.

He climbs up a small ledge, reaching out his hand, helping me up. Above us there are shelves and shelves of small smooth ledges, as though they have been carved specifically like manmade bunkers. I follow his lead towards a narrow alleyway between two shelves. 'You OK to go through?' he asks, checking on me again while I continue to try and take a hold of my thoughts. I'm trying to realign images of that night, picturing him forcing his way through the narrow ledge, not falling to his death five miles from here.

'Yeah,' I reply, my throat tight, packed with all the things I need to ask him. I look at the narrowing walls. I've never suffered with claustrophobia; if anything, I was more afraid of wide open spaces when I was a child, but life with Kit fixed that. Kit showed me how to take risks, how to enjoy everything the world had to offer. 'I'm fine.'

He beams at me. 'Good, because you're going to want to see this.'

We crouch down. Kit passes me a head torch from his bag, the two beams bouncing ahead of us like overexcited puppies, as we follow the path, our bodies ducked to half their height. All the sound inside this tunnel is amplified: our breath, the movement of our clothing against the rock, the scratch of our backpacks against the roof. It takes about ten minutes until light begins to step towards us, until we eventually break free of the tunnel's restraints and out into a cavern. It's huge: high walls, high roof, light splitting the darkness in a solid beam of gold from above. It's like a scene from *The Goonies*. I can imagine a pirate ship stranded in the pool of blue water. There is even a small waterfall, the water hitting the pool with a gentle rush.

'Wow.' The word echoes, a gentle whisper. Kit smiles at my reaction. He's never happier than when he's impressed me. My eyes roam around the cavern, my fingers sliding down the soft walls; the passing of time has moulded the sharp edges into smooth grooves. The stone is lighter here, a mink-grey. My eyes track the surroundings, landing on a smaller pool further up. Water pours in like its being poured from a jug.

'Want to take a dip?' he asks. My whole body is alight with questions.

'Yes.' I'm slightly breathless. 'Yes, I do.'

We undress, pulling on our wetsuits. The sunlight beams down onto the smaller pool and as I step into the water, it's luke-warm through the material. This place is deep within the rocks, the caves above sheltered from the wind, from the outdoors. The light is focused on the pool, warming it so that it feels more like a cold bath than the freezing temperatures that wild swimming brings.

The water comes up to my thigh, as I step in. Kit's wetsuit is unzipped, arms hanging down from his waist, his broad shoulders visible above the water line. I lean back, letting my hair dip. He puts his face in, dunking his head under, erupting back up, shaking the water from his hair.

'How did you find this place?' I ask. My voice feels like it's tipped with diamonds, clear and sharp.

I'm leaning against him, his arms around me, his back against the wall. From this vantage point, it looks like an infinity pool.

'Luck,' he says.

'Really?'

'No.' He laughs. 'I dropped my phone. It bounced through the crack in the rocks, I followed it and it led me here.' We're quiet, both lost in thought. 'It would be a great place to spend a few days hiding out, though, don't you think?' The water suddenly feels cold. 'You know, if you wanted to escape the rat race, be at *one with nature*.' He puts on a hippy voice, joking.

'Why would you want to escape?' I ask quietly, pulse racing.

'Everyone needs to escape at some time in their lives, Liv. We all need space from time to time.'

'But what if something happened down here? Nobody would be able to find you.' Maybe that's what happened. He *was* injured here: hit his head, lost his memory...

'True, but what a place to be stranded, eh?' He kisses the top of my head, but his words keep repeating themselves in my head: *great place to spend a few days hiding out.*

Did Kit purposely come here to hide? And if he did, then what or *who* was he hiding from?

I picture the days that followed. Was he hiding? Did he feel me and James searching for him close by? Did he care?

I wish James was here.

The thought comes into my mind, a yearning for the man I've spent the best part of the past decade with. He would love it in here too.

'Have you ever brought James here?'

'James?' he responds, curious.

'Yeah, I was just thinking he might like it here.'

He's quiet from behind me. 'Maybe,' he responds.

We stay in the pool for a while, letting our bodies relax and recuperate before Kit tells me we need to get back. The waterfall has begun to fill out, the pool now an inch or so higher than before.

I follow Kit's lead back through the tunnel. The sea is filling up the smaller cave, the ledges that were high up now only skirting the water's surface.

We wade through, the sea up to my thighs already. The flicker of panic diluted by Kit guiding me.

As we exit the cave back into the sun, I turn my back, picturing this place, a blank space in my answers around Kit's disappearance now starting to feel secure in my mind.

There is no other way out from this cove other than up. Kit harnesses me.

'You ready? I'll be right with you,' he says smiling and looking deep into my eyes. I nod, feeling that oh so familiar and yet distant feeling of always being safe when I was with him, no matter how high we climbed, no matter how far we fell or jumped or dived. I nod and begin the climb.

16

TWO DAYS AFTER I LEFT HER

The great outdoors. I feel like a cartoon: head down, shopping bags buffeting out behind me, heavy coat, thick hat.

By the time I shoulder-barge my way through the wind and make it to the narrow path leading to the cottage, I feel like I've been battered. Deep-fried. Crispy on the outside, a soggy mess on the inside. I drag myself and my shopping to the cottage, the key rattling in the lock before I'm finally through the door. I lean my back against it. The shopping bags at my feet. My heart feels like it's jack-hammering into my ribcage.

It was just one trip into town, but the loss of Liv and everything I have sacrificed pierces through each second that I'm away from her, through every one-word answer I gave.

New to town?

Yep.

Staying long?

No. A shake of the head and eyes focused on the money in my hand.

Cash.

Not a debit card, actual cash. It really is like I've stepped into the setting of a *Famous Five* book. But without the other four. Famous One... what a sad state of affairs.

The warmth of the cottage is making my cheeks flush. Cold sweat runs down my spine. I unbutton my jacket and sling it on the back of the sofa.

The sun is streaming through the windows in the kitchen as I begin to unpack. I flick on the radio, twisting the dial, an *actual* dial, until I find a station that isn't fizzing, that isn't Easter bunny-hopping onto another station, and begin unpacking the shopping.

* * *

I tread carefully across the paddock. Mac has his back to me and is emptying some kind of fodder into a tin trough. I clear my throat. Mac straightens.

'Thought you could do with an Irish coffee?' I say, offering the mug, with a double shot of whisky inside. Mac's thick eyebrows narrow but then relax.

'Nice of you,' he says, taking a deep swig of his drink. He holds it in his mouth, his eyes widening and his Adam's apple seemingly lodged in his throat before dropping with what looks like great difficulty.

I take a sip of my own drink in case I have accidentally added something I shouldn't have, but it tastes as it should: half-decent coffee, well... as decent as you can get without an espresso machine, whisky that was mid-price, not the cheap stuff, and full-fat milk. Liv would always insist on it: *Life's too short to spend your life drinking half of anything.*

Mac looks into the mug and swirls it around a bit. His gaze flicks from the mug and back again. He seems lost in his own thoughts.

'Feeding the sheep?' I ask.

Mac takes another swig of his drink, swallowing it with difficulty again before placing the mug onto a tree stump with a nod.

'Can I... do you want some help?' I ask.

Beneath the beard, I can see the hint of a smirk.

'I'm not busy. But' – I shrug – 'I guess you have your own...'

'You can take this.' He lands a bag filled with something that looks like the middle of a liquorice allsorts next to me. 'Head up to the second field, past the third gate. Second turning on the left.'

'Second field, second left... third gate. Got it.'

'Aye.' I can see a smile twitching beneath the beard. I find myself questioning if the stories about him are true. Connor McDonald is a liar, of that I'm sure. But, on first impressions, he doesn't strike me as the type of man to destroy someone's life.

So why did he?

'Right.' I shift the bag against my chest and carry it back through the paddock and out toward the second field.

I'm no closer to finding the answers I need, but if feeding sheep is what it takes to get the truth out of him, then feeding sheep is what I'll do.

17

FOUR DAYS BEFORE HE LEFT ME

I wake with a start. A montage of the day before dashing through my mind: the drive, the lay-by, the car park, the hike, the cave.

I know where he goes, I know how he disappears, and yet I still don't know why.

We'd been tired when we got home last night, full of fish and chips, cheeks aching from smiling, thighs pleasingly humming with the warmth of a workout. I'd hung our coats over the banister to dry, thrown our gear into the washing machine ready to turn it on this morning. I'd been too tired last night and couldn't face it. I'd fought sleep again, watched him for as long as I could until I drifted off. I'm quiet as I shift away from him. I need to find out who Rebecca Bevitt is; I need to find the answers before it's too late.

'Don't go,' he mumbles, his nose digging into the back of my neck. I turn my body to face him. He opens one eye, a slow smile on his face as he rolls onto his back. I begin to smile back but then my whole body locks.

The scratch is gone. I reach for his neck, running my finger over the place where I'd drawn blood.

'Your neck,' I say.

'My neck?'

I sit up, turning his head from side to side, examining his skin, but there is nothing there, not a blemish.

'Liv?' he asks, confused.

'Kit, did we go to the beach yesterday?'

'The beach? No, I was working and—'

I throw the sheets off the bed and rush into the kitchen. Pots and pans are scattered around the surfaces, the remains of something that looks like a pasta bake glued to the outsides of a glass Pyrex dish.

'Liv!' he shouts from the bedroom.

I spin around in a circle. Our coats aren't hanging on the banister. I rush back into the kitchen and open the machine. It's empty – no wetsuits, no towels. I hurry down the stairs. Our walking boots aren't covered in sand, and my backpack is in the small cupboard at the foot of the stairs. It's empty: no half-drunk bottle of water, no leftover bar of Snickers.

Yesterday didn't happen.

At least not for him.

We didn't go to the beach, he didn't show me the cave, we didn't go to the bay in Pembrokeshire.

I didn't change anything.

The thought comes into the flat like a wave. It rushes through the open doors, floods through the windows, the doors; I'm drowning in this realisation, my throat tight, my lungs trying to gulp down air.

Memories of yesterday flicker and fade.

My legs carry me to the lounge, hand reaching for the corner of the table to steady myself. I'm shaking as I begin leafing through the books on the table, all tidied away, all with sticky labels and asterisk signs. A small shopping list sits atop a Post-it pad next to the pile of folders, ingredients for playdough for the science lesson I have clearly planned for when I go back to work after the Easter break. Or rather, she had planned – Liv from back then, Liv who spent the day planning, not driving to the coast, not walking inside a cave, not sitting on the beach as the sun set.

I'm alone. Stuck in the past without being able to change a damn thing.

Memories from my childhood creep in. *You can't go out, Liv; it's cloudy. We can't go on the bus, Liv; we can't go to the shop. Can't, can't, can't.*

I can't stop him leaving.

The future has already been written. It's all there in permanent marker. I can't wipe it away; I can't erase any of it. I can't change my future. I can't make him stay.

I sink to the floor, wrap my arms around my knees and hug them, resting my head to the side.

'Liv?' Kit asks from behind me. I look at him over my shoulder. He's standing in his boxers, hair unruly. 'You OK?'

'You're going to leave me,' I say. The words fall out of me in a breath.

'What?' He laughs. 'Why would you say that?'

'Because it's true.' The truth is folding in on itself. He sits down next to me, taking my hands in his.

'I will never leave you,' he says, planting determined kisses on my knuckles. I let out a small noise that finds its way out from the lump in my chest.

'Unless... I mean is there something *you* need to tell me?' he asks, fear in his eyes, like I'm going to tell him something unforgivable.

I laugh then. I laugh at the mess I'm in. Yes, there is someone else. No, there isn't anyone else. Yes. No. Now. Then. Alive. Dead. Missing. Found. My life is like a map without place names. And I don't have a compass. I laugh again. James has a tattoo of a compass on his right bicep. He had it done a year after Kit disappeared. So he could always find his way back, he'd said.

I realise I haven't answered him. Kit's eyes are beginning to lose their shine. 'No,' I lie. 'There's just you.' And your lies. And your brother.

'Come back to bed. Let me make you a cuppa, OK? I haven't got a meeting until later today. We've got time.'

I almost laugh again. No, we don't, Kit; we don't have time.

He gently pulls me up, holds my hand until I'm back in bed.

I lie on my back staring at the ceiling. Then turn and reach for my phone. I type in: 'Is time travel possible?'

The first answer that comes up is 'Yes'. It's on the NASA website.

NASA. It must be true if NASA say so, right?

I shift up and adjust the pillows behind my back. '*Although humans can't hop into a time machine and go back in time, we do know that clocks on airplanes and satellites travel at a different speed than those on Earth.*'

Am I travelling at a different speed? Is this version of me real and I've, what, fast-forwarded to my past then reset? Like a broken alarm clock?

'Tea and toast. Extra peanut butter,' he says with an exaggerated shudder and a smile. He places the breakfast on the bedside cabinet and carries his tea to the other side, climbing in between the sheets. I slip my phone beneath the pillows. 'Come here,' he says pulling me towards him, putting his freezing cold feet against mine. I let out a little yelp.

'Your feet are freezing!'

'Sorry.' He pulls them away but I hunt them out beneath the sheets with my own, warming them.

'So what's this about me leaving you?' he asks.

My breathing has calmed. There is a strange numbness inside my chest now, like I'm floating, watching this all happening from a distance. 'I just... I had a dream and it was so real, Kit.' I turn to him, my hands running back over the place his neck should be marked.

'What happened in the dream?' he asks softly, pulling the palm of my hand to his mouth and kissing it.

'You went for a hike... and you never came back.'

I watch his face closely, looking for a reaction, a hint that would make him realise that I'm on to his plans, but there isn't even a blink. He would beat a lie detector hands down. But then I think back to his reaction the night it snowed. I don't think he knows, in fact, I'm sure of it. He isn't planning to leave me, at least not yet.

A horrible thought comes to me. Maybe I am the *cause* of his disappearance? Maybe all of this is caused by me and my big mouth. *Let's go to Pembrokeshire and find the perfect place to hide, Kit; you go on a hike and never come back.* I chew my bottom lip. No. The scratches have gone. There is nothing that suggests anything I say or do will have an effect on the future. I'm not changing anything. But still, the thought rolls around.

'Well, I have absolutely no plans whatsoever of going on a hike and never coming back. In fact, the only plans I have today involve you and me, this bed and work while you go to your mum's, that is if you haven't tired me out too much.' He plants a kiss on my mouth and sits up, reaching over and biting a piece of toast, his face pulling into disgust. 'Ugh, this is foul.' He swallows with difficulty, reaches for his cup and washes down the toast with his tea.

My mind is spinning plates, trying to keep yesterday's events balancing.

I still don't know who Rebecca Bevitt is. He doesn't know I

know about her. He hasn't deleted his messages because I was never at the boxing club that day. This time I'm not going to ask about her.

The plates keep spinning while I try as hard as I can to recall what happened this day seven years ago, but all of the days merge into each other: mornings, afternoons, breakfast, lunch with Mum, dinners with Kit, shopping trips with Ava.

The plates keep spinning as I sip my tea, as I eat the toast that scrapes and tears at the inside of my throat.

Kit's scrolling through his phone now. I examine every movement he makes, every intake of breath, watching for a sign. Then I see it. It's a flicker, a frown, a glance in my direction then a smile. He closes the screen and brings me closer so I'm lying on his chest. His heart beating quickly, his lies hidden inside.

I'm getting ready to go to Mum's when there's a knock on the door.

'I'll get it!' I say, already heading down the stairs.

James is standing in the doorway. I feel a rush of love, of need. In my mind, I throw my arms around him. *I think I know where he goes,* I say, and his face is full of relief. *Where?* he asks. *I'll show you...* He pulls me under his arm and I'm covered in the warmth of him. But I don't do any of those things, because James is looking at me as he waits for me to say something.

'Hi,' I say. It comes out in a croak and I have to clear my throat. I stand there staring, rolling my hands into fists to stop myself from touching him.

'He in?' His expression is neutral, no smile for me, no look of absolute love and devotion anywhere near his eyes.

'Oh, yes, he's upstairs.' I step away from the door, letting him in. 'Kit!' I shout as James takes the stairs two at a time as though he can't get away from me fast enough.

'I'll see you later!' I shout after him, them.

'Love you!' Kit responds.

'Me too.'

I close the door behind me, and begin walking to Mum's.

I get to the end of the road when it starts to spit with rain. Last time I'd checked the forecast and had an umbrella. I make an about-turn and head back to the flat to grab it, slowing my pacing as I hear James's voice. It's raised, angry. I step closer, pressing my back against the wall like a low-budget spy.

'I mean what the fuck!' James shouts.

'I've got it all under control.' Kit's response. 'It's nothing to worry about.'

'You'd better!' is all James says before he walks out of the door, slamming it behind him. I watch as he strides away, hands through his hair. He stops, turns as if to go back, shakes his head and continues to his car, starting the engine and practically two-wheeling a three-point turn.

James has never told me he argued with Kit just days before he left. He's never uttered a word about it. What has Kit got under control?

I slip my key into the lock, charging up the stairs to confront him. I step into the lounge and he has his head in his hands. Sensing me, he looks up, reforms his expression. 'You OK?' he asks.

'Why were you and James arguing?'

'What?'

'I heard you. I think most of the street could hear you.' I nod to the open window.

'It's nothing, just James being James.'

'What do you need to get under control?'

His face blanches slightly. 'I can't talk about this right now, Liv. I've got a meeting.'

There is a snap to his voice, which he immediately softens on registering my reaction.

'Kit.' I walk forward, taking his hands in mine. 'Tell me what's going on. If you're in some kind of trouble, I can help. You don't have to do this... whatever this is, alone.'

'I'm not in trouble, I promise.' But he doesn't meet my eyes; instead he kisses the top of my head, grabs his things and leaves.

'Kit, wait!' I chase down the stairs after him. 'Just tell me the truth. I know something is going on with you. Please just tell me.'

'I know your dream spooked you, but Liv—' He puts his hands on my shoulders, smiles that smile, eyes glinting. 'There is nothing going on. I love my brother, but you know... he can kind of be a dick. He's overreacting to something Mum said and as always I'm stuck in the middle, trying to make peace.'

'What did she say?'

'It's not my place to say. Now please, stop worrying, OK?' He kisses me on the mouth, leans his forehead against mine. 'I've got to go. Love you.' He kisses me again and closes the door behind him.

I pull up outside the boxing club and walk in. It's strange seeing the place like this, the before, the after. James is going hell for leather against the punch bag in the corner of the room. It's not there any more in our timeline; there are two treadmills in its place. I stride over. He's got his earphones in, loud angry music tsk-tsk-tsking outside the sound of his gloves pounding the bag. His eyes widen when he sees me. He throws another couple of punches before stopping.

'Can we talk?' I ask him.

'What?' he says. I reach over and pull out one of his earphones.

'I said, can we talk?'

'Why?'

I inwardly sigh. I'm reminded of the battle I used to have with James, how hard it was to get a conversation out of him.

'Because I know you're pissed at Kit and I want to know why.'

'It's not your business,' he replies.

He pulls off his gloves and heads over to the skipping area. I hurry after him, old anger resurfacing at 2016 James. He picks up the ropes and unwraps them.

'James!' I say, my voice louder than I intended. Heads turn our way.

'What?'

I lower my voice. 'Look, I'm worried about him. I think something is going on and I need to know what you know.'

He stretches out the skipping ropes, pulling them tightly.

'Why don't you ask him?'

'I did, but he says everything is fine.'

'Look, Liv...' He continues unwrapping the rope. 'I don't know what you want from me. If Kit's got shit going on that he doesn't want to tell you about then it's none of my business. Now if you don't mind, I've got half an hour to train before my double shift at the pub.' He pushes the earphones in, turns his back, and starts to skip.

2016 James is a complete and utter dick, I decide, marching out of the club.

18

THREE DAYS AFTER I LEFT HER

I sit on the bed, looking in the mirror on the inside of the wardrobe: clean jeans, clean navy jumper, bloodshot eyes from that tiny matter of RUINING MY WHOLE LIFE.

I stare at my reflection. At the outfit Liv chose. My stomach hardens. I force myself to exhale, reminding myself that I'm doing this for *her*. I try not to think of my brother, try to ignore his betrayal, but I can't. It's festering away deep inside my core. My hand punches the wall before I've even registered I'm standing, a crack in the plaster splintering like a vein.

My knuckles sting as I knock on Mac's door. He invited me for dinner as payback for feeding the sheep yesterday as he 'dinnae expect folk to work for free'. He'd also told me to pour 'that dram' down the sink as it was 'offensive'. Again, this makes me question if I'm on the right track. Being invited for dinner. Bringing over food parcels. None of this fits with the image of the man who left so much destruction in his wake.

'It's open!' he yells. Caesar bounds towards me, immediately sniffing my crotch. I nudge him away and head towards the familiar sound of Elton John's 'Your Song' coming from the kitchen.

Caesar loses interest, returns to his place by the fire. Mac is at the sink, hands in soapy water. The room is bright, the wall a Lurpak-butter colour. There is an Aga like the one at the cottage, but it's cream. The cupboards are painted dark blue and each one seems to be brimming with contents, not unlike the lounge. The fridge is large. American. It looks out of place with the rest of the room. As he opens it, I can see that it is filled with pies of all shapes and sizes. He catches me looking.

'What? A fella can't bake pies?'

Elton has moved on to 'Bennie and the Jets'. Of all the thoughts I've had about this man, not once did I imagine him baking pies. This is a man who shows no mercy. Not a man who *bakes* and listens to Elton John.

'It's just a lot of pies for one man,' I reason. Caesar yelps from the doorway, making me jump. 'Sorry,' I say over my shoulder. 'One man and his dog.' He sinks down onto his paws but remains in the doorway, eyeing the provisions.

Mac shakes his head, a snort coming from beneath the beard. 'They're not all for me. I sell them at the farmers' market.'

'Right.'

He takes out a pie with high pastry walls and lands it on the table before returning to the freezer section and plonking a large ice cube into a whisky tumbler. He closes the freezer door with his backside. Returns to the counter. He pours two inches into both glasses, passing me the one with the ice.

'Thanks.' His eyes glance towards the grazes on my knuckles but he doesn't comment, instead he pulls out the chair opposite and sits down. I take a sip as he opens a jar of chutney. The whisky is really good, smooth, hints of honey.

Mac nods towards my plate while he takes a bite out of the pie. I take a slice and slide it onto my plate. It's like a quiche but super-powered. The pastry is rich, the insides filled with cheese, with a bite of mustard and something I can't quite place.

'So you sell at the farmers' market... Any other businesses?' I steer the conversation.

'No. This keeps me plenty busy.' I take another sip. 'The writing not going well?' he asks with a glint, wiping his beard with a folded napkin.

'It's fine. I'm getting plenty of thinking time in,' I say in explanation and reach for a slab of ham and a piece of thick bread smothered in butter.

'And?' he asks.

I pause, the bread halfway to my mouth. 'And?'

'What have you been thinking about?'

Liv.

But I don't say that. Instead, I take a mouthful of bread, the butter creamy and salted, and I rack my brains for a response. 'Zombies,' I reply.

'What about them?'

The bread lodges in my throat and I reach for the whisky, taking a large sip.

'How they, um, eat brains and why.'

'Sounds riveting,' he replies.

We both know I'm lying.

'So...' I place the tumbler back on the table. 'Have you always been a farmer?' I ask, all innocence.

He meets my gaze, unwavering. 'Aye.'

I look away first, spearing two rounds of thick circles of tomato onto my plate.

'What brings you here, really?' he asks, my eyes drawn back to his. 'You can't write about' – he looks away first – 'zombies in... York?'

'I can, but you know... a change of scene can help... fill up the creative well.'

Creative well?

'Right.'

I take a mouthful of food.

Mac chews thoughtfully then swallows. 'You know' – he mounds more bread onto his plate – 'I've always wondered why zombies eat brains.'

'What?'

'Zombies? Why do they eat brains?'

'They... need it for their, um, intelligence.'

'Really? Not for the vitamins needed to keep them walking about?'

'No. Mine are clever. Clever zombies.' I finish the food on my plate and knock back the whisky. I'm drinking too quickly. Mac swirls his in his glass as if to make a point. He waits. I wait. He swirls the glass some more. I look down at the plate, the flecks of tomato juice, the ripple on the top of the quiche-pie looks like it's smirking at me.

I heap more salad on my plate to counter the carbs and continue eating. He finishes his glass and gets up. I sit there wondering if this is my cue to leave, but Mac places the bottle on the table and turns to retrieve what looks like bread and butter pudding from the oven. He scoops out a portion and passes me a plate then gets a jug of cream from the fridge.

'I don't like custard,' he explains gesturing to the jug. 'And if you're going to keep knocking back the drinks you'll need more than that bit of salad.' He tops up my glass as I sit here with my head spinning. My life is falling apart amidst a farmhouse, good whisky, and bread and butter pudding.

I straighten. The whisky has taken down my guard and I need to focus.

'How did you end up living here? I mean it's pretty remote,' I probe, shovelling pudding into my mouth. He pauses, a spoonful halfway towards him. He stares at me before leaning over the spoon and chewing slowly. I swallow. 'No properties anywhere else?' I ask, taking another bite.

There is a spark behind his eyes but it's extinguished quickly. 'Mam and Dad died. I inherited. That's about it.' He tilts his head, assessing me. 'So... what really brings *you* here?' he challenges holding my gaze. Neither of us blinks. Elton has finished playing. The burr of the fridge is the only other sound in the room and, for a second, I think he knows.

I think he knows *exactly* who I am.

19

FOUR DAYS BEFORE HE LEFT ME

Kit is asleep on the sofa when I get back.

I'm exhausted from my trip to Mum's. I'd tried to tell her what had happened to me, but the minute she saw how upset I was, when I began to try to explain, her anxiety had already kicked into action. I had backtracked, told her I was hormonal, that I was just tired and then spent the afternoon eating cheese scones while surreptitiously trying to find out something about Rebecca Bevitt, but she is a ghost. I had gradually made my way through the list of names committed to memory, looking for anyone who sounded suspicious – in any way, shape or form – but there was nothing there except a few pictures of Kit with them back in the day, or friends that Kit had made on his travels years ago. There are no more suspicious messages and I can't get into his Gmail account on my phone.

I hesitate next to him. This really doesn't look like someone who has the weight of the world on his shoulders, white shirt open at the collar, deep and peaceful in sleep. I unshoulder my bag and watch him for a moment. His eyes are moving beneath his eyelids, mouth slightly open, freckles in the shape of a tick. I crouch down beside him, feeling the warmth of his breath against my face. I fold my legs beneath me, the stripes of the cheap carpet already making an impression against my skin. I lay my head on the edge of the sofa and close my eyes, as I listen to the sound of him. He shifts, his hand finding its way onto my scalp.

'Hey,' he says, his voice thick with sleep. I smile and turn my head to him. 'You're back early.'

'I missed you,' I reply, looking up at him.

'Come here,' he says.

I climb onto him, laying my head against his chest as he wraps his arms around me. My head lifts and rises with each breath. 'I love you.'

He kisses the top of my head in sleepy acknowledgement. 'How was she?'

'Fine.' I blink back the image of Mum's face, the twisting of her hands, the fear of danger. 'How did the meeting go?'

'Good. They sound like they're going to take me on.'

I turn myself over to kiss him. I let myself be her, the real her from seven years ago, with short hair and clear skin, eyes less tired, body more supple. It's so easy to fall into the rhythm of his kiss. Everything is so familiar: the heat that rushes through me at the taste of him, the way I instinctively know how to kiss him. His hands tighten around me and I feel the pressure of him beneath me. Time falls away as he begins to pull my top off, the knot of questions – the whys and what ifs – all pushed away.

His hand cups my breast, his mouth moving along my collar-bone down towards the edge of my bra. My hands bury themselves into his hair as my back arches, my fingers instinctively reaching for the buckle of his belt.

James.

The moment shatters into pieces, the sound of his name inside my skull like a vase being thrown at the wall.

'Stop,' I say. I pull back.

Kit looks up at me, his eyes somewhere between confused and aroused.

'I... need the loo,' I say.

He flops backwards. 'Talk about ruining the mood,' he says, but he's smiling, safe in the knowledge that he has nothing to worry about. He knows how much I love him.

I climb off, my legs shaking. 'I'll be back in a sec.' Something in my voice, my expression, mustn't ring true because he grabs my hands gently as I move away.

'Is something wrong, Liv?'

I plaster on a calm smile and lean back over him, kissing him gently on the mouth. 'I'm fine. You know how quickly coffee goes through me.'

'You sure?' he asks as I pull my top back on.

I try not to show the thick green of betrayal coating my thoughts. 'Honestly, just my usual weak bladder.'

Did I have a weak bladder back then or did that come later once I stopped exercising so much?

I close the bathroom door behind me, my old *young* reflection staring back from the mirrored bathroom cabinet. I walk towards her, the old me, and trace the outline of my face, leaning my forehead against the cool surface until I hear our doorbell ring.

I turn and open the bathroom door a crack, watching him exit the lounge and make his way down the stairs. I analyse every movement. He's not rushing; he doesn't look worried at all. In fact, he's humming, out of tune again, to 'Seven Years' – I wonder if time travel has a sense of irony. I open the door further and pad along to the top of the banister, standing back so as not to be seen.

The door opens. A man. Tall. Blond. Suited.

The man then leans in, his words quiet. I step forward and it's then that I see the change in Kit. His shoulders pull back; his stance is firm. He steps forward, casts a glance towards the bathroom and steps out, closing the door behind him.

Now I have a flash of memory. I remember looking out of the window. I'd been at the desk again. I'd been preparing reading comprehension questions for the Gifted and Talented group in Year Six. I hadn't gone to Mum's as planned; I'd been too busy. I remember knocking my head on the roller blind and wondering who was at the door.

I rush to the lounge window, moving past my ghost self, trying to get a closer look. The blond man is smiling. I remember that smile. That's all I'd seen: a tall blond man in a suit. I'd paid no attention to Kit, standing in the doorway. I'd been too relieved that I'd almost finished writing the questions. This time I pay more attention.

Kit has folded his hands in his pockets and his head is lowered. A series of nods, no eye contact I see. I scan the road outside. Parked on the edge of a kerb is a blue BMW, a personalised licence plate: K8N WYT1. The car is new. Expensive. It seems to match the person talking. Kit's head flashes upwards, a knee-jerk of a reaction that seems to make the blond man smile. No, smile isn't the right word. But sneer wouldn't work either. It's a 'gotcha' smile, a 'you know it' and 'I know it' expression. Kit's body changes. Gone is the strength of his stance. His hand gestures show that he's now asking for something.

I make my way down the stairs and open the door.

Kit's head turns towards me, his easy smile in place.

'Thanks, mate, but we're renting so not interested.'

The blond man's demeanour changes. He takes a step forward, a hand outstretched. Kit sucks his breath in. The sound is quiet, almost a click, but it has a bite to it, like he's got a boiled sweet tucked against his molars. Kit's arm slopes around my shoulders.

'Kane,' he says, clasping my hand long enough to make me feel uncomfortable. 'Sorry to have interrupted your evening.' He drops my hand, with his eyes back on Kit. 'Remember that this is a one-time offer.' He flashes his non-smile in Kit's direction.

'Um, sure.' The man takes his leave. Kit's arm is tight around my shoulders.

'What was all that about?' I ask.

'Nothing. He's trying to sell us double glazing. Talk about giving it the hard sell, I couldn't get away from him. Arsehole. Christ, I'm starving. Fancy a takeaway?'

Double glazing. That's what he'd said last time too.

I'm about to say we had takeaway last night. We had fish and chips and if I carry on eating like that I'll soon lose this size-eight body, but we didn't, did we? We had some sort of pasta bake. 'Sure,' I say. It's not like it'll make a sod's bit of difference – anything I eat doesn't really exist. 'Let's have extra sides and some cookie dough too?' I add.

'That's my girl.' He releases me and walks back into the flat. I watch as the BMW pulls away. Kane catches my eye and gives a small salute as he pulls off the kerb. There is something in the way he looks at me that makes me feel like I need a shower.

Later, full and bloated, I try to bring the conversation back, but Kit just shrugs and changes the subject to the TV, then goes and grabs us two cold beers from the fridge.

We go to bed. I make excuses as he tries to touch me... Too much pizza and beer, I say.

I wait until I can hear his breathing regulate then creep from the bed. I tread quietly to his side and retrieve his phone, locking myself in the bathroom.

I close the toilet seat and open up his phone. One new message from Rebecca.

REBECCA

Can we meet?

KIT

Yes. Tomorrow. Usual place?

REBECCA

See you there.

His Gmail account reveals nothing suspicious between the lines of IT talk, so I slip back into the room, replace his phone, and slide in next to him. Before I go to sleep, I turn my clock around so that it's facing away from me. Something that says I was here, that I was present today. My mind begins to drift and just when I'm at the edge of sleep, about to slip back into the past, the thought comes like a blow from a hammer: the stickers are still on the corners of our windows. The double glazing was only replaced a few months ago. So why would a double-glazing salesman knock on the door of a flat with new windows?

20

FOUR DAYS AFTER I LEFT HER

I begin sanding down the bedroom wall ready to replaster, but it feels like my energy is caught somewhere I can't reach. Like I need to untangle the leads to get the power back on.

Every time I feel a fizz of energy, it trips and I'm back to square one. Everything I've done runs through my mind in quick, mortifying succession. Like a series of *You've Been Framed* clips without the canned laughter. Without the cute kids and drunken grannies falling on the dance floor. No, my reel of *You've Been Framed* moments starts and ends with Liv and the life I've just demolished.

I flick open the tub of filler. Mac didn't ask why I needed it, just told me to help myself from the shed. The edges of the tub are dry but it'll do. I pick through the rubble – through the remnants of my life – while the shadows of early morning slide along the wall. Christ, I miss her so much it hurts – like, actually hurts my stomach. But I need to find a way to move on without her.

The morning unfolds. I make breakfast, try to distract myself.

I've got enough money to tide me over for a few weeks. Then

I'll have to go back. Not that she'll have me back. Not after this. I wonder how she'll react when I turn up on our doorstep. Will she slam the door in my face?

How can I have fucked up so monumentally?

There's a knock on the door, startling me.

Mac is standing there. 'I need your help.' The words come from beneath his bushy beard. I'm still no closer to understanding his motivation.

'Let me grab my coat,' I reply.

* * *

Half an hour later and I'm knee-deep in mud, holding a mallet, whacking it against a wooden stake, trying to get it out of a piece of land that it has clearly been rooting into for decades. I wipe the sweat from my brow and look up. Mac is taking large bites out of an apple, watching me as he leans on another piece of fence.

'Any chance of you helping?' I ask, giving the base of the wood another whack, narrowly missing hitting my thumb instead.

'Can't. Low blood sugar. You don't want me passing out, do you? I doubt very much an ambulance will be able to get to these parts in under an hour, and as handsome as you are, I don't want the kiss of life from you.'

He finishes the apple, throws it with a hefty swing more suited to a javelin thrower and crouches down beside me. 'Move over,' he says taking the mallet from my hands. He gives the post three bangs to the left. One to the right. Lifting it out of the earth with ease.

I let out a long sigh. 'If it's that easy, then what did you need my help for?'

'Two-man job,' he replies, throwing away the fence. He strides over to the back of his trailer where he pulls out a long roll of wire mesh and a new fence post. He passes the roll of mesh to me, hoists the wooden pole onto his shoulder.

'Who normally helps you with the two-men jobs when I'm not around?' Something passes over Mac's face. 'Tim, but he's in charge of lambing, unless you want to help with that?'

I try not to outwardly shudder.

'And I don't need an extra pair of hands.'

'And why's that?'

'You're here.'

* * *

For the next hour, he gives me instructions. I follow them, but he does most of the job himself. Apart from holding each stake in place, I can't fathom why he wants me helping him. I'm clearly more of a hindrance.

'You have a girlfriend, boyfriend?' he asks out of the blue. One minute he's telling me how to make hot-water-crust pies and the next we're delving into my love life.

A memory of Liv's face as she chopped an onion: a pair of swimming goggles on to stop her eyes watering. I'd joined her in the kitchen once wearing a snorkel mask. Neither of us acknowledged it and we continued cooking the dinner. Setting the table without a word. We'd finally sat down to eat and I couldn't get the food in my mouth. She'd laughed so hard that she ended up with hiccups.

'No.' I shut down the image. 'I'm recently... separated.'

'Sorry to hear that.'

'Thanks.'

'Why did you separate?'

'We... just weren't meant to be.'

'And why's that?'

'I'm not what she needs in her life.'

'And you have the right to make that decision for her, do you?' he asks. 'Hold that steady,' he growls as the wind tugs and yanks on the mesh that he's trying to secure into place. 'You have the God-given right to make that decision on her behalf?'

'It's more complicated. You wouldn't understand.' My voice is taut.

'Oh, you think you know everything about me too, do you? Well excuse me, Mr I write about zombies and I'm from *York*.'

'What is your problem?' I say, anger raising my voice, the wind almost swallowing it at once.

'I don't have a problem. You're the one with the problem or else you wouldn't have run off here rather than facing up to things with your missus.'

'That's not why I'm *here*. And if your life is so perfect, then why do you keep knocking on my door?'

'I never said it was perfect,' he responds. 'There you go again, thinking you know everything about everyone.'

'Do you know what, Mac?' I squeeze the bridge of my nose. 'I don't need this shit.'

'Oh, yes you do. You think you're the only man who's made mistakes, has regrets?'

His words are spoken with a chipped edge. I stop to look at him.

Now we're getting somewhere.

'What are you saying?'

'I'm saying...' He grunts as he tries to hold the post and add another tack to secure it; I grab the post and wait for him to continue. '...that you're not the only man alive who can make mistakes.' He stands and folds his arms, eyes narrowing. Like he's daring me to say something. 'You have time to fix your mistakes. I doubt I've got much of a chance to make amends now.'

I pause for a moment. My mouth opening then closing. 'You could try.'

He ignores me. 'Does she love you?' he asks.

'Yes.'

'Do you love her?'

'Yes. But... it's complicated.'

'So, you keep saying. If you love her, she loves you, then whatever it is that's complicating things. Fix it.'

And with that he calls Caesar to heel and stomps away.

I kick the post a couple of times to make sure it's secure. It's rock solid. I lean on it, watching the great hulk of a man heading downhill and wonder if he has any idea of the implications of his 'mistakes'.

Regardless of his regret, he doesn't deserve my forgiveness.

At least, not yet.

21

THREE DAYS BEFORE HE LEFT ME

I open my eyes; the clock has returned to its position and is facing me.

I have a sinking feeling, like the bed is too soft and I'm cocooned in the memory foam. The shower is on. Kit is singing to 'Stitches' by Shawn Mendes. I roll over to his side of the bed, reaching for his phone. My eyes are stinging and, as I try to focus on the screen, I realise I'm still wearing my mascara. My head is banging and the inside of my mouth has all the tell-tale signs of one too many glasses of wine.

Then I remember. In 2016, I *had* been out last night. I have a fleeting memory of meeting Ava after I'd finished writing my comprehension questions. We'd hit the wine bar down the road from here. I ducked out once she started chatting to Pete Simms and it was clear where the night was heading for them both. Pete had gone to school with us and had always had a thing for Ava. She'd liked him too, although I could never understand why – he gave me the ick. It's not that he was bad-looking, just a bit of a knob. He came across as insincere, sometimes being cruel to the other kids to impress the popular gang. But Ava, being Ava, sees the good in everybody and even though I'd tried to talk her into coming home, I had known my battle was lost.

Kit had made me a coffee and a sandwich, had listened to me lament all the reasons that Ava shouldn't sleep with Pete, and put a bottle of water beside the bed. It's still there, untouched, which explains the headache.

I go shopping with Ava today.

I remember we'd both been worse for wear and we'd consoled our pounding heads with lunch and by spending more vivaciously than usual. I'd bought the coat I'd wear a week after while I was standing in the cold, with the police. I had replayed today, wishing I was living it again rather than a day that involved me looking for Kit's body. The day had started the same: Kit in the shower, me with a hangover. Kit had gone to work. He'd been tired when he came home, and we'd argued about money, something we never usually did. He'd commented on the coat, on Ava's choice of restaurant for lunch. He'd gone to bed on his own that night. I'd stayed up, feeling angry with him. He'd woken me the next morning before work with a tired-looking daffodil that he had been outside to pinch from the house over the road's garden.

I remember thinking he was almost gunning for a fight, but then I had put it down to the fact that the coat *was* expensive; I had felt a tinge of guilt myself when I bought it but it had fitted me so well. But of course, back then, I didn't know he'd arranged to meet Rebecca Bevitt. He stops singing and I quickly check his messages. They've been deleted.

Kit comes into the room, towel around his waist, a coffee in one hand and two paracetamol in the other. 'How's the head?' he asks with a smile.

'Like there's an elephant shoving its tusks into my eyeballs.' I shuffle up the bed and take the coffee, swallowing down the pills.

Double glazing. Rebecca Bevitt.

'I was thinking,' I begin as Kit gets dressed, 'why would a double-glazing salesman knock on our door when we've clearly got brand-new windows?'

'No idea,' he says stepping into his trousers and zipping them up.

'Did he look familiar?' I ask.

Kit sighs loudly, his eyebrows drawn in tightly. Kit rarely looks angry. 'What's with the twenty questions? How the hell should I know?'

I can feel the shock of his response registering with him. He opens his mouth, closes it as though he's about to apologise, then starts opening and shutting drawers. Kit sits on the end of the bed and pulls on his socks. His shoulders sag a touch. 'I'm sorry,' he says, his back to me. He turns his head. 'I'm just in a rush and I've got another Zoom call this morning, then a meeting in town at one, and if I don't land this account then I'm screwed.'

Meeting in town at one.

'What do you mean, screwed?'

'It just means I need to land the account, that's all.' He's short with me again. Kit was never short with me. I don't think I've ever seen him like this.

My head is pounding. I try to replay this morning in its original form. I'd stayed in bed. Kit had still brought in the coffee and pills, but I'd groaned and he'd said go back to sleep.

'Kit, is there something worrying you?' I shuffle forward, wrapping my arms around his neck.

He relaxes a touch, leaning his head against mine. 'I'm being a dick. Sorry, I had a crappy night's sleep... You were snoring by the way,' he says, but there is a smile there.

'Sorry.'

'And you smell like Jaeger.'

'Jesus, what was I thinking?' I enjoy the normality of this for a second before the thoughts of random men knocking on the door and strange women asking my boyfriend to meet them take over.

He looks at his watch. 'I've got a Zoom call.' He gets up and hesitates at the door rushing back to me, taking my face in his hands and kissing me. 'Wish me luck?'

'Good luck.' He kisses the top of my head three times and then he closes the door to his office.

* * *

I knock on Ava's door. The curtains are still drawn; I'm early. I knock the door again. There is still no movement inside. I've run here. It was like a gentle stroll to my younger body. Even though I'm hungover, I barely broke a sweat. I make a vow to get back into proper shape if I ever get home. I've told Kit I'm still going shopping. Today I know he's going to meet Rebecca Bevitt.

Ava opens the door, mascara smudged, her face green. Her blonde hair is crimped, a hangover from a set of plaits she would have worn the night before.

'For Christ's sake, Liv. You're two hours early.' She turns her back, tying a pale pink dressing gown around her, long tanned legs heading into her kitchen.

'I know, but this is an emergency.' I close the door behind me.

'It had better be.' She blasts water from the tap and downs it from a Bulmers pint glass. She wipes her mouth with the back of her hand as I begin pacing up and down. The glass is refilled and her eyes track me back and forth as I move from one white surface to the next. I give myself a nod and clutch the back of the stainless-steel stool next to her kitchen island.

'So... something has happened. It's going to sound like I've lost my mind. I might have actually lost my mind, but just listen, OK?'

I spill the events of the past seven years in a hyphenated rush of words. Her eyes widen, her mouth opening and closing at moments where she wants to interrupt but I just hold up my hand and keep on going.

'We need to get you checked out. You might have had a stroke, or an aneurysm or something...'

'No, we don't. We need to follow Kit.'

Ava leans on the island, sleeves pushed up to her elbows.

'Last night you slept with Pete Simms,' I say.

Her eyes widen and then narrow. 'Who told you?'

'You did. Not for a long time, but eventually you did. I mean, Pete Simms? He's such a slimeball, Ava.'

'He's not that bad.' She looks at me with suspicion. 'And that doesn't prove a thing.' But I can see that I'm getting through to her. She clicks her fingers. 'You could have guessed that or, or you could have found that out on social. He didn't put anything on Insta did he?'

'Not yet. But he will. If you don't believe me, how about the fact that he broke your favourite purple thong and you had to walk home with it swinging about like a baby's nappy under your skirt?'

'Holy shit.' She holds her head in her hands then looks back up at me. 'Now that I'm looking at you, your heart chakra is off, like its bouncing between two magnetic forces.'

I try not to roll my eyes. 'That's about the size of it.'

'So... hold on. You're telling me you're a time traveller? Wait. I'm still asleep right?'

I reach across the island and pinch her on the arm. 'Ow!'

'Does it feel like you're asleep now?'

She rubs her bicep and scowls at me.

'Let me make you a coffee.'

She watches me move around the kitchen. I pull open a

drawer and slide a packet of paracetamol in her direction as well
as a tub of vitamins. She takes them as I make the coffees and
join her.

'I can't get my head around this; you're from the future? How
come you don't look any older?'

'It's not like that. I didn't hop in a DeLorean. It's more like,
my... I don't know, spirit? Is here.'

She nods, as though the cosmos is talking to her directly.

'Believe me, I don't look this slim in seven years' time.'

'Why not?'

'Life changed. I work long hours; I don't do all the things I do
now. Once Kit disappears, it all kind of fizzles out. And there are
always biscuits in the staffroom, and James is a good cook.' I
ignore the way her eyebrow quirks when I say his name. 'And life
is just... slower. I can't actually remember the last time I went for
a run in my timeline. But I do still use the gym. We bought it. The
boxing club. So I still use the punch bag, but more often than not,
I just sit in the office catching up on work. Marking books. James
is still fit though.'

I think about the way he'd been with me yesterday, the tone of
his voice when he pretty much told me to mind my own business.
Ava looks like she's about to blow a gasket.

'Can we... just rewind a bit? So let me get this straight. Kit
goes... where?'

'One of his favourite hikes in Pembrokeshire. On Good Friday,
in three days' time. He never comes back. No body, he doesn't use
his bank card, his car is left in the car park. But the thing is, I
think it was all deliberate. Leaving the car in a popular spot,
being seen on a common trek, making sure someone saw him
setting up the rig, ropes in hand. But I don't think he climbed
there. Now I think he hid in that cave. We couldn't look for him

there. The cove is tiny, not a clear enough route for the lifeguards.'

'You seriously think he planned to that extent?'

I nod. Tears in my eyes. 'I just don't know why, why he would put me, us, through it all. We thought he was dead; he made sure that's what we would think. That he'd had a fall or that he drowned. But we held out so much hope, for so long... that he was lost, or hurt, that he'd got amnesia. You have no idea how long we hoped he would come back.'

She blows over the top of her cup, eyeing me.

'Don't look at me like that. I'm not crazy. You're the one who has just slept with Pete Simms; maybe you're the one who needs to see a therapist?'

'Touché. Although... he wasn't *terrible*.'

'I'm sure... if the carpet burns on your back are anything to go by.' I quirk an eyebrow.

'How did you know I've got carpet... time travel. Right.'

'Have you checked your phone this morning?'

She shakes her head and gingerly sips at her coffee. 'Why?'

'Just check your phone.' She gets up and unplugs it from the charger by the silver bread bin.

Her eyes widen as she reads the several messages I know she will have already received this morning. Her face blanches.

'Let me guess, five messages and a missed call?'

'Nope. Two missed calls and three messages.' She begins plaiting her hair over her shoulder and closes her phone screen.

'You need to tell him it was a one-nighter. Trust me. This is just the beginning.'

Pete had hounded Ava for weeks after, turning up with flowers, constant messages and phone calls asking for a second chance. He gave up eventually, but I didn't know all of this when it was happening. She never told me until a year after, once I'd started to climb out of my grief.

'I will. Anyway, enough about that. I want to know more about what the fuck is going on with you. This is batshit. So Kit leaves, and you hear nothing from him until...'

'My wedding day.'

'Can we just talk about that? You're marrying James? *James*. James Palmer. Brother of Kit Palmer. The man who is, what did you say last week?' She makes quotation signs. '"A self-absorbed arsehole?"' I flinch at my words. I really, really didn't like him back then, but now I've experienced his avoidance of me this week, I can understand why I would have said that.

'Things changed when Kit left. We... needed each other. Nobody else knew how it felt. We did everything we could to find him.'

'You and James. *James*?' Then she makes a face that is something like impressed.

'What?'

'It's just that... I know you're not his biggest fan and everything, but I've always wondered...'

'Wondered what?'

'Nothing.'

'No, go on – what? Today doesn't matter. Everything you or I do or say will be wiped clean in the morning. We'll have gone shopping, I will have spent a ridiculous amount of money on a coat and you won't have told me a thing about Pete Simms, so you may as well tell me what's on your mind.'

'All that is on my mind is if someone slipped something else into my tequila last night and I'm high.'

'You're not high.' I glance at the clock and drain the last of my drink. 'We need to get going.'

'Where?'

'I don't know, but he said he had a meeting in town at one. We need to follow him. I need to find out what's going on.'

* * *

An hour later and we're parked beside a tanning salon. I'm wearing Ava's grey cap and she's rubbing her temples behind a pair of sunglasses.

There he is. My stomach swoops. I'm still getting used to seeing him in the flesh. Not a shadow, not a smudge of memory: Kit. He climbs into his car, starts the engine, turns right. I keep my distance, at least two cars behind, as he heads out of town. It gets harder to follow him as he makes his way along country A roads.

'Where *is* he meeting her?' I say.

'No idea, hon. So if you're right, he's going to meet the woman from his Facebook messages?'

'Yep.'

She sighs and I can see her looking at me through the corner of her eye. 'Tell me about James.' She shifts in her seat, adjusting the seat belt. 'About your relationship with him.'

'James is...' I smile. I can't help myself. 'James is great. At least, I thought he was.'

'Run through the morning before you ended up here, again. Just so I can have this alternate universe in my mind. But first please tell me I'm your bridesmaid?'

I grin at her. 'Maid of honour.'

'Naturally. So you're in your hotel room? Where?'

'The Grange.'

'*The Grange*?' she asks slightly aghast.

'It's close to Mum,' I say in explanation.

'OK. So you're in the hotel room, then what?'

'I wanted to call Mum, but I couldn't find my phone charger.'

She scoffs. 'Some things are the same, then. You still don't know your arse from your elbow. Sorry, so you're looking for the charger and you find the necklace in James's hoody with a receipt from the week before and a note?'

'Yep.' I keep my eye on the road. There are two cars in front of me, Kit leading the way. 'Which means...' I pause, still not wanting to believe that James knew. But the more time I spend here, the more I think that he must do. He had the necklace.

'Could James have kept the necklace from before? Now? Jesus, this is all making my head spin.'

I shake my head. 'The note was new. And then there is the date on the receipt. Kit was going to get it engraved *this* week, not seven years in the future.'

'Do you trust him? James?'

'Yes,' I say without hesitation.

'And now?'

I think back to yesterday, to the argument. He never told me about it.

'Now I think that... maybe he knew? If not all of the details, I think he knew something was going on with him. Or maybe they've both been lying all along.'

'Why don't you ask James? Straight up. Tell him everything you've told me.'

I snort. 'Can you imagine how he'd react? Hi, James, I know we can't stand each other but in the future we get married.'

But, she has a point, maybe I should speak to James, tell him the truth.

'The thing is, James was... distraught. He was grieving. You can't fake grief. Or maybe you can.' I crunch the gears.

'Careful!' she says as we bounce over a pothole.

'Sorry, it's been a while since I've driven a manual. We've got an automatic. James took some convincing, but he came around.'

She's quiet. I imagine she's trying to picture me and James, our life together.

'And you *really* love him? James?'

I pause. 'You have to understand that I'm different now. Losing Kit, it changed me. Changed us. I think I lost a piece of me when he left... I wasn't in a good place when he died. I moved back in with Mum.'

I try to force down the blocked-up entrance of my memories to that time, where danger whispered through the cracks in the walls; when I didn't go to work, didn't go to the shops, didn't leave the house unless James was with me.

'James was there for me in a way that no one else was. That's not to say you weren't there for me too. You were, but...'

'I hadn't lost him in the same way as you two had?'

'Yeah.'

I think of Ava, sitting on my bed, refilling mugs of cold tea, urging me to leave the bedroom; the terror I'd felt when she'd asked me to go for a walk; the void that hung dark and threatening over the threshold from the front door to the kerb. And James. The way he helped me step over it, the way I felt like I could leave the house if he was with me.

'We're good together, James and I. We make a good team.' I push down gently on the brakes as we head into a bend, the steering wheel light beneath my hands.

'Can I ask you a personal question?' She shifts, pulls at the seat belt, readjusting it.

'Sure. You won't remember any of this anyway.'

'How soon did you get together with James?'

'Three years,' I say. I glance at her as she analyses my words. She's not looking at me with judgement, just as though I'm a puzzle that needs solving. 'It was intense. We got caught in this bubble that nobody else could be part of and it just developed from there. He's not who you think he is,' I add.

'And who do I think he is?'

'Grumpy, indifferent, moody?'

'Actually, I think he's pretty decent. It must be hard being Kit's brother.'

'Shit, we're going to lose him,' I say edging out so I can see past the cars.

Kit's car turns onto a retail park: Tesco, Next Home, Costa.

I slow down and flick on the indicator. Kit turns right at the small roundabout. I slow down, circle the car park and pull up next to a white van, edging the bonnet forward so we can see him but keeping the rest of the car hidden.

'Slouch down,' I say to Ava as he gets out of the car, locks the doors and runs his hands through his hair. He looks agitated. Kit hesitates before looking both ways, crosses the car park and heads towards a small café, but he doesn't go in; instead he gets in a car with a woman at the wheel. We sit back up, both of us watching his progress through the glass windows. He leans in, kisses her on the cheek.

My mouth is dry, my pulse strumming through my veins.

'Do you recognise her?' Ava asks, turning to me. My whole body is shaking.

I nod. I know exactly who she is.

I shake my head trying to clear my thoughts. She's a bit younger than the last time I saw her at Kit's funeral. Her hair is cut into a bob, brown not blonde. 'It's Becky Thomas.' Her name is a nettle sting on my tongue. 'Kit's ex-girlfriend.'

I watch as Kit talks. She smiles at him as he speaks, leaning in as she listens to him. I can't lip-read; I can't hear what he's saying, but whatever it is he says means that her whole body relaxes. She laughs and nods.

Rain starts to fall onto the windscreen. I flick on the wipers. The action feels so automatic, *so normal.*

My whole body is fighting against what I can see, resisting the implications of how comfortable he looks, how they're interacting. He can't be doing this to me. Can he? Of all the scenarios I have volleyed back and forth in my mind, the multiple reasons he would leave me, another woman never even made an appearance. He leans forward, gives an encouraging smile, then she laughs, nodding her head. They are holding each other now. I don't know who made the first move, but Kit's eyes are closed, his face a picture of contentment. They pull apart and she starts the car. I grapple with the door handle, stepping out of the car but they are already driving away. I run across the tarmac.

'Liv, wait!' Ava says chasing after me, but I'm too late.

We stand in the rain, watching the indicator tick as they pull onto the main road, the red tail lights merging with the traffic.

'Liv?' Ava says, trying to hold her coat above our heads. I don't answer her; instead I stand there in the rain. Both of us speechless. Both of us unable to believe his betrayal could be so monumental.

Ava drops me home, against her will; I need to be alone.

I stand in front of the door to our flat, but I can't face going in. I need to get back. I need to get back to the present day. I can't do this. I'm not strong enough. Is this why I'm here? To find out that he was in love with someone else, that he was having an affair?

I begin running, a jog at first, but my feet begin pounding harder and faster as I follow the roads towards the Grange Hotel. The rain continues but I don't care. Maybe if I go back to room 307 it will break this spell. I have my answer. This all makes sense to me now. I can understand why James wouldn't tell me; he knew Kit having an affair would break me. I don't forgive him for lying to me, but at least I can understand why he would.

I hurry up the steps, the same steps that had taken me into the building that I had walked into full of laughter and excitement. I ask if room 307 is available, ignore the looks I'm getting in my saturated state, and pay for it on my card, before walking up the stairs.

I stare at the hotel door. I touch the metal, tracing the numbers like reading Braille.

'Take me back. I just want to go home.'

I take a deep breath, place my hand on the doorknob and turn.

Please let this work, please let this work.

I hold my breath in my chest and walk through.

22

THREE DAYS BEFORE HE LEFT ME

The room is different from the last time I was here. The walls are lilac; the bedding is grey.

I'm still here. In 2016. Will I ever be able to get back?

I sit down on the edge of the bed, my head in my hands as I begin sobbing. I lie face down and pound my fists against the mattress.

Kit's face as he got in the car, the way they looked at each other; Kit shrugging his backpack on; standing with my coat wrapped around me as police dogs and the search party combed the hills and crags of the Pembrokeshire coastline; Rebecca, *Becky*, her face as she approached me at the funeral, red eyes, soft hand on my forearm. There was something in the way she looked at me that was off, I remember now, but then the next person was sorry for my loss, and the person after that, and the person after that.

I close my eyes: the image of myself in my wedding dress and James. James. The security being with him brings me, that feeling of safety, of being protected, his smile; the way he looks ten years younger while he sleeps; the look of joy that would pass his face as I took a mouthful of something he'd cooked. All of it feels raw, all of it real, not real, lost but found.

There is a message on my phone. I play the robotic voicemail introduction and listen to the voicemail from Mum: *Hi darling, just checking in to see how you are. It feels like I haven't seen you for weeks! I hope everything is OK? Give me a call when you're free. Love you, bye. Bye.*

I feel the uselessness of my endeavours again. Mum has no recollection of the afternoon I spent with her where I tried to explain everything that has happened. On the flip side, this is a good thing. At least she didn't spend yesterday afternoon shaking and wracked with anxiety that her daughter was either losing the plot or about to jump headfirst into imminent danger.

I don't know how long I lie on the bed, but it's dusk when I sit back up. I take off my clothes, letting them fall to the floor, and step into the shower. I close my eyes under the water, resting my palm against the cool tiles.

I need him. I need James.

I dry myself off, pick up my phone and dial his number.

'Hello?' he says. His voice has an edge to it. Gone is the familiar, 'Hey, you'.

'It's me. Liv,' I say redundantly as if my name wouldn't have flashed up on his phone screen.

'I can't talk. I'm at work.' I can hear the sounds of the bar, picture him with his phone on his shoulder as he pulls a pint.

'Can we meet?'

'Meet? *Why?*' He's blunt and there is something in the shock of his voice that makes me want to laugh. 'Hold on—' I hear a thanks, a beep of a card reader. 'This isn't a good time.'

'I... I just need to talk to you. It's about Kit.'

'Is he OK?'

Oh, he's fine, I almost say, *he has probably been having an affair with his ex for God knows how long and is about to do a runner.* Did he leave with her? If he did, they didn't stay together because she was at the funeral. Or maybe they were still together and she was there to scope it all out, to check that we really did believe he was dead. Jesus, is this really happening? Was he sat outside waiting in a car for her so they could drive off into the sunset? Maybe she grinned at him as she got in, Kit wearing a fake pair of glasses and a hat. 'They bought it!' I imagine her replying then kissing him passionately before he turns the key, gravel spinning out behind them as they drove away laughing at their plan working.

'Liv?'

I push the thoughts away. Kit wouldn't do that to me. *He wouldn't.*

'I just need to talk to you about something. Can you meet me?'

'Can't you just tell me over the phone?'

'No. It's important, James. I wouldn't be asking you otherwise.'

That seems to strike a chord if nothing else I'm saying does.

'Fine. I'll come round after work.'

'I'm not home. I'm at the Grange Hotel. I'll explain why when you get here. When do you get off?'

'In about an hour.'

'Perfect. Thanks. Thank you. I'll... I'll see you then? I'll be in the bar. And James?'

'Hmmm?'

'Don't... Could you not mention it to Kit?'

He pauses. I can hear the noise of people in the background, a muffled sound as he moves the phone, a door closing behind him, the conversations around him dulled.

'Liv, I'm not interested in getting mixed up if you two have had a fight.'

'We haven't... I just, I need your help with something. Please, James. You know I wouldn't ask if it wasn't important.'

'I'll be there in an hour.'

* * *

I sit nursing a glass of wine. I've ordered James the same. His frame fills the doorway as he scans the room. I smile. His hand moves, flexes by his side.

'Hi. I've got you a drink,' I say, pulling at my ear. It's such a strange feeling, to be nervous talking to a man who I know inside and out. His brows furrow but he sits down and takes a sip.

'So what's this about?' he asks, his delivery blunt.

I swirl my drink, already half empty. 'What can you tell me about Rebecca Thomas?'

His eyebrows rise in surprise. 'Becky? Why do you want to know?' Just beneath the table his leg is bouncing up and down. To an outsider this would symbolise nerves, but James's leg bounces even when he's relaxed. But pulling and messing around with the cuffs of his shirt, that's nerves.

'Because I think Kit's having an affair,' I say.

James laughs, leans back in his chair, shaking his head.

'You think it's funny?' I ask, heat rising in my cheeks.

'Yes.'

'Well great, I'm glad you think there is something funny about it, because let me tell you, James, it's not. Not in the least.'

'Kit's not having an affair.' He takes a sip of his drink, his focus roaming around the hotel lobby.

'So why did I just see him driving off with her?'

His eyes dart back to mine, uncertainty in them.

'Look, as far as I know, Becca and Kit have been over for years. She married Nate, moved on. End of story.'

'But it's not the end of the story because this afternoon Kit met with her and, let me tell you, they looked pretty comfortable together.'

He avoids my eyes, tugs at the hair at the nape of his neck. I try to ignore how I know that it's softer than it looks, how it feels between my fingers.

'Look, Liv, I honestly don't know anything about this. But Kit's not having an affair. It's not his style.' He's telling the truth. At least I think he is, but if he's been lying to me about his brother being dead, then what do I know? 'Have you asked him?'

'No. I...'

'Is that why you're here?' He gestures to the hotel bar. 'You've left him before he's even had chance to explain?'

'Yes and no.' I take a sip of my drink, while James's eyebrows draw in. 'Would he tell you?' I put the drink back down. 'If he was having an affair? Would he confide in you? I mean, it's not like you're my biggest fan.'

He leans back in his seat. 'I don't know. What my brother does with his private life is his business.' He's saying the right words, but his demeanour has changed. He's upset. Hurt.

'Would you tell me if you knew?'

He keeps his eyes on mine. Long lashes that I've watched closed as he sleeps, lashes that have touched the inside of my thigh. A conversation runs through my mind. I'd been watching him, head dipped between the pages of a magazine: *If you were an animal, you'd be a giraffe.*

A giraffe? I think you mean a tiger or lion... a bear.

Nope. A giraffe. It's the eyelashes.

He'd fireman lifted me, running across the heath. *Take it back.*

No! I'd been laughing, squealing as he spun me around, dog walkers smiling and nudging each other as they watched these two people in love.

'It's not my business.' His reply rips the memory apart, screws it up and throws it to the floor.

'So that's a no?' My voice wavers. 'You wouldn't tell me if I'm being lied to?'

'Look, Liv.' He pushes the drink aside and shoves his chair back. 'I don't know anything. As far as I know, you're the fucking love of his life. So if you're asking me if I think he's having an affair, then my answer is no. I don't know why he would be meeting with her, but I sure as hell don't think my brother is capable of lying to us both.' He pushes the chair back and stands. 'Thanks for the drink.'

'James, wait!'

He hesitates, his hand on the back of the chair.

'You're wrong.'

He frowns.

'He is capable of lying to us because in a week's time he's going to leave. And he won't come back for seven years.'

James tilts his head, his eyes narrowed. 'What are you talking about?'

'Can you... can you just wait for a moment? I can explain. Please?'

He looks towards the door, back to the seat and sits down.

'Thank you.' I drain the rest of my drink, take a deep breath, then begin. 'I'm going to tell you something now, and you're going to think I'm making it up. But I'm not.' I fold my hands on top of the table. 'I've been here before,' I begin.

'What do you mean?'

'I'm from the future.'

He stands immediately, anger making his fists clench and unclench. 'I don't know why you're messing with me, but accusing my brother of having an affair and then telling me you're what... Marty McFly? It's not funny.'

'I'm not trying to be funny, James, I—'

He pulls out his wallet and throws a ten-pound note on the table. 'For my drink,' he says and strides across the room. On the TV above the bar is the six o'clock news. Memories come flooding back. I chase after James.

'James, wait!' I grab him by the arm. 'The charity football match!' I say, slightly breathless. 'Man U and Arsenal.' He frowns. 'Both teams are allowed to have a wild card player.'

'Wild card player? Jesus, what is with you?' He shakes his arm free.

'Just listen.' I point to the TV above the bar, the news subtitles running along the bottom of the screen in yellow. I remember the news coming on later that night, just before we had our argument. 'I'm telling you the truth. I've lived this day before. Watch the news and I promise you, you'll see. The wild card player for Man U will be injured and his replacement will come on and score three goals. Four. But one is disallowed. He's only sixteen. His name is Steven Watts.' I look at my watch. 'In about four hours, this will be on the news. I know you don't believe me. I wouldn't believe me either, but I promise you, James. This *will* happen.' His eyes search mine, anger, confusion all there. 'Look, I'm staying in room 307. If you change your mind and you want to listen to what I have to say... I'll be waiting.'

* * *

I'm watching the news on the hotel bed. Kit rings my phone again. I've sent him a text telling him I'm staying at Ava's, too many Proseccos while we were shopping, I say. I can't face him, not until I've spoken to James again. There is a knock, and I turn down the sound, opening the door a crack.

'OK,' James states. 'You have my attention.'

I push the door wide. He walks into the room, the door slamming behind him.

23

THREE DAYS BEFORE HE LEFT ME

James hesitates at the door then strides past. 'Tell me how you knew about that match.' He's pacing the room.

Where do I start? I want to say, but the tension radiating from James needs to be tamed first.

'Let me make you a drink. Coffee?' I head over to the hotel kettle. It's an older version than the one on my wedding morning. The hotel has since gone under new management and it shows in the quality of the lilac bedding, the chip in the small white bowl containing the drink sachets.

'I don't want coffee, Liv. I want answers.'

'Right.' I sit and gesture to the bed but he continues to stand as I sit down. 'I don't know where to begin.'

'How did you know what was going to happen?'

'I told you—' I watch his broad frame, the V between his eyebrows. 'I've lived today before. In fact, I've already lived the next seven years.'

'Is this a joke, Liv? I swear...' He runs his hands through his dark hair and sits down, thick thighs filling the base of the chair; the chair that just a few days ago, he had hung his jacket on; the jacket with a locket that should never have been seen on my wedding day.

'It's not a joke. Look, I don't know how much time I have here. I could be here for the rest of today. I could be here for another week. I could be stuck here forever, so I'm going to cut right to the chase. This Friday, Kit is going to go for a hike and he won't come back.'

James looks up at me, eyes almost black. 'What do you mean, he won't come back?'

'He... I know how this is going to sound... We think he dies, but he doesn't.' James's face relaxes a touch at that assurance. 'Me and...' I swallow. 'And you. We spend the rest of the year looking for him. We spend days walking the coast, checking his social media accounts, searching the newspapers for any clue or hint that he's been found. The evidence of him dying is strong enough that he's officially pronounced dead. But he's not. I think he planned the whole thing.'

James's leg stops bouncing, his dark eyes boring into mine. 'What? Kit wouldn't do that.'

'I could be wrong. I mean, I suppose he could have had amnesia or something but there are things I've learnt that make me think he planned it. Faked his own death. He goes for a hike in one of his favourite spots. His car is left in a car park he doesn't usually use, but it's busy. He walks a track that is popular, where he knew people would be able to say they'd seen him. I'm fairly sure he hides in a cave that search and rescue can't get to, that we never found. He doesn't use his bank cards ever again. His bag is found further down the coast. He doesn't come back for seven years, James.' I watch his thought process crossing his face.

'But he does come back?'

I nod. 'On the morning of my wedding' – James's eyes flash

towards me – 'I find a necklace he bought me in... my fiancé's jacket. It's engraved and there is a note from Kit.'

'What does it say?'

'*I'm sorry. I had no choice.*'

'And the engraving?'

'*Just jump.*'

I let the significance of the words sink in. James has heard me and Kit saying this to each other plenty of times in the past.

'That doesn't mean he's not dead though, does it? He could have bought that and had it engraved before he goes missing?'

'There was a receipt in the box dated the week before.'

'So maybe your guy knows something about why he left. Did you ask him?'

'I didn't get chance, because I opened the hotel door and found myself here. In 2016.' I turn to him, aware of the time ticking by on the hotel clock. 'James, you have to think, is there any reason you know of that would make Kit do this?'

He shakes his head. The action less determined than before.

'Yesterday, you went to our place... you and Kit had an argument. What was it about?'

He looks at me with surprise. 'It was nothing.' So he's still not going to tell me.

I pause then continue. 'Could he be having an affair with Rebecca?' I ask.

James looks taken off guard but still shakes his head. 'No. He wouldn't do that to you.'

'Just consider what I'm asking, James, just for a minute. If he was' – I swallow again – 'having an affair, would he tell you? Was that what you were arguing about?'

He rubs the back of his neck, sighs, looks to the door as though he's about to bolt.

'Please, James, this is real. I need to know why he left.'

'This is crazy.' He gets up and starts to move across the room again.

I can see him mentally battling with everything I'm telling him. I can see him trying to weigh up the facts of the ten o'clock news and everything I'm saying.

'Let me think this through.' He continues pacing. 'You found the necklace in your boyfriend's jacket?'

I nod.

'So that means he knows, right?' James sits next to me, his leg bouncing again. 'He must know Kit is alive if Kit's given it to him to give to you?'

Tears blur my view for a second. I blink them away. 'I think so, yes.'

'Well, that's your answer. You need to speak to him. He must know where Kit goes.'

I chew my bottom lip. 'I have. He doesn't know anything.'

'You're certain?'

'As certain as I can be given he doesn't like me very much right now.' I give him a sad smile. 'We haven't fallen in love yet.'

'Maybe you should ask him again?' James continues. 'Ask him if Kit has been acting weird, or if he's asked for any favours?'

I meet his eyes, steadying myself. I reach for his hand. James's body goes rigid and he stares at my fingers, beginning to link through his own. His eyes travel back up to my face. The room is still. Outside a door opens and closes. A TV in the next room switches off. I squeeze his hand gently.

'I *am* asking him.'

24

THREE DAYS BEFORE HE LEFT ME

The air is charged as my meaning lands. James snatches his hand away. 'That's not fucking funny.'

'No. No it isn't,' I say, still reeling from the speed he's pulled his hand away. He stands, begins striding back and forth across the room. I continue, 'I know it's hard to believe, that we... you and I' – his mouth opens and he makes out a 'hah' sound, interrupting me – 'but I'm telling you the truth.'

'This is bullshit. You and me?' He shakes his head with such disbelief that I feel myself tense up. I knew it would be hard for him to take but I never expected his reaction to be so resistant. Is it really so preposterous to him right now?

Libby's words come back from the day before we got married: *duty, always picked up Kit's mess.*

'Just stop.' I stand and grab his hands. He's breathing quickly, eyes still darting around the room. I look up at him, squeezing his hands firmly. 'You don't like having your ears kissed because it gives you goosebumps. You sleep on the right side of the bed. You love listening to Smooth FM when you're in a bad mood because it perks you up, but you would never let the boys at the club know that.' His eyes stop roaming around the room and he settles on me. I soften my voice. 'When you were thirteen, Kit let your dog, Busker, off the lead and he got run over. Kit told your parents it was you.' His body is stilling. 'You never told them the truth and you took the blame.' He takes his hands out of mine and sits on the bed, head in hands. I sit next to him.

'I've never told anyone that,' he says quietly.

'I know. But you tell me.' He looks at me with caution, trying to work out if I'm a fraud.

'Kit could have told you that story.'

'He didn't.'

He takes a deep breath, holds it in his chest then exhales slowly. 'Tell me something else, something that no one else could know. And if this is a wind-up, Liv, I swear...'

My voice is calm, quieter as I begin. 'You once heard your mum saying that she wished you'd never been born.' His eyes meet mine, unwavering. 'You were six years old,' I continue. 'You were standing at the top of the stairs and your mum and dad were arguing. You were wearing Power Ranger pyjamas and wished you could be as strong as them when you grew up so that you could fight, so that you could take care of yourself.'

He drops his head again. I place my hand on his back, rubbing along his shoulder blades. James tenses at first, but then his body relaxes and he turns his head to me. 'I tell you that?'

'You tell me everything... at least, I thought you did.'

'Thought?'

'You had the necklace, James. I think you know Kit is alive. You argued with him yesterday and you never told me about that either.'

'That was nothing. He hasn't paid for his gym membership and Ian came to me asking me to give him a nudge. It pissed me off. That's all.' He rubs his knuckles across the inside of his palm.

'And now? Now that I've told you something is happening to Kit, something so huge that he plans his own death? Is there anything you can think of that might help us understand why?'

He scratches the back of his neck, and exhales.

'I don't know, Liv. Honestly. I don't know.'

We sit in silence. James's leg bouncing notches up. I need to calm him down.

'Do you want to know some good news?'

He shrugs, drags his hands through his hair.

I smile. 'We own the boxing club.' I smile at him. 'It's ours, James. Fighting Fit is ours.'

His chin jerks up. 'We call it that?'

'Yep.'

'I've had that name in my mind for years.'

I smile up at him. 'I know.'

He looks pleased in that self-conscious way that means he hides his smile by rubbing his hand across his mouth. I used to pull it away, kiss the palm of his hand, tell him I loved his smile.

'This is insane.'

'Yep.'

'So, what now?' he asks.

'Well... I'm here for a reason, so I'll keep looking, keep trying to find out why he did it, see if I can somehow stop it happening.'

Minutes tick by. I wait to let James come to terms with everything I've told him.

'Penny for your thoughts?' I nudge him with my shoulder.

He frowns, deep in thought. 'I was just thinking... what if him not paying Ian isn't Kit just being, you know, Kit? What if he couldn't pay?'

I shake my head. 'Kit wasn't in any money trouble. It was all checked out by the police. There was nothing suspicious.'

'But what if he's in trouble before he goes?'

I nod, tugging at this thread of thought.

'Maybe check his accounts,' James suggests, 'find out if there is anything unusual? If he planned to leave, there must be a trail somewhere... He can't have started a new life without money.'

'You're right.' We're quiet for a moment before I refocus the conversation. 'If you knew Kit was alive' – James looks up at me, dark eyes, dark lashes, his expression somewhere between hurt, confused and guarded – 'why would you lie to me, James?' I chew my bottom lip. 'I know this is a hard concept for you to grasp...' I look down at my hands, running my finger over where my engagement ring has been sitting for over a year. 'But you *do* love me.' I look up at him. His eyes widen a touch and then focus across the room into a future that he's trying to imagine. He continues looking off into the distance. 'I think you lie to me though, James.' His focus returns to me, puzzled, hurt, sceptical. 'And if you did, then you let me grieve; you let me search for him.' He shakes his head. 'Why would you lie, James?' I ask again.

He squeezes his eyes shut, pushes his fists into his sockets. His shoulders slump. I wait. Someone in the next room flushes a toilet. A door opens and closes further down the corridor.

'There is only one reason I can think of.' His words come from deep inside, like it's someone else speaking on his behalf.

'And?'

He moves his fists away, his eyes glassy as he looks at me. 'To protect him.'

25

THREE DAYS BEFORE HE LEFT ME

James is still processing, our conversations and theories lobbing back and forth. We've checked out Rebecca Thomas on his Instagram page. She works at Barbers and Co – an insurance firm. She used her maiden name to contact Kit. To keep the messages secret, I'm presuming.

'You should go to her, tomorrow, ask her straight out what she is doing meeting him,' James suggests.

'Would she tell me though? I mean, if they are having an affair?'

James gives me a look that reads, 'I've told you that's bollocks.'

'Well, she's hardly going to tell me, is she?'

'I still think you should confront her.' He blows out the air from his cheeks. 'Do you have anything stronger than coffee?' James asks, rolling his neck from side to side.

I look at the clock. It's gone midnight. 'No but I can order room service?' I pick up the phone and order a bottle of red wine, Merlot, James's favourite. I ask if they have any mixed nuts but change the request to just peanuts.

'Why did you change it from mixed nuts?' It's a test, even after everything I have told him.

'Because you think walnuts look like hamster brains, which makes you feel queasy.'

There is a small smile hiding in the corner of his mouth as I say this. I feel warmth in my solar plexus. He likes that I know these things about him.

'And the Merlot?'

'Shiraz gives you a headache.'

He laughs. The sound taking him and me by surprise. He groans and lies back on the bed, his head hanging off the end. I join him, our hair hanging upside down. He turns to me. 'This is the weirdest day of my life.'

'Weirder than the day you turned up in fancy dress to your friend's birthday party when you were thirteen and no one else was dressed up?'

His eyebrows rise again.

'And yes, you do tell me that you had a crush on his older sister and that she told you your Mario costume was *cute*.'

His hair hangs there. I want to reach out and touch it, to feel the thickness run between my fingers.

'It's gone midnight,' he says. 'Shouldn't you have disappeared or something?'

I turn to him. 'No. The next day only starts after I've fallen asleep.'

I lift my legs and give my toes a wiggle. 'Just so you know, I'm not this fit in our future.'

I notice his Adam's apple travelling up and down. He sits back up on the bed. 'We need to find out some answers.' He gets up and starts opening the drawers in the bureau opposite. I know what he's looking for; he needs to write a list. I open my handbag, pull out a pen and a receipt. 'I need to make a—'

'List. I know. Here you go.'

He frowns briefly then takes it from me, sitting back at the desk. 'Number one, is Kit in trouble with money?' I make my way over to him, looking over his shoulder as he underlines it twice. 'Number two, Becky. Number three, dodgy double-glazing man. Number four, motivation.' He underlines that too. Then adds 'Why did he leave?' and on the line below… 'Why do I lie?'

A lump forms in my throat as he underlines 'I'. It's interesting to me that he's questioning his own motivation as much as Kit's. James is an honest man, a good man. He knows that it's out of character to behave that way.

'Have you tried calling him since this afternoon?'

I shake my head. The image of him inside the car with his ex is too visceral right now.

There's a knock on the door and James gets up and answers room service, then pours us the wine. He knocks back half of his glass in three large gulps. I take the other glass from his hand. He sits down heavily and opens the bag of peanuts, offering me one before shaking out a handful and loading them into his mouth.

'Can I ask you something?' he says between chews. He crosses his legs and we sit opposite. He swirls the wine in the glass.

'Shoot.'

'How do I cope?'

'With Kit leaving? The same as me. We're both wrecked, we—'

'No, I mean about us. I betray him. Being with you.'

I take a moment, my mind wandering back to those weeks where we would laugh at the same thing then reset our faces as though laughing together was as much as admitting we'd given up on him. The moments where we'd cook together forming a natural rhythm, the times where our gazes lingered on each other for a fraction longer than would be polite.

There was a night in a busy wine bar. We were squeezed in together, a fairy-lighted brick wall behind us. I had felt the warmth of the outside of James's thigh next to mine. It was a few weeks after the call I had made to Ava, from the morning I had dropped the water and realised I was in love with him. We had stayed that way for a few seconds. I had been trying to ignore the pull of attraction, was still trying to deny my feelings for him, still unsure of his feelings for me. He had shifted, a pencil width away, and I had worried that I'd misread the signs. The tiny gap between us felt as though it was vibrating, like I was being pulled towards him but pushed away in the same moment. I had moved closer so that our legs were touching. This time he didn't move away. As the night had worn on, we stayed that way, heat burning through the fabric of our clothes. James and I didn't fall in love. We climbed into it, each step towards each other met with resistance, fraught with danger.

'You fight it at first. We both do. But then we both learn to forgive ourselves.'

He nods, his finger running around the rim of the glass.

'It's real,' I say and he meets my eyes. 'What we have, James.' I look down into my glass. 'I love you.' I can only imagine how weird it must be for him to hear it from me. 'I love you both,' I add.

'And now?'

I meet his eyes. He's watching me closely.

'Now? Now I can't stand you.' I laugh.

'Oh, don't I know it,' he says, but he's smiling. 'But I meant now, now that you know he's alive? Will you still marry me – future me?' He grimaces at the words but there is weight to his question even though to him, this must all seem very hypothetical. He holds an expression I've never seen on his face before, almost self-conscious. Our declaration of love for each other was never shy; it was visceral, raw, painful, *beautiful*.

'Honestly?' I reach for a nut and chew thoughtfully. 'I don't know. If you've lied to me, James...' I shake my head. 'If you *know* Kit's alive, I'd find it hard... to trust you again.'

'I understand.' He pauses. 'I feel sorry for him, future me.' James takes another long sip of wine. 'He can't compete with Kit coming back. He would know that. Me. Future James. He would know you would choose Kit.'

I can feel tears welling up; I blink them back. 'You don't know that. *I* don't even know that. I love you as much as I love him, James. It's just a different kind of love.' I pause. 'Can I ask you a question? Can you picture us together, at *all*?'

'I... no. Not really.'

'Don't sugar-coat it for me, will you?' But I'm teasing him.

'It's not that I don't. I mean, you're not *hideous* to look at or anything.' He bites back a smile.

'If it makes it easier... if the roles were reversed and you were telling 2016 me that we were about to get married, I would think you were off your bleeding rocker.'

He snorts, gets up, retrieves the list, places it between us on the bed, tops up our glasses and stares at the paper. He taps the top of his glass with his pen. Catching me looking at it, he stops. 'Sorry.'

'You don't have to be sorry. You fidget all the time. After a while it's just like white noise.'

We're quiet for a moment, both of us lost in the what ifs and maybes. 'Can I ask you *another* question?' I say. He nods. 'Why do you hate me so much?'

James swirls the wine again and takes another sip. 'I don't *hate* you, Liv. I just...'

'Find me irritating? Can't stand to be in the same room as me? Wish you'd never taken a summer job at Waterways?'

He laughs then. 'No. I wouldn't wish that. I've never seen Kit as happy as the day he met you. You are irritating though.' He smirks. 'Sorry.'

I laugh then. 'It's fine. We get past it.'

'Right. Let's see if we can work out why he leaves, then maybe all of this won't matter anyway.'

I don't correct him. I don't remind him that Kit will still leave, that I can't stop what is about to happen.

We move the conversation back to the list; we finish the wine. The clock is edging towards two a.m. I yawn. James notices. The weight of what will happen if I fall asleep presses into the room.

'Do you want to get out of here?' he asks. 'Go for a walk? You can't fall asleep while you're walking, right, and we need to keep thinking.'

'Sure, good idea.'

The hotel is dimly lit. Outside the air is cool. It's a clear night. The moon is almost full and the sky is full of stars.

'Cassiopeia,' he says pointing to the sky. 'It's named after the—'

'Vain queen Cassiopeia. She boasted about her own beauty.'

He digs into the pockets of his jeans. 'I've used that line before I'm guessing?' Our feet are crunching along the gravel as we head out of the hotel grounds, along the narrow road. I shiver, do up the top button of my jacket, still damp from my run earlier. This is the same road that I had looked out at on the morning of my wedding, as I'd pictured James running along, his ear pods in, grey hoody on.

'No, I just knew that fact.'

'Oh.'

'I'm messing with you, James. Yes, you've used that line on me before. Wait. That was a *line*?'

'Of course it's a line,' he says with a small laugh. 'It's the only fact I know about the stars.'

'What's your success rate? With that line?'

'Not bad and I hear that it'll be pretty successful in a few years.'

'Is that so?'

'Well apparently she agrees to marry me even when she discovers that I know nothing about constellations.'

The breeze runs through the trees lining the road, leaves rattling; hedgerows alive with nature, unmuted by the cacophony of daytime sounds.

'So, what's changed? What is the future like?' he asks, our breath coming out in puffs of mist.

I decide against mentioning the pandemic. He doesn't need to know and I want to save him from it all. 'Nothing much, really. The world just keeps ticking on. We do have an electric car though.'

'You're shitting me?'

'Nope... and it's an automatic.'

'Now I'm questioning everything you've told me. There's no way I'd agree to an automatic.'

'Well, you do.'

'Why?'

'I have many powers of persuasion.'

He clears his throat and I realise I've just taken things a step too far. I have to remind myself that this is the old James. Thinking of me in that way must feel so strange to him. I yawn.

'Think back to today.' He brings the conversation to why I'm here. 'Do you remember anything at all, anything out of the ordinary?'

'We argue, me and Kit, when I get back from shopping with Ava.'

'What about?'

'My coat.'

'Your *coat*?'

'Yeah, or rather...' I stop walking. We argued about the cost. 'Money.' We both have the same expression as the thread begins to unwind. Not only was Kit late paying Ian at the club, but he also brought up money with me, which was something he never did.

'Do you normally argue about money?'

I shake my head. 'No. You know what Kit is like: he *likes* to spend money. I remember thinking that it felt like he was gunning for a fight, that something must have happened at work to put him in such a bad mood.'

James veers to the side where there is a gap in the fence. He climbs over the ditch, turns and puts out his hand, and I think the action startles us both; 2016 James should have just walked on ahead. He wouldn't have put out a hand to help me.

I'm quiet.

'What?' James asks, glancing at me out of the corner of his eye.

I realise I'm smiling. 'Oh nothing. It's just that, well, if you want to know how our relationship started, then this is a pretty good demonstration. This is what we do after he leaves. It's kind of how it all starts.'

We keep walking, going around in conversational circles as we try to make sense of it all until we're back inside the hotel.

We take off our coats and sit down. 'What now?' I ask him, yawning again. He sits next to me.

'Now you have a place to start looking, you need to connect the dots. Look into his bank accounts, speak to Becky. If Kit's in trouble, there's only you who can save him. You're the only person he trusts. You can do this, Liv. You're stronger than you think.'

My stomach drops, his words bringing back the morning I stepped over the void and onto the pavement, James's hand outstretched. *You can do this; you're stronger than you think.*

He turns to me. 'Liv?'

'Hmmm?'

'I... I need to tell you something.' He exhales deeply, eyes looking at the door then back to me. 'I don't hate you. I... fuck me.' He scratches the back of his head. 'I can't believe I'm going to tell you this but it doesn't matter, does it? All of this won't happen?'

I'm about to open my mouth to remind him that it will still happen to me; I will still remember today.

He takes my hand in his; my eyes widen in surprise. He's shaking, just a gentle tremor.

'It was me who swam you back, that day on the river. Not Kit.'

'It was your voice I heard?' I frown, looking up at him. 'You saved me?'

He nods, squeezing my hand. 'Yep.'

What?

My memories of that day become scrambled. I was unconscious when it happened but when I think of that day, it is always Kit that I imagine holding me as he swam me back to the river bank. It was always Kit's face, Kit's voice. The image changes slowly, Kit's green eyes replaced with James's brown ones; Kit's shoulders and arms powering through the water rubbed out, James's tattoos and dark hair taking the lead role.

'Me that swam you back, me who told Kit to stay with you while I tried to radio for help.'

'Why wouldn't he tell me that?'

'And destroy your version of the great lightning bolt love story? Not a chance.'

I think back to that day, the weeks and months after, the way I told the story as if it was fate that we'd met; how I would tell anyone who would listen, that I knew from the first time I heard his voice that he was the one. How must it have felt to James to hear me saying those words? How did Kit feel, knowing that our meet-cute wasn't actually ours?

'Why didn't *you* tell me?'

His thumb is running over my knuckles, eyes focused on the rhythm.

'What would be the point?' His eyes lift. 'I saw the way you looked at him, how you couldn't take your eyes off him. Telling you the truth would have achieved nothing.'

I can feel this information filling in the gaps in my history that I never knew were there.

'And that's not the first time I saw you either,' he continues after a breath.

'It wasn't?' I tilt my head but he's staring straight ahead, as though lost in his memories.

'I saw you earlier, in the car park with Ava... and I thought' – he swallows, eyes dragging back to my face – 'that you were the most beautiful girl I had ever seen.' His words slam into me. His voice is tight with emotion. 'I've been in love with you for years, Liv.'

He lets go of my hand, rubbing the heels of his hands against his eyes like a toddler who doesn't understand why he can't have his own way. James holds himself, arms crossed and wrapped around his torso, the tops of his arms flexing and moving as he tries to contain the emotions inside. He buries his head deep in his chest, so I can't look at him.

'You can't be. You don't even like being *around* me,' I say gently, leaning forward.

'No,' he says, his head lifting. 'It's just hard being with you. And... hating that I love you. I hate that I'm *in* love with you.'

Everything starts to shift.

Libby's voice: *He always wanted what Kit had.*

I don't know what to do with this information. This is a different version of the man I fell in love with. The man I fell in love with grew to love me, changed during our time together, fell in love with me at the same time as I fell in love with him.

'Liv.' He shifts. I can feel the warmth of his hand hovering over my shoulder blade before he drops it and takes my hands in his. 'Please understand that I would never tell you this under normal circumstances. This is my burden. Not yours. Not Kit's, mine.' His eyes are fierce. 'And if I don't tell you, then it's because I'm too ashamed to admit that I've been in love with my brother's girlfriend since the first day they met. Until tonight, I've not even really admitted it myself. Do you have any idea how hard it is for me to not look at you? To not let my feelings slip. Being in love with you is... *exhausting.* It eats away at me like a parasite. I try to stay away from you, try to focus on your faults.'

'My faults?'

'Yeah, you know... how you section your dinner so you eat one part at a time. How you turn over every chip separately on the baking tray instead of going at them all with a spatula. And how you are always, *always* late. But... it's never enough, because then I notice that perfect crease between your eyebrows as you concentrate, or I'd realise that you're always late because you've grabbed an extra snack for us, or because you've sent your friend some flowers because they're having a tough time... You make it *impossible.*' The final words come out of him in a long breath.

He drops my hands. Gets up, pulling on his coat. 'Come and

find me tomorrow,' he says, his voice above mine. 'Tell me about the Power Rangers pyjamas. And if I still don't believe you, tell me all of this.' He heads towards the door then turns. 'If I go back to avoiding you, tell me this first.

'I'll believe you because I would never say this to you, under normal circumstances. I would never betray Kit. I guess that's why I never tell you, even when we're about to get married.' He gives me a sad smile. 'But maybe I can help you get back to him.'

I look up and reply, 'And back to you.'

The air in the room thickens as he looks at me, and I see it. The look I've seen a thousand times before: the way his eyes darken yet soften, the seriousness behind them that lets me know he loves me.

James loves me.

Now.

Not just in the future, but right here in 2016.

I get up, stepping towards him.

'Come and find me,' he says again, his hand on the door. 'You're not alone.'

26

FIVE DAYS AFTER I LEFT HER

I'm heading down the hill. The sun is shining. The sky clear. No hint of the storm that brought me here. Caesar is barking. He circles a few times, then on seeing me he bounds across the field, stopping in front of me, barking again. He turns. Bounds back towards the house. Hesitates and barks at me again like a scene out of *Lassie*.

Something is wrong. My insides start to thrum, like my veins are wound too tight. Like they could snap. I start running after Caesar. 'Mac?!' I shout. 'Where is he, boy?' I ask just as I see Mac inside the work shed, planing some wood.

'Jesus Christ, Caesar, you've just given me a heart attack.' Caesar's brown ears are pulled back. He's still in a state of warning. Or maybe I'm just spending too much time on my own with a grumpy Scot and his dog for company.

Mac looks up at me, the plane falling from his hands. I step forward. His eyes are off focus. Like he's already been on the whisky. But it's only nine in the morning.

'Mac?' I say stepping closer.

'Fucking wind nut's eaten the chopper,' he says. I try to make sense of the words. This could very well just be Mac being Mac, but his skin looks clammy. Caesar barks again.

'Mac, I think we need to get you inside.'

'You don't get to tell me what to do!' he snaps and steps forward. His movements are clumsy and he's leaning to the side.

'Actually,' I say bracing myself and wrapping my arm around his waist. 'I do.'

'You do?' he says. He's starting to lean his weight against me. Caesar is barking again.

'Pipe down!' Mac shouts.

I look over to Caesar whose snout is rummaging inside a canvas bag on the floor.

'Yep, how about we get you sitting down, eh?'

I'm panicking. If he's having a stroke then I need to get him to a hospital.

Caesar does another circle and barks again. I pick up the bag, rummaging through. Empty cans of Diet Coke, and a paperback, and some tissues, and tin foil screwed up. My hand hits on a Tupperware box. I open it. Inside is a Mars bar, a carton of orange juice. Glucose tablets.

'Mac, are you diabetic?' I ask. Ryan had a similar stash in his bag when he would sometimes come over after school. I never really paid any attention to it back then.

'What?' he shouts as if I'm hard of hearing.

I crouch down beside him. 'Mac, are you diabetic?' I repeat.

'Yep.' He gives me a strange smile.

'Right, fuck, I don't know what to give you!'

I recall Ryan drinking orange juice, so I go for that first.

'Drink this.' I puncture the carton with the straw and lift the box to his mouth.

'Give me that.' He snatches it from my hand, sucks on the straw and eyeballs me. I stand and look around the workshop.

Spotting Mac's phone on the side. I quickly google what to do if you're hypoglycaemic and dial 999. According to Dr Google, it will take about fifteen minutes for the juice to work.

'Emergency services, how can I help?'

I explain the situation and they stay on the line while they instruct me to give Mac four glucose tablets until he starts to feel better. He dutifully chomps through them and after ten minutes he starts to lose the glassy look in his eyes. 'I'm all right. Stop making such a fuss. There's folk who need that line open.' They recommend I take him to the doctor's to get him checked out. I thank them and end the call.

'Let's get you inside, eh?'

I go to help him up, but he shrugs me off. 'I'm diabetic not a bloody invalid,' he says then immediately stumbles.

'Could you stop being a git for a minute and let me help you?'

I put my arm around his waist. Guide him into the house.

'I'll be fine. You've got zombies to get to.' He rubs the space between his eyebrows.

'Headache?'

'Aye.'

'We need to take you to the doctor's.'

'No need. I've been through this before. I just need to lie down and I'll be right as rain.'

'You go up to bed and then I'll grab you some water and painkillers.'

'Fine,' he says like I've told him he needs to eat his sprouts.

I stand at the bottom of the stairs. Watch as he climbs them. He hesitates. 'I can feel you watching me.'

'I'll... go and get you some water.' Mac shakes his head and continues up the stairs. Caesar waits until he's reached the top and then bounds up after him.

I head into the kitchen, pour water into a pint glass. I open a few cupboards and grab some painkillers.

At the top of the stairs, there are three rooms, each with heavy wooden doors and stable latches.

I knock on the open wooden door and step in. Mac is lying on his side, hand stroking Caesar, telling him he's a good dog.

The room is surprisingly light, even though the furniture is dark. There are two wardrobes against the wall. A large sash window with pale green curtains. A writing bureau and bedside cabinets. I step into the room, placing the glass and pills down. There is a photo next to the clock. Mac is laughing, his arm slung around another man. He's taller. Blond. Wealthy-looking in that home grown, good teeth, good hair, kind of way. I lean in closer, scouring the blond man's face.

My heartbeat quickens.

I can feel my version of Mac changing. As if I'm adding water to the pages of a magic painting book that I had as a kid. Grey pictures suddenly transforming into colour.

He's watching me like he's daring me to say something.

'Good-looking guy.'

'Aye. He was. Too good-looking for the likes of me, but he loved me anyway.'

'Where is he now?' I ask, bracing myself.

'I don't want to talk about him, just now.'

I walk over to the bureau and reach for another photo. Mac, with a boy of about a year old on his knee. Mac is pointing at a green kite above them, his hand holding the plastic spool. The boy isn't looking at the kite though; he's looking at his father. I can feel Mac's stare from the bed.

I don't remember this.

I don't remember being pulled onto his shoulders, can't

remember the feel of his hair in my hand as I gripped on as though he was a horse.

I look over at Mac. And then I realise. He's always known. Right from the moment I turned up at his door and claimed to be a writer from York.

'You never liked holding it on your own, thought you'd fly away.'

I swallow hard and turn to him. A thousand questions in my eyes. 'What?' He tilts his head and I feel nauseous. 'You think I don't recognise my own son?'

27

TWO DAYS BEFORE HE LEFT ME

The first thing I think of is James's voice, running through me like electricity. *I don't hate you, Liv. I've been in love with you for years.*

Kit comes into the room quietly, his eyes apologetic, a sad-looking daffodil in his hand and breakfast on a tray.

'I've come to beg your forgiveness.' It takes me a while for my thoughts to settle.

James was already in love with me? How can that be? How did I not spot the signs? 'Sorry I was such a dick yesterday,' Kit says. He's talking about the argument about my coat, the comments about spending money. Not about meeting up with his ex-girlfriend. Not about hiding something from me.

Back then, I had forgiven him. I'd said that I would forgive him if he went and fetched me some peanut butter for the toast.

It was nothing on that Wednesday. I had forgiven him in a heartbeat. We'd had make-up sex, he'd put on his suit for a meeting and I'd gone over to Mum's.

He smiles at me – that confident smile that makes his eyes spark with that mischievous look that has everyone falling under his spell. It's only now that I notice a translucent shadow over that expression, a gossamer-fine coating. He has bags under his eyes. There is a tension to his smile that I never noticed before.

'I saw you yesterday,' I say, the words already out. 'With Becky? Becky Thomas?'

'Yeah?' he says, reaching over and taking a sip of my tea, before standing up and opening the wardrobe doors, playing for time.

'You were in a car together. I was out with Ava. I saw you,' I prompt.

'You never said?'

'Well, I'm saying it now.'

'Blue or white?' he asks holding up both shirts with a smile, anxiety being hidden behind the mundane, the ordinary.

I ignore his question. 'I didn't think you were still in touch.' He replaces the white shirt and begins pulling his arms through the sleeves. 'I wasn't... She sent me a message out of the blue. She wants to start up her own company.' His eyes are focused on his fingers manipulating the buttons. 'She asked me if I'd set her up with a decent website. I agreed. It's no big deal.'

'It looked like a big deal. You had your arms around her.'

He frowns briefly, then resets. 'She's having a tough time. It was nothing. I felt sorry for her, that's all. Her mum's just died. Nate, her husband, is being a bit of an arsehole and I wanted to help her out. He always was a jealous dick.'

Was he? A thought sparks. Maybe Nate has something to do with why he goes missing.

'You've not mentioned Nate before.'

'Why would I? He's harmless, but can be a bit of a knob where Becks is concerned.'

Becks. The familiarity of the name burns the back of my throat.

He tucks in his shirt and looks back at me. His mouth twitches at the side. 'Are you jealous?'

The way he is deflecting unsettles me.

'I'm just wondering why you never mentioned it. That's all.'

'It's nothing, Liv. Honestly. She asked if I could do her a favour and I said yes. She's married... We're not having a sordid affair.'

On seeing my expression, he softens and crawls across the bed towards me, nudging my nose with his, his eyes sincere. I feel myself softening despite all the thoughts in my mind, the lies I think he's telling me. Is this how it always was? I think back to our relationship, the days where I didn't want to go off on whatever adventure he had in store, how he would always win me over with a smile, with a kiss, with a promise of whatever he had planned being something I wouldn't regret.

'I'm sorry. I should have told you. But I promise you' – his gaze is intense – 'I would never be unfaithful to you.' There is fire in his words, conviction.

Every part of me wants to believe him. I'm yearning for it to be the truth; I'm overwhelmed by my insatiable need to believe him, to believe *in* him.

'So why didn't you think to mention that you were meeting up with your ex?'

'Honestly?' He's still leaning over me, his hair falling forwards, his breath on my face. The freckles running along his cheek like a Nike tick. 'She asked me not to. Said Nate would throw a fit if he knew she'd asked for my help. But you're right' – he kisses me gently on the mouth – 'I should have told you.'

Kit climbs off the bed and bends down in front of the mirror. He tames his hair with his hand, and grabs his tie from the end of the bed, knotting it.

'I'll make it up to you,' he says hesitating at the door. 'Why don't you meet me for lunch?'

I think back to this time in our lives. There was no suspicion between us. I loved him; he loved me. We were steadfast.

I shake my head. 'I can't... I've got to do some more work.'

He frowns. 'I thought you'd finished?'

'So did I, but it turns out I have another lesson left to plan.'

The lie skips from my mouth, bouncing and dancing across the room without a care in the world.

I've never lied to him before and the ease with which I do shocks me. Without even thinking about it, without planning which muscles to use, my face lies too. It looks disappointed. The lie unfolds without my control. 'I've got to teach them the basics of algebra.' My mouth forms words. It adds layers to my deceit, a scenario about word problems, an idea of making the lesson more practical.

'Well, have fun with your algebra.' He hesitates at the door. Can he tell? Or has the lie become solid, a fixed truth?

'Kit?' I sit up. 'Why were you cross about the money I spent on the coat? Is there something else going on?'

My words seem to startle him. He frowns but I can see there are things he wants to say. 'Tell me, Kit.' I get up and walk over to him. 'You can tell me. Is something on your mind? Are you having money trouble?'

He pulls a confused expression, a 'what are you talking about, everything's fine' look.

'Nothing for you to worry about. I was just tired, that's all. Problems with one of my clients not paying on time. I shouldn't have taken it out on you. I'm sorry.'

Money. James's words from last night. *You just have to connect the dots.*

Kit bends down and kisses my forehead. 'I've got to go. I've got a presentation at eleven with that tech company. If I get this then we can book that weekend trip to Amsterdam.'

He winks, kisses me again, knocks on the door frame three times, then he's gone.

'Love you!' he shouts from the bottom of the stairs.

The door closes before he hears me saying it back.

I let out a long breath. The muscles along my back are tense.

I've just lied to him about a fake lesson plan and I feel the weight of it pressing down on me. How must it feel when he leaves? How must it feel to him to lie about his own death?

I start opening and closing drawers. I upend his underwear drawer onto the bed. I throw open the wardrobe door and stuff my hands inside his pockets. I check his work jackets; I throw each item onto the bed, one by one. I'm breathless as I stand and look at the state of the room. The fire burns inside my stomach, the fire of grief that I went through the last time I did this. But today, something else is fuelling the flames. The truth is here somewhere. It has to be.

I storm into his office. His filing cabinet is locked and I rattle each drawer before spinning around on my heels looking for the key.

We hadn't looked into his accounts after he died because the police had, and there was nothing to suggest that Kit did this deliberately. He'd had an accident; he needed to be found. He couldn't be dead; he just couldn't.

My hands run around the inside of his desk drawers before pulling them out and shaking the contents onto the floor.

I get on my hands and knees and begin sifting through his stationery. I scour old receipts that he keeps for his tax bill, a new monitor for the computer, and receipts from business lunches over the past year. Each one with a hand-scribbled note at the top: Kingwood Team x 4 – WH; The Topmire Account x 3 – L; Jenkins x 6 – PP. On and on they go. Could this be something? But what can I do with this information? Ring the restaurants? Ask if they remember Kit being in there months ago?

There are no bank statements. Kit did everything online. He was always looking at ways to save paper. He loved the world we live in, was always conscious of our carbon footprint. I log onto his computer, opening up his banking, but I have no idea what his password is, or his PIN.

'Fuck!' I shout, pushing myself back on the desk chair.

You don't have to do this alone.

I reach for the phone and, just like yesterday, I ring James. The conversation is similar to yesterday, only this time I understand the forced way he's cool with me, reluctantly, agreeing to meet.

I shower and sit in front of the mirror. My make-up choices were lighter back then: pale pinks and greys for my eyes, liquid eyeliner that my fingers automatically remember to flick at the edges. I step into a pair of skinny jeans. I hold up a cold-shoulder black jersey and automatically reach for a bra but then remember I didn't wear one with this outfit. My cup is three sizes smaller right now. I replace the bra, pull on the top and sit in front of the mirror and blow-dry my short hair. I add a pair of silver hoop earrings and try to calm the nerves running through my body.

I'm going to have to watch James learn to accept the truth again.

I pick up the clothes scattered around the room and hang them back up; I smooth down the duvet. I stay there for a moment, my hands splayed against the soft fabric, my head bent over as I think about last night – the weight of James's feelings for me – then I pull myself up, throw on my leather jacket and leave.

* * *

James is already at the bench by the river. He stands as I approach him: dark hair, dark eyes, a wary look.

'Thanks for meeting me,' I say. He nods, sits back down. I pass him a takeaway coffee. 'Flat white, right?'

He takes the cup, the distance between us is back, space that pulses, expands and retracts, full yet empty. 'Thanks.'

'No problem.'

'So, you needed to talk to me?' he says, leg bouncing, eyes focused in the distance.

'I do.'

He nods, eyes focusing on the pewter surface of the river, hair unruly, the wind tugging it.

'James?' I go to reach for his hand. He looks down at it like it's a wasp. But now I understand his reactions. He can't for one minute let me know the truth about his feelings. I pull my hand away and take a sip of coffee instead.

Then I begin. Again.

28

FIVE DAYS AFTER I LEFT HER

I look at Mac, my fist clenched as though all of the words I want to say are held tightly inside. We eye each other, all sidesteps and punches waiting to be thrown.

'Why didn't you say anything?' I ask Mac.

'I'm not the one trying to hide anything. Why didn't you say anything when you turned up at my door, Mr I'm-a-writer-from-York?'

I'm still standing. The photo clutched in my other hand. I turn my back and stand it on the bureau. From behind, Caesar yawns and shifts. 'I didn't know if... if you'd slam the door on me.'

'Shut the door on my son? Why would you think that?'

I turn back round. He looks genuinely confused.

'Oh I don't know, Mac.' I flex my hand. 'Because you walked out on us, when you never wanted to be in our life. And you lied too. I asked you if you've ever lived anywhere else and you said no, so you can get right off your high horse.'

'No, you asked if this had always been home. I answered you truthfully. This is my home, the only one I've ever had.'

'And what about the house you shared with us?'

'That was never home.'

'Well that's just great. Thanks for clarifying that for me. I feel much better about my father walking out.'

'I didn't walk out; I was pushed.'

I laugh at that. I barely recognise the noise that is coming out of my mouth. I imagine Mum trying to force this great hulking man through the door. She's about seven and a half stone wet.

'You could have written, visited, sent birthday cards.'

'Aye.'

'So why didn't you?' There is such venom in my words it feels like I'm spitting them out.

'Because you were better off without me.'

'Better off? Are you serious right now?'

Mac rubs the space between his eyebrows. I lower my voice a notch remembering the laboured way he had climbed the stairs.

'I'm sorry for that,' he says.

'Yeah, well. It's a bit fucking late for that now isn't it?'

'Now is not the time to talk about this.'

I snort and shake my head. 'Right, well. You just find a space in your diary and let me know when you can pencil me in.'

'Pencil you in?' Mac shifts up the bed. 'Do you want to get off your own high horse for a minute, eh? Let me catch my breath? *Pencil you in.*' He rolls his eyes. Actually rolls them. 'Look, I've got a bastard migraine, I feel half dead and so this is no conversation to have just now. I can talk to you later, when you've had time to calm down and I don't feel like I'm about to puke my innards out, all right?'

I take in his appearance. He's pale, and the grey hairs of his beard stand out amongst the black. I take a breath. 'Fine. Get some rest,' I say.

'That's what I was trying to do until you started throwing your arms around like an air traffic controller.'

I don't respond. Instead I stride over to his bedside, pick up his glass and refill it from the bathroom tap. When I return, he's already asleep. I stand there looking down at him.

'I can't sleep with you standing over me like a fishwife,' he says.

'I'm going. I'll... I'll talk to you tomorrow.'

'Aye, you will no doubt talk at me, but you might want to take a moment to listen too.'

'Just...' I want to say more, but all that comes out again is: 'get some rest.'

29

TWO DAYS BEFORE HE LEFT ME

Just as before, James had accused me of making a sick joke. He fought everything I'd said, until: 'She said she wished you'd never been born.'

I'd wanted to tell him the truth, that we're getting married, the consuming love we feel for each other, that I know he's already in love with me, all of it, but I'm don't tell him that today. Today I decide to keep to the facts as best as I can. I won't tell him about us; I'll make this easy for him.

Now, we're climbing out of the car and facing the building where Rebecca works. It's tall, white-faced amongst a row of similar offices: accountants, estate agents, a bank. I've convinced him that it would be best if he tries to find out the truth rather than me. After all, if she's having an affair with Kit, I'm the last person she is likely to be honest with. 'You know there is no guarantee she'll speak to me, right?' he says. James had hinted that they had history but wouldn't tell me any more, saying it was a long time ago.

'I know, but it's worth a shot. I just need to know why they met up yesterday. I'll wait here.' He nods, fiddles with the neck of his sweater and pulls on the cuffs of his jacket. That's the same jacket he'll be wearing next week as we stand in the rain watching the lifeboats bumping across the waves.

'Right then.' He eyes the pavement then turns on his heel and walks into the building. I hover outside, not knowing what to do with myself, other than lean against a lamp post like a spy. Do spies hang around lamp posts? I have no idea. James is at the reception desk. I watch the body language from behind the counter, all smiles and hair flicks. It's funny to see how women respond to James when I'm not around. James isn't stop-you-in-your-tracks good-looking – broken nose, scar at his lip – but Jesus is he sexy. And then, when he smiles, his whole face changes, and there is this light – like the goodness inside him comes pouring out. I didn't see the attraction in 2016, when he was all scowls and abrupt replies. I was so wrong.

He walks over to sit on the sofa, glancing in my direction. Then he stands, says something to the receptionist and hurries out of the doors. He looks left and right, crosses the road, hand through his hair.

'What are you doing?' he asks.

'Nothing. Waiting.'

'You can't wait here. She'll see you and she's not going to open up about Kit if she can see his girlfriend hovering there like a private detective.'

'Ha! I was just wondering that: do spies hang around lamp posts?'

'What?' His eyebrows quirk and he glances back to the building. 'Just... find somewhere else to wait. Somewhere less conspicuous. She's coming down in five minutes.'

'Righto, boss.'

He frowns again. This must be so strange for him, for me to be so friendly, so familiar. James begins to turn.

'By the way...' I interrupt his movements. 'That receptionist is into you, just in case you're wondering.'

'I... I wasn't.' But I can see the flush around his neck. Oh he knows all right. I bite back a smile.

'I'm just saying.'

'I need to get back.'

The right side of his collar is flicked up. I reach over to straighten it and he pulls away.

'Sorry.' *Old habits*. His eyebrows corrugate, confused.

'I need to go back,' he replies.

He turns and strides across the road, straightening his collar as he goes.

I step along the street and sit at a bistro table outside a wooden coffee bar, just far enough to be out of sight but allowing me to still be able to see the reception area.

James stands as she approaches, hand raking through his hair. Her arms are folded across her chest. She sits down with her back to me as they begin speaking. James is leaning forwards, his hands accompanying his words. I see her shaking her head, glancing back to the receptionist. She gets up to walk away. James stands, hands in his back pockets. She stops, then gives him a small smile. It looks like she's saying a parting word of advice, before she closes the door behind her. James stands and exits the building, crosses the road glancing up and down until he spots me. He walks quickly, eyes down, until he pulls out a chair and sits across from me. He looks agitated.

'Well?' I ask.

'Kit did meet her yesterday.'

'I know. I told you. I saw them.'

'But... it's not what you think. He's not seeing her, at least not romantically.'

'So why did they meet?'

'She's investing in his company.'

'What? That's not what Kit said; he said she was setting up her own company and needed him to do a website.'

'Well, he's lying.'

'How can you be sure *she's* not lying?'

'I can't... and I know you don't much care for my opinions.' I open my mouth to interrupt to tell him I do, but in 2016, I used to think he was always too cautious, always finding reasons not to go anywhere with us. I close my mouth. 'For what it's worth, I believe her.'

'How much money is she investing?'

'She wouldn't say, only that he got in touch, suggested they meet and then asked her, but I get the impression it was a big ask.'

'And did she give it to him?'

He reaches for a packet of sugar, fiddling with it before replacing it and picking up a napkin, folding the corners into a boat sail. 'James?'

'Yes.'

I let this information sink in. 'But that doesn't make any sense.'

'You say that there was nothing out of the ordinary with his finances? But maybe there is before he disappears?'

'The police looked into it, when he first went missing. There were no big deposits, no big withdrawals. So if what Rebecca is saying is true, what happens to the money?'

'Maybe he needed it to... to start a new life?'

'But Kit doesn't know he's going to leave. I believe him.'

'This is messed up. Kit loves you; he would do anything for you, Liv. I honestly don't think he would leave you intentionally. Which means...'

'Maybe he didn't mean to leave for good? Or maybe he

intended taking me with him?'

'Maybe.' The sugar packet is back in his hand; he rotates it against the top of the table like a square wheel.

He's silent, but I know the clashes and clambering thoughts that will be going on inside, that noise of the what ifs and the whys that only ever quietened when we were together, only starting to ebb with the passing of time and the slow acceptance of his death.

On the table behind him, a baby starts crying.

James and I talked about having children. We are going to start trying next year. I wonder how he would feel if I told him that right now?

We bumped into an old friend of his a few weeks back, before all of this happened. She used to come to the gym and had recently had a baby. We all chatted on the pavement, ended up sitting down for a coffee. I'd gone to the counter and when I'd looked back, the baby was in James's arms, his mother rifling through a changing bag. I'd stifled a snigger at the way he was holding it like a trophy, arms outstretched. He glanced up, a look of alarm on his face. By the time I'd returned with the drinks though, James had the baby against him, asleep on his shoulder. Something had passed between us, a softening of a conversation that had seemed so hard to approach, suddenly becoming easy.

'Did we...' James begins. 'During our time together looking for him...' The together is soft, a trace of a concept, not real, not to him. 'Did we ever suspect anything was, you know, amiss?'

'Honestly? No. There is nothing that made me... made us think that. He was fine, James, is fine. At least on the surface.'

Of all the herculean events that I'd thought of – the drowning, the falling, the starving in the dark – this was never one of them.

'And you said the police checked his finances?'

I nod.

'So there was no reason we would suspect that he was in trouble?'

'No. None. It was an accident, a horrific, terrifying accident. We didn't suspect anything. There really was no reason to.'

My stomach rumbles; James glances at it. I fold my arms across my torso.

He lifts a finger at the woman clearing the table next to him. The action is confident and yet unobtrusive. The girl joins us, a notepad in her hand, blowing her red hair away from her eyes and smiling.

'Can we have two coffees and—' He looks to the folded board outside the door of the hut. 'Two BLTs?' He raises his eyebrow at me. I nod.

'Sure,' she says and scribbles it down, heading inside.

'Thank you,' I say. He doesn't say anything, but he smiles.

There you are, James.

* * *

James finishes the other half of my sandwich and we make our way back to the car. It all feels so normal as we walk through town. It's funny, isn't it? How most towns look the same but all hold different lives: the woman talking quickly into the phone, sidestepping a man bending down to tie his shoelace; a window cleaner swiping across a café window; a postman smiling as he passes; a father bending down and wiping away the tears of his son; a group of three women, all wearing similar smiles, the same curve of the chin that gets passed down generation by generation. So many lives, so many stories, the same but different all over the world. This feels the same as my real life: walking along, James next to me, the aftertaste of coffee, of lunch.

'Where does Kit go tomorrow?' he asks as we continue walking.

I shake my head, trying to push away the thoughts throbbing behind my eyes.

'A team-building thing. He went last year. The company that invited him is Broomfield Photographic Associates, BPA. He had worked for them last year and they did the same kind of thing. The previous year it was in the Cotswolds. Kit was in charge of their computer security system and they had paid him a retainer for the rest of the year. It's one of those all-expenses-paid team-building places.'

'Where?'

'In Monmouthshire or something like that.'

'Was there anything unusual about him when he came back?'

'That's what's so hard to understand, James. Nothing was out of the ordinary, nothing at all.' I sidestep a mother who is trying to console her toddler. 'He came home around eight in the evening, happy – exhausted but happy. We ate dinner; he told me he'd had a good day. Made some good connections, new clients. They'd played mini golf. There was nothing about anything he told me that sounded different. He's been to these things count-less times before. I didn't pay it much attention after he went missing. Why would I? He was fine.'

'But he's not, is he?' James asks as we reach Bertha. 'Some-thing is going on.'

I nod, tears in my eyes.

We're both quiet as he begins driving us back. 'You said you and Becca' – *Becks* – 'had history. Were you two involved?'

He pauses, his shoulders dropping.

'No. Yes. It's complicated. Ancient history.' The engine ticks over as we wait at a set of traffic lights.

'But today doesn't happen, James. We don't have this conversation. So it doesn't matter. You might as well tell me what happened between you two.'

Duty, rebound, always wanted what Kit had.

The lights turn green. 'We, Becky and me,' James continues, shifts the gears and indicates. 'We were kind of together. In sixth form. Before she met Kit. It was casual, nothing serious, at least from her point of view. Then she met Kit when she called for me and I wasn't in. And that was that. I didn't take it too well at the time.' A small smile as he turns the steering wheel. 'I was young, hot-headed. Called them both a few choice words when I got home and saw them sucking faces on the sofa. It's not something I'm proud of.'

As he talks I remember this anecdote about James's old girl-friend. It was all laughs and ribbing each other but hearing James now, I realise it cut deeper than he's ever let on.

'Has that happened before? You've been with someone and Kit…'

He looks to the right, scar at the back of his head just a stretch away from my hands.

'Like I said, it's ancient history.'

'Did Kit know? That you two were…'

'No. I mean, I don't think so. It was probably me just reading the signs wrong. We'd only gone out a couple of times; I hadn't even made a move. Kit didn't waste any time though.'

I let this sink in.

James always wanted what Kit had. What if it's the other way around? What if Kit always wanted what James had?

He parks outside our flat, Bertha purring.

'Do you want to come in?' I ask as though this is the end of a first date.

'No thanks, I've already made an excuse not to go to Mum and Dad's for dinner. If Kit sees me, he'll know I've ducked out.'

'Dinner? Oh crap.' I'd forgotten that we go to their parents' for dinner tonight.

James holds a small smile as I say the words. 'Not as big a fan of Madame Palmer as you make out, huh?'

I chew the inside of my mouth. 'No, you could say that. She doesn't take it well when I meet someone new. She thinks I've betrayed Kit's memory... or words to that effect.'

'Figures.'

He taps the steering wheel, but I hesitate for a few seconds. I don't want to get out of the car; I don't want to lose him all over again. 'Could you come over later?' I blurt out the words.

His eyes widen a touch, and he pulls at his earlobe. 'Sure, I mean, if you think it'll help?'

'I think it would. We can have a debrief. I could always get rid of him, um, send him to the shops or something?' The words come out flippantly, as though lying to Kit is something I do on a daily basis. Great, now I sound like a woman who is used to lying to James's brother and I'm just one step away from fluttering my eyelids and telling him we'll have the place all to ourselves.

He bites his bottom lip then nods.

'Or maybe you should come to dinner? See if you can spot something going on?'

As soon as I give him another option, he seems to grab on to it. 'That might be a better idea, actually.' I can see him resisting being alone with me again.

I want to reach out and kiss him. I want him to wrap his arms around me and tell me we'll find out the truth. I want him to tell me I'll be coming home soon.

What if I'm not? What if I'm stuck here? What if I have to go through the pain of losing Kit all over again? I shiver, despite the warm air in the car, the feeling of being trapped, of not being able to get out rises from my feet to the top of my head in a rush, the fear of a swirling void outside the car door: one misstep and I'll be consumed by it.

'What if I'm stuck here?' I say. 'What if I never get back?' I turn to James, his image blurred as I blink.

'Isn't that what you want? To save him? To stop him doing whatever stupid shit he's about to do?'

Is that what's going on? Maybe I do stop him, maybe I do stay here with Kit. I don't want to, I realise. I don't want to stay here with Kit. I want to get back to James. James is my future; James is the man I want to spend the rest of my life with.

The thought is warm, like melted butter, like honey. I love James. I learnt to live without Kit, but as I sit here now, the idea of not having James, of not spending the rest of my life with him is like ice burning my skin.

'I'll see you in a bit, then?' he adds, prompting me.

'Yeah, see you later.'

Kit's home. I can hear the kettle boiling in the kitchen as I step through the door.

'Hey!' he shouts. 'Fancy a coffee?' Kit comes out of the kitchen. 'What's wrong?' he says taking in my appearance. I get to the top of the stairs and he pulls me close. I clutch to him tightly, trying to pull apart the strings that tie me to him. Because it's not Kit's arms I want around me; I know that now.

'You OK?'

I nod into his chest, this man who I always, deep down, felt that I should be with, who has been hiding in the background of mine and James's entire relationship.

I take some deep breaths. 'I'm fine; had a few cross words with Ava, that's all.'

Another lie – how easily they come.

'You sure? We don't have to go to my parents' if you don't want. I can cancel?'

'God no, and face the wrath of your mum?'

'It would be cutting it fine. You know how she gets but I can call her, tell her you're ill?'

I exhale loudly.

I have a job to do.

I'm here to find answers. I only have one more day until he leaves. I have to help him before he makes the biggest mistake of his life. I just hope that by doing that, by saving Kit, it's enough to send me home.

30

FIVE DAYS AFTER I LEFT HER

I go back to the cottage. I'm wired. I change, tie my feet into my runners, and slam the door behind me.

I run through the past. Taking myself further into the hills. I try to shut it all out. Instead, concentrating on the burn in my legs. The sun is now hidden away behind a vast expanse of lard-coloured sky, widening the higher I go. I run through memories with Alan, the man I have called Dad all my life: the way he would pick me up if I fell, his gentle manner as he put magic cream on my grazed knee. Alan would let me go first if we were playing a board game too. Because Alan is a good man. A good father.

The sky swirls above me, cream mixing with slate-grey like a paintbrush has been dipped into an artist's water pot. Rain starts to fall in sharp needles as I push my way further up into the wilderness. Higher and higher. All signs of manmade life fall away so it's just me, and my memories, and the mountains, and spasms of shame.

With each mile I run, old memories that I have folded away

open and flutter in front of me. The day I found my birth certificate. Twelve years old. Me and my brother looking for hidden Christmas presents. He'd been the one to read it first, his eyes flashing towards me, his hand shaking as he passed it me. *Name of Father: Connor McDonald.* Old McDonald did indeed have a farm.

I let my feet take me higher and higher into the hills. Bright greens sink into sage, and army greens. I breathe in through my nose. Out through my mouth. My breath hot in my throat. I can feel his arms around me: it doesn't matter, we're still brothers. Mum had walked into the room, looked at us, at the paper in my hand. She dropped the laundry in her arms, snatched the paper. It had left a paper cut along the inside of my palm. I'd picked and picked at it so even now there is a pale scar, a reminder of that day.

'Connor McDonald left us,' she began, his name like a hiss. 'Like the spineless man he is. And good riddance. He's corrupt, immoral, the worst of men. He is a man who you are never to see, do you hear me?' She'd held my shoulders tightly, nails digging into my skin. 'You are not to bring that man back into our lives. Or so help me God...' She looked up as though God himself was nodding, giving her permission to speak. 'Just leave it be. For all our sakes.' She'd walked out of the room.

The rain is coming down heavily now. I push on through. I push past the night I told Liv, the way she had held me telling me that just because he didn't want me, didn't mean I wasn't good enough.

I've reached the top. I'm surrounded by space, rocks and fields; the view stretches out, forest green hills, burnt-lemon-coloured grass. Below the cliff edge and in the distance there is a lake, the surface pewter, the sky now bruised and angry, the rain pummelling against its surface. I rest my hands against my knees.

The memories are compressing inside my chest. I scream into the air, tears running down my face. With the sound escaping my body, I feel a small sense of relief since the morning I left Liv.

The morning of our wedding.

The morning Kit came back.

31

TWO DAYS BEFORE HE LEFT ME

We arrive at Lynn's. Lawn trimmed to within an inch of its life, gable-fronted house with windows that are reflecting the sun so brightly it's a wonder it's not setting off little fires everywhere. Cleanliness is next to godliness.

She opens the door, pulling Kit into an embrace the moment he crosses the threshold. My throat tightens. She never hugs James. Lynn pulls back, places a hand on Kit's cheek, radiant in her love for her favourite son, her golden child.

'Olivia,' she announces, drawing me into her embrace. I lean down. Lynn is only five foot, incredibly slim and fit: all squash-playing sharp shoulders and elbows, brutal backhand. 'So good of you to come.'

When Kit left, she was all warmth. She took care of me, packed my things, guided me to the car, took me home to my mum, to where she knew I'd be looked after. It was like she was pouring her love for him onto me.

'Hi, Lynn.' I smile, and pass her the bunch of flowers that we'd bought from the garage on the way.

'How lovely, such unusual colours.' She sniffs them and walks through to the kitchen.

'Something smells nice,' I say. Kit takes my coat as I take off my pumps, putting them in a neat pair by the door.

'Oh, it's nothing.'

Beef bourguignon and dauphinoise. I remember it being delicious.

I follow Kit into the lounge. This is where James and I had been standing when she told us to get out. The minute she saw him take my hand in his, as he told them we were a couple, is still scarred on my retinas; the look of disgust and the visceral hatred that had poured from her mouth was unlike anything I had ever experienced.

Alan is sitting in the armchair with a newspaper. I feel myself relax as I step into his embrace. I've missed him. He seems lighter, the lines around his eyes softer, the curve of his spine more fixed. Alan had tried to stay in touch with James once we got together, but James had pulled away. It would be easier for him, he would say, when I saw him ignore Alan's name on incoming calls: *Mum would never forgive him if she found out; it's better for him to stay away.* I'd bumped into Alan a few weeks back, shocked at the way he looked: greyer, shrunken. He'd insisted on buying me a coffee, had told me it was the least he could do. I'd told him about the wedding. He'd asked if we were happy, and I'd told him the truth that we were, but that we were sad he wouldn't be there. He had seemed grateful for my time, wished us luck, asked me to tell James he was only ever a phone call away. Looking at him now, I wonder if it is just the loss of Kit that changed him so much, or the loss of James too.

'Villa are having a good season.' He jumps into sports talk with Kit, both of them all smiles and banter at their team's performance. There's a knock on the door and I hear Lynn striding along the hall. James's voice rumbles through the walls, thrumming up my spine.

She follows him into the room, sharp-angled brackets around her smile. 'Looks like he could make it after all. I just hope the beef will stretch.'

'Jimmy!' Alan pauses the conversation, the recount of the team's last match half finished. He pulls James into a bear hug, landing his hands on James's shoulders. 'Of course there's enough beef; you cook enough to feed an army!' He rolls his eyes at the boys conspiratorially. They both sit down. James glances briefly at me then away.

'Let me get you some drinks. What'll it be?' Alan claps his hands together.

'I'll get them. You boys catch up,' I say with a smile, standing and leaving space for James to sit next to his brother.

'Kit?'

'I'll have water thanks. Need to keep a clear head for tomorrow.' He winks.

'James?' I ask, my voice tentative.

He meets my eyes. They're shuttered, and his true feelings for me are kept locked away. 'I'll have a beer, thanks.'

I look away quickly. 'Al? What are you in the mood for?'

'A nice stiff whisky, to be truthful, but the lady of the house can't abide the smell.'

'Glass of wine?' I coax.

'Oh well, only if you insist,' he replies with a wink.

I head into the kitchen. Lynn is at the island, snipping the stems of the flowers and arranging them in a vase.

'They look lovely,' I say as I approach the fridge. 'You have such a way with flowers; I never know how far to cut them down.'

'Thank you, dear, roses aren't my favourite; they always have an air of something sinister about them, all those hidden thorns.'

I open the fridge. She glances at me with a fleeting look of disapproval as I pull out a bottle of beer. 'James, I take it?' She shakes her head glancing at the clock. 'It's not yet five. Perhaps a cup of tea?' Lynn takes the bottle from my hand and replaces it in the fridge.

'Oh, let's live a little,' I say and she raises an eyebrow at my suggestion. 'Oh, and Alan fancies a glass of red.'

Her responsive smile doesn't meet her eyes, but she pulls out a bottle from the rack. 'Well I suppose it's got some health benefits.'

I pour a healthy amount in a glass. 'Do you fancy one?' I ask her, shaking the bottle a little. 'Go on, it'll put hairs on your chest.'

'Well, that's not quite the right phrase to convince me, but it will go with the beef. Thank you, Olivia, just a drop now.'

I pour a glass for myself and resist the urge to neck it in one go.

'Kit's after water. He's got a work function tomorrow, needs to be on his "A game".'

The pride on her face suggests I've just said he's going to walk on water not drink it. 'Here,' she says opening the fridge and taking out a bottle of Evian, then she goes about slicing a lemon, flowers left dripping from the counter. I surreptitiously open the fridge again, take out a bottle of beer, twist off the top and carry Alan's wine and the beer through. James's fingers touch the tips of mine; he retracts the bottle quickly. Lynn is hot on my heels, passing Kit his water like a trophy. She does a second take at the bottle of beer in James's hands; I feel a smug sense of satisfaction.

Dinner is frustratingly delicious and the conversation is easy-going despite James's determination to barely acknowledge me. How exhausting loving me must have been for him.

'That reminds me,' Lynn says, placing her knife and fork in a neat line at the side of the plate. 'Kit, I need your help with my new phone. It's all gobbledygook to me.'

'Sure,' he says as she smiles back at him. They begin talking about the apps that she'll need.

'How's the training going, James?' Alan asks, leaning forward.

James chews a piece of potato. 'Good,' he replies.

'Don't talk with your mouth full,' Lynn snaps. James stares at her, swallows, opens his mouth to show her the food is gone and continues. Kit hides a smirk behind his hand.

'Good thanks, Dad. I need to get my weight up a bit, but I should pass the physical.'

'When do you fight?' Alan asks.

'The NAC qualifiers start in a month.'

'You'll smash it,' Kit says.

'A little old to still be fighting at amateur level aren't you?' Lynn raises her eyebrow.

I look to her sharply. She doesn't notice, just concentrates on slicing her beef.

'There is nothing amateur about the way our boy fights,' Alan cuts in. 'This is going to be your year, Jimmy; I feel it in my bones.'

I swallow a piece of carrot with difficulty. James won't go to the physical; he won't ever get to professional level. He stops training for it once Kit leaves. All of his time was taken up looking for Kit and looking after me.

James is watching Kit closely throughout the meal, eyes darting back and forth. I pick apart everything that is going on around me: the way Kit is talking to his mum as he sets up her phone. There is nothing in his demeanour that hints at the catastrophic choice he is about to make.

'You free tomorrow, Kit?' James asks.

I look down at my plate, at the rich gravy mingling with the cream of the dauphinoise.

'Ah no can do. Work gig. Team building, which usually means free booze and networking.'

'Right. Where are you going?'

'Hmmm?' Kit says, filling his mouth with food.

'The gig, where is it?' James repeats.

Kit reaches for his glass of water, looking over at James. He puts the glass down. I stare it him. He frowns at me then sticks out his tongue as if this is all a big joke. Usually I would return the insult, but I don't; I continue to stare at him. There is a slight shift in his body language. He rubs under his eyes then cuts another piece of meat. 'Wales. I'm getting the train tomorrow, early doors. Monmouthshire.'

'What's the venue?'

He pauses. 'Huh?'

'The venue?'

'Call of the Wild or something like that. One of those places where we're all supposed to help each other across rivers and stuff. I'll check the itinerary when I get back.'

Kit had told me there was mini golf, a clown with a mouth that kept getting the ball stuck. I feel myself frowning as James continues.

'Fancy a run when you get back?' James asks, focusing intently across the room at his brother.

'Maybe, I'll give you a bell when I'm on the way home.'

Pudding of apple pie and custard is eaten; playing cards and coffee are brought out. Lynn's eyes fill with a spark as she wins at gin rummy, and at Kit's laughter as he wins the next round. There is no hint of regret, no extra hugs and kind words to his parents.

'James, will you put down your phone for just a minute? This is family time,' Lynn says.

'Actually, I'm going to make tracks.'

'Well, it was nice of you to *drop by*,' Lynn says, her focus back on the cards in her hand.

Alan gets up, pulls him into a hug. James drops an airbrushed kiss on Lynn's head, nods at me, raises a hand to Kit, then leaves. My breath is rock-hard in my chest.

I stand up, leaving them to the games as I begin washing up.

'Liv?' James is back, his voice making the rock in my chest knock against my ribs. 'Could you move the car forward a bit? Someone has sandwiched me in.'

'Sure,' I say, my voice overly keen. I dry my hands on a tea towel and ask Kit for the keys. He holds them back with a challenge and a glint in his eyes. I roll my eyes, kiss him and then he passes me the keys.

I follow James along the hall and step out onto the path, shielding my eyes from the setting sun. He turns on his heels. 'There is no Call of the Wild venue in Monmouthshire.'

'Maybe he has the wrong name?'

'I can't find anything that sounds even close to it.'

'You're sure?'

James puts his hands in his back pockets and looks down at his feet.

'You think he's lying?'

'Looks that way.'

'So where does he go?'

'Beats me. Anyway...' He pulls out the keys in his hand. 'I thought you should know.'

'Thanks.' He nods and begins walking away.

'James?' I take a few steps forward.

A rush of winds scatters the remains of autumn leaves across the lawn, mixing with the daffodils beginning to open: the old circling the new.

I want to step closer to him, to put my hand on his shoulder, but I remain in the same spot.

Tears threaten again. He turns towards me, eyes scanning my face, the car door open. 'Thank you,' I say. 'For today, for everything.'

He meets my eyes, searching them briefly. 'Can you save him?' James asks. 'Can you save my brother?'

'Yes,' I say even though I have no idea how. If I don't save him in this timeline, I vow here and now that I will help him in the present.

He gives me a slight nod. 'Keep your phone on. I'm going to see what I can find out and if I can't find anything today... Call me tomorrow? Tell me again. I'm not going to lose my brother.'

'Thank you.' He taps the top of the car, climbs in and drives off.

He really doesn't know.

James doesn't know what Kit is planning to do.

But then I remember his words from the other night: *there is only one reason I can think of, to protect him.*

Does Kit ask him for help tomorrow?

The games are finished, and we all say our goodbyes. I analyse Kit's actions. His farewell is brief, his eyes on his phone, distracted. As far as I know, this is the last time he will see his parents and yet there are no lingering hugs, no final last words, no sadness.

Kit pulls me close to him as we walk to the car, my head leaning against his shoulder as we walk away.

I tighten my hold on Kit's waist, I need to save him, keep him safe.

My phone buzzes in my back pocket. A message from Ava.

> What time are you getting here? If you don't get
> a move on we'll miss the trailers and you know
> that's my favourite part.

I'd forgotten about tonight. I'd left early, didn't stay for cards or pudding. I'd got a taxi and Ava and I had watched *London is Falling* and I'd made myself feel sick by having too much Ben and Jerry's after the meal.

James didn't come for dinner. I remember the beef, the flowers. James had sent a text to Kit asking if he wanted to go for a run. Lynn's eyebrows rose at the fact he was free for a run but not for dinner with his family. Did they go for a run while I was at the cinema?

Kit lets go of me, waves to his family, his hand already tapping out something on his phone. No lingering glance as they stand in the doorway, Alan's arms around his mother.

I look at Kit. I need to stick to him like glue for the rest of the evening. I reply to Ava telling her that I've got an upset stomach but to go ahead and spend the night with Gerard Butler without me.

As Kit drives us home, I think about James and my suspicions that he must have known Kit was alive. But I know now that he had no idea, at least not today.

Kit reaches for my hand, holding on to it even as he shifts gears. He smiles, brings my hand to his mouth before frowning in the rear-view mirror.

I hear the crunch of metal on metal.

Our bodies slam forward against our seat belts; Kit's foot hits the brake.

The car swerves, clipping up a kerb, coming to an abrupt halt. Kit's instant reaction is to check me.

'Are you OK?' He unbuckles his belt, leaning across me. I'm breathless, but unharmed. 'Liv?' His voice and hands are shaking.

'I'm fine, I'm...' And then I see the car that has just run us off the road. A blue BMW: K8N WYT1

'You sure?' Kit continues. I nod, unable to reply.

The tail light of his car had been smashed. Kit had told me he'd reversed into a lamp post.

Another lie.

He didn't reverse into anything. I wasn't in the car with him when this happened; I was safe on the way to the cinema. Kit hadn't been shook up when I got home; he laughed about being such an idiot. Laughed, brushed it off, said he'd get it fixed next week.

He didn't tell me that Kane, the double-glazing salesman, had run him off the road.

The flickering of fire is back in my stomach, the breath held in my lungs to stop it igniting.

What did you do, Kit?

32

FIVE DAYS AFTER I LEFT HER

The bath is cold. My legs tight from my run earlier. I'm spaced out. The beer in my hand is lukewarm when I hear the knock on the door.

'James!'

Oh now he wants to talk. Now when I am knackered and have made short work of the six-pack that has been festering in the back of one of the kitchen cupboards for God only knows how long.

Caesar barks.

'James! Open the door!' Mac's voice from outside the bathroom window is determined. He's not going anywhere. I drain the last of the warm beer, pull myself out of the bath, wrap a towel around my hips and head downstairs. I yank open the door. My wet skin accosted by the cold wind and Mac's stare. He glances at the tattoo of a phoenix etched around my ribcage.

'What's that supposed to symbolise?' he asks, walking past me, a large shopping bag in his hand. 'Rising from the flames of what?' He gestures to my torso with his head, as he starts emptying the contents onto the counter. Tinned tomatoes, capers, lamb chops among other things. Water is still dripping from my hair as I close the door behind him, Caesar nudging my thigh.

'It doesn't symbolise anything,' I answer, reaching for the last beer from the counter.

Mac looks better. Face back to a normal shade of Scot. 'Bullshit. Nobody gets a tattoo that big for no reason.'

'That's what you came here to talk about? Not the fact that you're my father, or so it claims on my birth certificate. That you walked out and left me to be brought up by a woman who, by her own admission, thinks I ruined her life?'

'Aye, well, that conversation needs sustenance, more than a packet of Doritos' – he pinches the bag in question as though it's poison – 'and a six-pack at any rate.'

Mac lands a packet of spaghetti next to the tins.

'What does it mean?' He nods to my still-dripping torso.

I think back to the day I got it. The day Kit asked Liv to move in with him and the piercing cold feeling that had made my bones ache.

'There's no hidden meaning; I just liked it, that's all,' I reply, remembering the pain after I had left the tattoo shop. The heat from it thawing the chill inside. Mac looks up to the ceiling, a 'give me strength' expression.

He pulls out the chopping board and starts smashing cloves of garlic. 'Are you going to put some clothes on?'

Jesus Christ. I swear I get whiplash from our conversations.

* * *

By the time I return, the air in the kitchen is garlic-filled. Caesar is napping beside the range and Mac has poured two glasses of red wine. A breadbasket is sitting in the middle of the table. Bob Dylan is playing in the background: 'Lay Lady Lay'. I tear off a chunk of bread, chewing quietly while I watch him chopping and stirring.

'I never wanted to leave you,' he says, lifting a lid, steam billowing around him as though we are midway through an already established conversation.

I swallow. 'So, why did you?' I say, reaching for the wine, taking a large gulp.

'Because I was weak, because I believed your mother, because I was in love with a man... take your pick.'

'Oh, come off it, Mac. None of that explains why you left. Why you didn't stay in touch.'

The beers have erased part of my filter. He grates parmesan, putting it on the table next to the basket of bread.

'It doesn't?' he asks as though his answer explains everything in detail. Even more jarring is the look of surprise on his face.

'No, Mac. It doesn't.'

'I didn't want to leave you; you're my son.'

'Yes, I am. But you still left me.'

'Aye. And not a day has gone by that I didn't wish I'd fought harder to stay in your life.'

He turns. Begins plating the pasta. Ladles sauce on top. He brings the plates to the table, sits opposite, spoons cheese on top. I cross my arms, eyeing his actions.

'Eat.' He gestures to the plate, slurping spaghetti into his mouth. I pick up a fork, cramming some in my mouth. He grinds more pepper over his plate. 'I wasn't in a good place back then. I started a relationship with Lynn to hide what I knew about myself. I thought that if I just tried harder, I would fix myself.' He takes a sip of wine.

'Fix yourself?'

'Aye,' he puts the glass back down and twists pasta onto his fork. 'Fix my predilection for tall blonds with knackers instead of knockers. And who better to guide me than a God-fearing woman like your mother. It was a mistake.'

'Nice to know I was a *mistake*,' I say bitterly.

'Nothing about you is a mistake, James. Well, apart from running away from the woman you love.'

'We're not talking about my mistakes, Mac.'

'No, not just now, we're not. But don't think that conversation isn't going to be had.' He slurps more food into his mouth, gets up, pulls some kitchen roll out, and dashes it against his whiskers before returning to the table.

'I did right by your mother, married her, stayed for two years, a year before you came along and a year after. I tried to make it work. She wasn't all bad you know. She had a wicked sense of humour and we liked the same music, the same films, but... she changed when you were born, when she discovered the truth about me and my *sinful* ways.' He smirks when he says sinful, as though this is all a big joke, but I can see there is more to it than that, more hurt behind his eyes. He takes a sip of wine. 'I tried... for a long time, to bury the truth. I hated the man I was, the men I was attracted to. I hated God, my parents.' Mac leans back, glass in his hand, eyes focused on the contents as he tips it left and right. 'And when Lynn found out my *preferences*' – he takes a large gulp – 'it was like she amplified every last bad thought I had ever had about myself.'

I hesitate as I imagine the hurt and turmoil he must have gone through.

'I'm sorry,' I say. 'That you had to go through all of that.'

'Aye. Well, I'm not the first to be judged for my taste in men and I doubt I'll be the last. To be fair to your mother, I think it was more the fact that I'd slept with another man and had humiliated her, rather than the fact that I'm gay, that she took issue with.'

I nod. 'But that still doesn't explain why you left me.'

'Left you?' he shakes his head. 'That's what she told you?'

I push the plate away and nod.

His eyebrows furrow, a look of pain there. 'I didn't leave you, James. I tried to see you. I came around every weekend, worked three jobs to live close by. But she wouldn't let me see you.' I can't remember a time where I have considered Connor McDonald as a man who regretted leaving us. The image Mum had forged was of a man who had walked away without the merest notion of regret. But it doesn't change the fact that he's since had plenty of other opportunities to get in touch with me.

'So, you just accepted that?'

'No. I went to a solicitor, filed for joint custody. Lost, of course. What judge would allow a man, a *wife beater*, to look after a one-year-old boy?'

I feel sick, the food and wine sharp at the back of my throat. 'You hit her?'

'Och, did I bollocks, but she's a clever woman, your mother. She told close friends at church that I was violent. She even suckered poor old Alan into her lies. He was on the scene before your second birthday. After I lost the custody claim, I kept working, sent them money, tried another solicitor but couldn't get anywhere near you. I went off the rails a bit. Turned up pissed at the door on your third birthday. A well-meaning neighbour called the police and I spent the night in jail.'

A memory. Fleeting but there. A dark shadow at the door. Shouting. Police lights. 'I think I remember that.'

'Aye. That was all I could picture when I sobered up. The way you looked at me, tears down your face, Alan holding your hand, Paddington Bear under your arm.'

The memory takes on a more solid form. The smell of Alan's sweater and the soft brown synthetic fur of the bear. Mum's large stomach beneath her navy dressing gown. I remember the fear of this large looming man stumbling on the lawn. Blue lights were flashing as he was pushed face down. The neighbours' curtains had let shards of light onto the street.

'Nobody was going to believe I never hurt her after that, or that I was fit to care for you.'

I twist the stem of the wine glass, eyes focused on a splodge of sauce on the table.

'I left for a while then. Dad was sick; I was needed here. I came back, after a few months, met with Alan, tried to make him see sense. He's a good man, but he was just as duped as the rest of them. Told me that if I really loved you, I should move on. I sent you cards, presents. I'm guessing she never gave them to you?'

I shake my head. I have the mad urge to laugh. How many birthdays had I run to the door to check for a birthday card from the mysterious man who had left us?

He nods. 'I'd figured as much.'

'So, you never came back after then?'

He leans back, looks me in the eye. 'I came back lots of times, watched you playing with your brother in the garden, making sure I was never seen. You were happy, called Alan, "Dad". Even Lynn looked less... pinched. Calmer. It was best I stayed away. It was better for you... and for me,' he adds. 'I had to let you go, James. It hurt too much to be able to see you and not hold you, not teach you to read, or to swim, or tuck you in bed. I only caused you pain.'

'I'm sorry,' I say, even though I don't know what I'm sorry for. For me. For him. For Liv. For Kit.

'Lucas tried to convince me to come and find you again, a few years back.'

'Lucas? The guy in the photo?'

He nods. 'He found you on social media when you opened up the boxing club.'

'So why didn't you get in touch?'

'We found out he had cancer. It was quick.' His eyebrows furrow. 'Painful.'

'That... must have been tough.'

'Aye.'

Mac gets up and stands next to me, a firm hand on my shoulder. 'He'd have liked you. He was hot-headed, stubborn but had a heart of gold beneath it all. He was the best of men.' Mac squeezes it and I place mine on top of his. Tears fill my eyes as I hold on to his hand. 'I should have fought harder for you.'

And for the first time since I left Liv, something like contentment fills me.

33

TWO DAYS BEFORE HE LEFT ME

We get out of the car. My legs are shaking, heart beating loudly in my ears as Kit bends over, fingers inspecting the smashed tail light. His face is pale, but he smiles up at me. 'No harm done; I'll get it fixed tomorrow. That nutter needs to learn how to drive,' he says, walking back over to me, bringing me close, and kissing the top of my head. He pulls back, tilting my face left and right, running his hands over my arms and shoulders. 'You're sure nothing hurts?'

'I'm fine, a bit shook up. Are you OK?'

'Yeah, same. No harm done.' He pulls me against him, arms holding me close.

'I recognised that car. It was that double-glazing salesguy's.'

'Huh? You sure?' he says. I can't see his face, but his grip tightens a touch.

'Yeah, blue BMW. I recognised the reg plate.' We pull apart.

'There are lots of BMW drivers out there who are wankers with fancy plates. I don't think it was deliberate. The guy was on his phone, not watching where he was going, that's all.'

I let him lie to me. We drive home quietly, both of us lost in our own thoughts.

I'll wait until I get home until I tell him – tell him everything that has happened. Everything that will happen.

In our flat, Kit opens us both a bottle of beer. His hands are still shaking.

'We need to talk,' I begin.

He leans back against the counter, bottle visibly vibrating as he lifts it to his lips, his eyebrow raised. 'What about?' he asks.

'I know you're in trouble, Kit. And the reason I know is that I've lived this week before. I've already lived the next seven years.'

'What?' he asks, taking a deep pull on his bottle.

And then I tell him.

* * *

'This is ridiculous!' he says. I've gotten to the part where we search for him and then I tell him that I suspect he fakes his own death. I haven't mentioned James. I need to keep him focused.

'Why are you saying these things?' he asks. 'We need to get you to a doctor; I think you've banged your head.' He grabs his car keys. I stand and take them out of his hand.

'You borrowed money from Becky Thomas, Kit. The guy who you claim to be selling double glazing to a house with new double glazing just ran you off the road.'

His eyes widen, hands dragging through his hair. He starts pacing.

'Tell me what's going on. I'm begging you. Let me help.'

Something passes across his face, a hesitation. He opens his mouth but then stops. Anger or something else closing the hesitation down.

'There is nothing going on!' He throws up his hands.

'Yes. Yes there is. You're going to leave me; you're going to go on Friday and you never come back.'

'I wouldn't do that.' His voice is shaking. 'I would never leave you.'

'But you do!' I shout, all anger and pain and regret, hand gripping the back of the kitchen chair. 'You leave on Friday and you disappear. You go to a cave that is unreachable by search and rescue. You park your car in a place that you know it will be seen even though you don't normally park there. You run away, Kit.'

He shakes his head, pulls at his hair. 'This is such bullshit!' he shouts, but there is fear in his eyes. 'I don't know why you're saying these things to me. Is this a joke? Did James put you up to this?'

'You know it's not.' I calm my voice, step towards him, try to take his hand; he pulls it back. 'Just tell me, why would he run you off the road? Is it to do with money?' There is a flicker in his expression, a recognition. 'Why do you owe him money, Kit? I can help you; I can stop it from happening. Just tell me the truth.'

'I don't need to listen to this. Do you know how insane you sound right now?'

'Actually, yes. Yes I do.' I pull down the cuffs of my oversized cardigan.

'I don't know why you're saying this, but it's not fucking funny. I need some space.'

'Where are you going tomorrow?'

'I told you, I'm going to Wales.'

'You're lying. I know you're lying. There is no Call of the Wild in Monmouthshire.'

'I must have the wrong name. You want me to prove it to you?'

He storms out of the room and returns with his train tickets. 'Satisfied?' he asks as though this proves everything I've said to be wrong.

Kit grabs the car keys and storms out. I hurry after him, chasing him down the stairs. 'Kit! Just wait!' I try to take his arm but he shakes me free. I've never seen him like this before, never seen him so scared, so confused, so angry.

He slams the door behind him. I follow him. The sun is setting deep in the sky, but he's already in the car, the engine roaring, lights on, pulling away. I chase after him shouting his name but he's gone. I close the door behind me and stand there at the bottom of the stairs, back where it all began, where it all ended.

I'm dazed as I walk back into the lounge. I call Kit's phone. I sit there, calling and calling and calling.

An hour passes, then another, then another. It feels so familiar, this waiting to hear from him.

I dial James's number but it's almost midnight now. It goes to answerphone. I don't leave him a message; there's no point.

I walk into Kit's office and go through his drawers again; the receipts are all the same. I attempt to get into his online banking, but I can't; my eyes are gritty as I stare at the blue screen. At the sound of every car passing, at the lighthouse blink of light flashing along the contours of the walls, I look out of the window, but he doesn't come home. Where has he gone? Is he already driving to the coast? Is he safe?

My neck is stiff from the accident. I have a memory of Kit sitting on the sofa when I got back from the cinema, the same action, the same wince as he tilted his head – must have slept funny, he'd said.

I check his desk again, but nothing has changed. My focus roams the room, settling on one of his suit jackets hanging on the back of the door. I push the chair back. My hands finger the jacket, brush against velvet.

I pull out a box, my heart inside my throat. The box is different; I trace the gold lettering on the top of the box: *H&C*. I know what it will be, even before I click it open. I fold my legs onto the floor, the necklace glinting up at me. There isn't a receipt; there is no engraving. It's not the same box, but it's the same necklace.

I take it out, eyes heavy, body aching as I feel the familiar weight of it against my clavicle.

Another lie. Kit had told me he'd already taken it to the jewellers. He'd hinted at a surprise... I'd guessed that he was going to have it engraved, but had let him enjoy his ruse. In the aftermath of his disappearance, I'd wondered if he was going to ask me to marry him, if that was what was going to be engraved on the back, a simple: *Marry me*. But it's still here. It doesn't make sense. He'd said it would be ready to pick up on Friday morning. That's why all of this time I've pictured it on the bottom of the Irish Sea.

I have one more day until he leaves, one more day to find out the truth.

34

ONE DAY BEFORE HE LEFT ME

The events of the last few days flash like a croupier dealing out cards: the deck split into two – one half my past, the other, my present; both sides running into each other by imaginary hands: the river, Kit, James, Kane, Rebecca, Lynn, Alan, the jolt of the car, the necklace, Kit's furious denial last night, James's words, my wedding dress, Ava, the hotel door, Libby's words, the foot of the stairs.

I open my eyes. The bed is empty.

Kit has already left. I replay the real night before, the day that happened when we didn't get run off the road, well, not me at least. I'd got back from the cinema late. Kit had been on his laptop, researching the clients that are going to be at the function today. I'd been tired, turned in when I got home. Kit had ordered a taxi to pick him up early to save parking costs at the train station. I know that in the kitchen will be a note from him, it will say: *Wish me luck! See you later, love you. xxx* A few days after he disappeared I had torn open bin bags searching for that note, my fingers pulling apart the black plastic, hands covered in rotting food. I'd just wanted to hold something from him, something real. That's how Lynn had found me, the day she took me to Mum's.

Next to the note will be an almond croissant, a French press already primed and ready beside the kettle.

The weight of the future presses down on me.

I get up, see the note, the breakfast, my finger running along the indentations of his words. I make the coffee, sit picking at the croissant, taking it into his office. I stand still, eyeing the jacket on the back of the door. I walk towards it, my fingers reaching in the pocket. It's empty.

I take the jacket off, pull the pockets inside out: no box.

I have a flash from the tickets he'd slammed on the table last night. His train didn't leave until ten but he'd already left when I got up.

Finding the necklace started this. I know where I need to go.

I pull on a pair of jeans, throw my arms into a grey sweater, and grab the car keys, locking the door behind me.

The rain is falling as my fingers trace the dent at the back of the car, the brake light fractured into a spiderweb. I feel like I'm trapped in it, splintered and tethered to a web of lies.

I click the central locking and climb in.

* * *

The jewellers isn't hard to find, and is nestled between other high-street buildings only a short distance from the train station. I unbuckle my belt and take a deep breath. My eyes focus on the sign in deep blue, two letters in looping italics: *H&C*.

I climb out of the car, rain drumming against my hood as I stand outside the window: the necklace in the blue case glinting through the glass onto the street.

I look back up at the sign: *H&C Jewellers and Pawnbrokers*. The bell rings above me as I walk through. I close the door gently and push back my hood. The shop is split: to the left of me are glass cabinets, filled with everything you would expect from a jewellers. To the right, a more eclectic mixture of things: phones, electrical items. The man behind the counter looks up, a ready smile on his face beneath a moustache designed to be twiddled into a smile, as if it's there to emphasise his sincerity.

'Can I help you?' he asks, a salesman smile on his face.

'Yes, I...' My mouth is empty of words for a second. 'I'm interested in the necklace in the window?' The salesman smile ramps up a few notches. He floats towards the display, light feet, light hands as he retrieves it, placing it on the glass counter in front.

'A beautiful piece. Antique, original solid silver chain with mother-of-pearl insets.'

'Could you tell me where you got it?' My eyes are fixed on the locket, on the implications of it being here. Not at home in Kit's pocket, not with James: here, inside a pawnshop.

'I'm afraid I can't tell you that.' The moustache remains smiling above the hesitant mouth. 'But if you're interested I can give you a very fair price?'

The room is too hot; my head is spinning. I look up behind him, Harold and Cutler Jewellers and Pawnbrokers. *Pawnbrokers* pulses at my temple.

He's sold it. Kit's sold the necklace.

I find myself stepping forward, a hand reaching for the locket. 'How much?' I question.

'Seven hundred and fifty pounds.'

'May I?' I ask, fingers already reaching and turning over the locket. No *Just jump*; No 'K'; no kisses, no *Marry me*.

'Would you like to try it on?' My head is shaking in decline. I pass it back.

'It is an exceptional piece, and perfect timing I might add.'

'How do you mean?'

'Well.' He looks around the shop as though Kit is going to emerge from the shadows. 'He brought it in just this morning, and I expect it will get snapped up quickly. The early bird catches the worm, they say!'

His words drop, each one adding pressure to my skull. Kit's pawned it. I try to grasp at this new version of the man I had always believed was perfect.

'So if you're interested, you might want to snap it up quickly.' He unleashes his salesman smile again.

'No, I... no thank you. I thought it was... Never mind.' I start backing away from him, the necklace staring at me. I land myself back out onto the pavement with an apology.

He sold it. He sold my necklace.

* * *

Back home, I begin to frantically search Kit's office, the bedroom, the kitchen, his backpack, his coats in the cupboard at the foot of the stairs, anything that will give me a clue to what happens today and why he pawns the necklace.

I return to Kit's office, open his PC and check his calendar. The whole day is blocked out: 'Spring Celebration'.

I put 'Corporate Team Building in Monmouthshire' into the search engine. Just in case James missed something, just in case James knows more than he's letting on.

Five search results come up.

I reach for my phone. I don't know what I'm going to say. *Hi there, my boyfriend is on his way to your function and something may happen there to make him fake his own death. Do you have any idea what that might be?*

Someone picks up on the first ring. 'Hi, um, I'm coming to an event this afternoon and I can't for the life of me remember if I have the right day? I work with BPA?' I'm put on hold.

'Sorry, we don't have a BPA listed for today.'

'Oh, sorry my mistake.'

I ring the next on the list, then the next, then the next. Nothing for a function with BPA.

I begin scrolling, switching to images of Monmouthshire in case something jumps out at me. I've always been better at places than names. I scroll down, until a logo catches my eye. It's two horses pulling along a plough against a green background. I've seen that before. I click on the image.

Chepstow Racecourse.

Is Kit at the races?

I shake my head. He can't be. He'd told me everything about the event, about being blindfolded and having to follow team-mate's instructions, crazy golf, a lunch on a deck by a river. He'd laughed. He'd told me about the golf ball getting stuck between a clown's teeth. He'd told me all about it. In detail, the mouth opening and closing, having to put his hand in to grab the stuck ball. The food: Thai, good noodles.

The answers chime in my ears, a high-pitched ring.

One by one, images of Kit start to play. The way he pays atten-tion to the sports news, the look on his face when we were on the way to the caves as he heard about a player being transferred, his intensity as he watched sports on TV, the passion he had for a team or a player, or a match, the fight we had about my coat on the night of the charity football game. The way he knocks on the door frame three times, his smiling face asking me to give him a kiss for luck before he goes out to meet a client. Wish me luck, before he goes for drinks with potential companies, wish me luck when he heads off to deal with emails, wish me luck, wish me luck, wish me luck: the note he left me this morning.

Is Kit a gambler?

No. He can't be.

I would have noticed; I would have seen the signs. *Surely*, I would have seen the signs. I think to moments when I've returned to see him leaning forward watching the TV. I'd always assumed it was because he was so into sports. I think of the time he'd spend on his phone, the way he would smile or frown. Was he making bets? James and I used to tease Kit about being a sore loser, and he would take it in that flippant way that he has about him when his team didn't win or a player performed badly, but Kit has *always* been like that, taken himself away for a while. 'Go and have your strop time,' I would say and he'd kiss me, go for a run, go to his office, go for a ride. Often he would take me with him, but he would be quiet. But that isn't new behaviour; that is how Kit's *always* been.

Another image flashes: Kit and his newspapers, the intense way he sometimes looked when he read them, pen in hand. I push back the chair and go outside. The wind is already picking up, the beginnings of the storm that will hit us tomorrow.

I rummage through the recycling box, pulling out all the newspapers and carrying them back inside. I sit on the lounge floor, turning to the sports sections. The *Daily Mirror* on a Saturday morning. I'd do the crosswords while he read the sports section.

The room feels like it's closing in on me. I open the pages. There are red dots *everywhere*... next to football matches, rugby games, horse races, boxing. My mind is spinning. The air constricts around me as my finger runs down the horse racing fixtures.

I feel like laughing, crying, shouting, screaming.

I'm going mad; this can't be real. Kit's not a gambler.

I can't have missed this. There must be another reason. I'm

connecting the literal dots wrong; I'm creating a story that doesn't exist. He would have told me; he would have asked me for help, or James, his parents, anyone. Kit wouldn't fake his own death over a few misplaced bets. But then I replay last night. He had every opportunity to tell me, and he still didn't. And then there is the necklace, the best part of seven hundred and fifty pounds he's just got for it.

At the bottom of the page is an advert for William Hill bookies. Something about this pulls at me, a tug, as though someone has a rope lassoed to the base of my spine. William Hill... William Hill: WH.

I rush into his office, yank open the drawers, pulling out the receipts. *Kingwood Team x 4 – WH. Jenkins x 6 – PP.*

My fingers are shaking as I type in 'betting offices' into the search bar. There is a list, best betting sites: *Paddy Power.*

Jenkins x 6 – PP.

The Topmire Account x 3 – L.

Ladbrokes.

I keep searching, the initials correlating with betting shops, online sites. I lean back in my chair, my hand covering my mouth.

I think of the money he's had from Rebecca.

This is why he does it.

This is why he fakes his own death.

Debt.

35

ONE DAY BEFORE HE LEFT ME

It's taken me just over an hour to get to Chepstow. My mind is whirring with all of the information I've uncovered, all of the deceit. I've replayed times where Kit has been more subdued than normal, all of the days when he would be fizzing with energy after a meeting. I'm so angry, with him, with myself. The sky is overcast. The storm hasn't hit here yet but the sky spits at me as I make my way across the car park.

How long has he been gambling? How much does he owe? How much does he lose today?

I approach the barrier, pay for entry and begin searching for Kit. There is the smell of grass, of perfume, of fried food. There are hundreds of people here, the stand wrapping its way around the oval of the course.

A race begins, the horses' hooves thundering as I wander through the crowds, all cheers and whoops, smiles and arms thrown over heads urging the animals and jockeys on, the voice of the commentator on the Tannoy echoing around the white tiered stands. The adrenaline is pulsing through the atmosphere.

I know this is the type of place that Kit would love. He would be pulled along for the ride, shouting, cheering, forever optimistic.

I move from stand to stand, examining each face as they all eject from their seats as the winner clears the line.

Climbing up and down the steps, I scan along the rows as people begin filing out. It must be the last race of the day. I'm pushing against the tide as they head towards exits.

I make my way further down, closer to the track.

Then I see him. In the middle of a now-empty row.

He's wearing his olive-green suit, jacket folded beside him, white shirt open at the collar. His head has dropped to his chest, an unlit cigarette in his hand.

'Kit?' I say gently. He turns to my voice. The action is slow, like he's stoned: bloodshot eyes unfocused, hair curling around his collar. I expect him to be shocked, for his body to stiffen, but he just gives me a weak smile.

'Hey,' he says. I've never seen him look so broken. He doesn't ask me what I'm doing here. It's as if he was expecting me. In his other hand, a matchbook with the logo on. Now I know where I've seen it before. It was in his suit jacket; it had fallen to the floor. I'd been crying, remembering how he would occasionally have a sneaky cigarette: *there are times when you just need one perfect smoke to end a perfect day.* I'd been so wrapped up in that memory, of him, that I hadn't paid the slightest bit of attention to the logo on the front. He's opening and closing it, opening and closing: three matches missing. Three knocks on the door before he leaves, three kisses at the edge of his note. I sit down next to him.

'I've fucked up, Liv.' His eyes meet mine briefly before he looks away. Everything he hasn't told me – the lies, the shame, the defeat – seems to draw grooves into his skin. Bags under his eyes seem to fill. The laughter lines around his eyes are cut deep. The light behind his eyes that has always been there is dimmed, dipped, *faded*.

It hits me then. The Kit I thought I knew wasn't real. *This* is the real Kit.

'I know.'

His head sinks into his chest. 'Can you... take me home?' he asks, tear-filled eyes pleading with me.

'Of course,' I say gently, as if he's a child. He nods, and as he stands it's as if part of him has already disappeared. How did he hide this from me? He wasn't like this that night. He was laughing, joking, talking about the fucking clown and mini golf.

Kit doesn't speak as we walk across the car park, the sounds of the stands fading, swallowed by the heavy silence between us.

The rain is falling in earnest, now – wipers sweeping across the windscreen. Kit has closed his eyes; his head is turned away from me. The words he needs to speak fill up the car, like the mist on the windows. I turn up the fan, waiting for him.

'Do you want to talk?' I begin. The indicator judders into the silence. He shakes his head, this broken man beside me. And for the first time, I see a man who is desperate enough to fake his own death.

When we reach home, Kit still doesn't move. He's staring blankly out into the darkening sky, street lights glowing amber in the twilight. The engine clicks: metal contracting, heat evaporating. There is steam rising from the bonnet.

'Kit?' He turns to me with a look of confusion, as if he doesn't know where he is or why I'm here. 'We need to go inside,' I say. The words seem to reach him. 'And then you need to tell me – you need to tell me everything.' He nods, unbuckles his seat belt and climbs out of the car.

I guide him to the door, sliding the key into the latch. The wind is cold at the nape of my neck, rain coming down in gusty breaths, pulled back then exhaled against my skin.

The door closes behind me and follow him up the stairs: heavy feet, defeated shoulders. He walks into the kitchen, glances at the note on the table, the remains of the breakfast he'd laid out. Kit picks up the paper and rips it into pieces, stacks the parts on the centre of the table before opening the cupboard, twisting off the lid of a bottle of vodka and drinking it neat before pouring three inches into a tumbler. He doesn't look at me as I take off my coat and hang it on the back of the chair.

I follow him into the lounge, his eyes glancing at the newspapers on the desk. He stares at the pages. Sharp bursts of pain cross his face, like the red dots are being tattooed into his skin.

We sit opposite each other on the sofa, legs folded like the morning I came back here, the morning I came back to find the answers that were here all along. Everything I have discovered this week was already there for me to see, if I'd just read the signs more clearly: the interest in sports, the low moods when a team played badly, the relentless optimism, the times he would take himself into his office for hours on end to work, Rebecca at the funeral, the knock at the door from a stranger, the matches, the receipts, the necklace, wish me luck: it was all here, all hidden in plain sight.

'I first put a bet on the year I broke my leg,' he begins, swirling the clear liquid in his glass. 'It was a free bet of a fiver. I was bored, fed up of being stuck inside. It was hard for me, not being able to get around, to not have the freedom to run, to do anything but sit there.'

Kit had broken his leg in two places after he had been knocked off his bike, before his first year of uni. He'd already been signed up semi-professionally when he was seventeen, had been talent-scouted while he was in sixth form. He had a good future ahead of him.

James would often talk about the weekends he was left in peace as Lynn and Alan went to watch Kit play, how their Sunday hikes with their dad trailed off because they would go to watch him train. James said it gave him space to breathe.

'You have no idea how hard that was for me. Everything I thought about my future was lost, taken away from me in one afternoon. I lost the highs I would get when I played well, when I knew I was the best player on the pitch.' My whole body feels like its vibrating as he talks, like I've had too much caffeine. He glances up at me. There is darkness behind his eyes, a crack, an emptiness that widens as the words fall from his mouth.

'I missed it so much.' His fingers flick against the edge of the glass in beats of three. 'The rush, the purpose, winning, knowing that I was getting better in every game I played, hearing the crowd cheering, the pride on my parents' faces.' His eyes glint at that, that fire that I know so well.

'I started playing online a lot, after they dropped me from the team. My injury took me from being the best to barely being able to run up and down the pitch. I couldn't climb, couldn't walk. When I wasn't playing video games, I watched football and I tried to predict the outcome, see the flaws and the strengths of each player. I would take notes. I thought if I can't play, then maybe I could be a coach, you know?' But he's not asking me; it's as if I'm not even here. 'But when I started my degree, it wasn't like that. It was all biology and healthy eating and science. It bored me. It was too easy; it wasn't a challenge.

'Then I got talking to this lad about computer programming in the student bar. He told me about the money he was already making on the side, you know, setting up websites and stuff? I thought to myself' – a smile; a sparkle – 'I could do that. I was good at maths, I was good at computers, so I changed courses in my second year. My leg was almost fully recovered. I could play football again, but not to the standard I used to.' Kit hadn't talked to me about that time in his life much. All I know is that it took months to recover, that he deferred uni for a year, and that he changed course to computer programming. He's never talked about his time confined to bed. James had said it was tough on him, but listening to Kit now, it's clear that it wasn't just a small setback; it moulded him into this person, this person who gambles, who pretends he's dead.

'I was watching the football, and an ad came on for a free bet if I signed up. And I thought, why not? What have I got to lose?' He takes a deep sip of the vodka, his lip curling at the bitterness.

'I won.' He stares back into the glass. 'It was such a rush, that feeling of freedom, of taking a risk, winning. So I placed another bet, a different site, another free bet, and I won again. It was so fucking easy. I started climbing again, got the job at Waterways to explain my extra income, then I met you and then I was chasing a whole other type of high.'

He smiles at me, but my facial muscles remain impassive even though the thoughts are screaming inside my head. How did I miss it? How did James?

'Does James know?'

He shakes his head. 'God no. I mean, we went to a few casinos when we were on holiday with the lads; I wasn't in too deep back then. It was just fun.'

'Why didn't you ever tell me?' I ask him.

He reaches for my hand, but he stops, clasps his fingers around the glass. 'I honestly don't know. I think there was part of me that knew, that knew I was going to go down this road.'

'When did it get worse?'

'I don't know. It just became a habit. Saturday afternoon, I'd place a bet. Then it was Saturday and Sunday.'

For years this had been happening right under my nose.

'I started paying more attention to the news, to the games. Football and boxing at first, the sports I knew more about, then tennis in the summer. I watched how the players performed on different courts – grass, clay... the fitness of the players, the up-and-comers.'

'How much were you betting by then?'

'A tenner, twenty, thirty, and if I was really sure, fifty... Just at the weekend. It was like a treat, you know? Like a film and a bottle of wine on a Friday night.'

I don't move. Because I don't know. I have no idea.

'When did it start to get out of control?'

He chews the inside of his mouth. 'You remember the Ridley account?'

I think back to a moment two years ago: Kit coming home with a bottle of champagne, the big account he had landed that would set him up, allow him to expand. I nod. 'That was my biggest win up until that point.'

'So what are you saying? There was no Ridley account?'

'Oh, there was, but I used the money on a dead cert. Quadrupled the bet.'

He smiles, proud of his achievement. I feel like I'm going to throw up.

'I did well that year, started earning a nice income. I mean, I lost some but I was winning, making easy money. Then I thought to myself, how about the races? I could apply the same kind of research, looking at new trainers, jockeys, the tracks, the horses. I was still in control back then. I had a hard line; I was still only betting at the weekends. But I started losing more than I was winning. I started opening up more gambling accounts under different names, and betting on weekdays, using the fixed-odds betting terminals in the bookies. I started haemorrhaging money.'

'Why didn't you tell me?'

'I wanted to, but... I was too ashamed, too proud, I guess. It was like the words I needed to say were stuck in my throat and the more I did it, the more the lies just piled on top, pushing the words further and further inside my chest. I tried to stop. I *did* stop. For three whole months. I couldn't risk losing everything I had built; I made the decision there and then. I wouldn't use any money from the business. But then there would always be another game, another match, another free bet. You have to understand, I still had this hard line. I wasn't putting my business at risk, but I started borrowing from elsewhere.'

'Where?'

'Cash loans that I put on pre-paid credit cards, and I started borrowing from a few other people I knew.'

'Rebecca? And the guy at the door the other day: Kane?'

The air goes out of him. He deflates, shoulders sinking inwards, his spine compounded. 'Yes but no, not originally. I borrowed money from a small-time lender at first: Julie Donohue. She had a good rep. I'd checked her out, no mention of thugs with baseball bats or that kind of thing.' His half-smile twists. 'But when I couldn't pay her back, she sold my debt on.'

'Kane,' I say.

He flashes a look of surprise then nods. 'That's when the interest spiralled.'

'He's a loan shark?'

'I thought I could get myself clear, borrow from Rebecca. I just had to win big. I told myself if I just had one more win, just a good streak, I would be in the clear. I had no other choice,' he says. 'I was desperate, Liv,' he says, tears threatening.

'But you lost?'

He nods. 'I've lost everything. I didn't mean to. I knew the track was wet; I knew the front three didn't run so well on a wet course. I split the money, placed multiple bets, multiple races. I just needed one to win.' His eyes light up as he talks, and I can see the gambler in him; it expands into the room, this sphere of hope, swelling around him, the optimism making it grow so large that I doubt he is aware of how small he is inside.

'You have to understand, Liv, I had no choice.' The sphere wavers, the walls thin, unable to keep its form. 'It would have fixed everything, Liv. I'd be able to pay Rebecca, Kane…'

'How much do you owe? Altogether?' He hesitates, knocks back the drink in his glass. 'Kit, how much?'

'Seven-fifty.' The sphere pops, all the light and air lost around him.

My mind corkscrews, I feel like laughing. This all sounds so ridiculous. It *is* all so ridiculous. 'Seven hundred and fifty *thousand*?' He just looks at the empty tumbler, his eyes glassy. 'You borrowed seven hundred and fifty thousand pounds, Kit?'

'No. Yes. It's complicated.' He rotates his hands, an invisible cat's cradle of deceit and lies.

'So un-complicate it for me: how much do you owe Kane?'

'Four hundred grand,' he rushes on, 'but it didn't start off like that. I borrowed a few grand and then…'

'Then you borrowed more.'

'Most of it is interest. Every time I missed payment the interest went up. But I just need a couple of big wins, and I'll be out.'

The present tense hits me, like a window has been blown open, freezing air making my skin pinch. 'How much do you owe Rebecca?'

'Twenty. And there are… others.'

'So, this is why you do it?' I sink back down onto the sofa.

He frowns, his head tilting. 'Do what?'

'I know what you're about to do.'

'I don't know what you mean.' He tops the glass back to his mouth, a trickle of vodka hitting his lips.

'You're going to fake your own death.'

'What?' he asks, eyebrows shooting up, 'I'm not going to fake my own death, Liv. I'm going to make this right. I just need to—'

'Borrow more? Steal from me?'

'I've never borrowed a thing from you, Liv, I swear.'

'What about the necklace?'

His eyes widen. 'I'll get it back.'

'You're about to let me and your family believe you are dead, Kit. You let us grieve you...'

'What are you talking about?'

I get up, and pace the room. 'Do you have any idea what you are about to put us through? The damage you cause? You ruin our lives, Kit. Do you know that?'

'Liv, I'm telling you the truth! I have no idea what you're talking about!'

I'm processing all of this information. My life here is nothing like the life I thought I had. A thought stops me in my tracks. Something happened tonight that makes him disappear. Something that I can stop.

He must borrow from someone else. Someone who is much worse than Kane. I can fix this.

'You're going to borrow the money from someone else,' I say. The words concrete. He nods.

'I'm... I have to. There's no other way.'

'Who are you going to borrow it from, Kit?'

'I don't know.'

'Kit!'

'I don't know!' he repeats. 'Kane mentioned someone who I

could borrow more from but I don't know their name. I swear, Liv. I don't. I just have to call him and he said he could put me in touch.'

He takes my hand in his. 'I promise you, I'm not going to run away *or* fake my own death.'

'Yes, Kit. Yes, you are. Call him now.'

'Why?'

'Because I need to know who is the last person you saw before you disappear. But first, I need to tell you about the next seven years.' And I begin again, from the end.

36

THE DAY HE LEFT ME

It's early hours. We've stopped drinking. Kit is sitting at the kitchen table, his whole body sunken. He believes me this time, the pain and implications of his losses allowing the words to settle in the room, moving from hypothetical theories to facts, events, reality.

He's called Kane, but all Kane would say was that someone would be in touch. No name. No number for Kit to call. No answers.

'How long?' he asks, as I pour hot water from the kettle into two waiting mugs. His voice shakes. 'How long until you hear anything from me?'

My body stills, I put the lid back on the plastic bottle of milk; there are grains from the coffee on the counter, cooling water from the kettle starting to dissolve them, a brown stain that is growing across the surface. I turn to him, take the cups over and sit down.

'Seven years.' I blow over the rim. 'Not until the morning of our wedding.'

'To James?' He rubs his arms as though his brother's name is cutting his skin, as though scars are forming beneath the surface.

'Yes. To James.'

'When do you realise you're in love with him?' He forces the words out, each one seems to be painful.

'Three years after you go.' I swallow down that tightness at the back of my throat, tears stinging my eyes.

Kit leans back, dark circles under his eyes. The rain is clattering against the windows like gravel being thrown up from a teenaged lover. The clock is ticking, steam from the kettle settling around my words.

'And you're marrying him?'

'Yes.' He fights tears, wipes his nose with the back of his hand. I soften my voice. 'You were gone. He was the only one who could understand what losing you meant. I was the only one *he* could turn to. I love him.' His hands are shaking as he folds them on the table. I reach over, collapsing mine over his. 'But *you* were my first love.'

'Were?' he asks. It's more of a sound than a word: painful, fractured.

I nod, tears falling freely down my face now. I wipe them away with the heel of my hand. 'James is the man I want to spend the rest of my life with. I'm so sorry.' I take my hands away.

He stares at his cup, his head nodding as if everything I'm saying is what he deserves. I glance up at the clock, at the countdown to ten thirty a.m. when Kit puts on his backpack and leaves.

Kit fiddles with his watch strap, the one that was never found. He might even still have it.

'But I come back?'

I pull my focus away from the brown strap.

'Yes. You had the necklace engraved. There was a receipt dated the week before and you left me a note inside.'

'What did I have engraved?'

My voice is tight as I say, 'Just jump.'

'And the note?'

'That you were sorry and that you had no choice.'

He nods, and rubs the outside of his arms as though he's cold. 'That was one of the worst moments of my life, handing it over, pawning it. I swore to myself I'd get it back to you. I was going to...'

My eyebrows arch. 'What?'

He shakes his head, reaches for the cup. 'It doesn't matter now.'

Sadness fills me. For everything we could have had, everything that could have been.

'You give it to James, Kit. You *do* get it back to me.' Time continues to tick by, each second bringing me closer to the moment everything changes. 'Would you tell him? James? If you knew you were about to do it, right now... would you tell him?'

He chews the inside of his cheek. 'I make it really convincing? That I've died?'

I picture the orange of the search and rescue boat, the red of the backpack, our silver car left stranded, the grey complexion of the policewoman as she told me they were closing the investigation: missing presumed dead; the red-hot agony that burned inside for months, the kaleidoscope of pain. 'Yes.'

'Then no.' He meets my eyes, solid, convincing. 'What would be the point? It would be too much of a burden for him. I wouldn't do that to my brother.' Relief fills my chest.

I nod, the tension across my shoulder releasing. 'You must hate me,' he says.

'I don't know how I feel about you right now, but I don't hate you, Kit.' I reach for his hands, cold in mine. 'Not by a long shot.'

'I know you have no reason to believe me, Liv, but I honestly haven't thought of running away, of leaving you.'

'So that means something happened from the time you left the races until you returned home.'

'I suppose so. But we've stopped that happening, right?' There is a glimmer of hope behind his eyes.

'I guess, but Kit... nothing I've done has changed anything throughout the whole week I've been here.'

'So *far*...' He smiles, the green of his eyes is lighter, that optimism radiating from him. 'Maybe this is the moment? Maybe this is why whatever is happening to you is happening?'

'I don't know, I mean... maybe?'

'OK.' He grins, drinks his coffee quickly. 'This is what we're going to do. We're going to stay awake, we're going to have something to eat, we're going to pack up and we are going to drive far away from here. I'm not going to borrow money, I am *not* going to fake my own death.'

'And then?' I ask, the thought of losing the life I've been living, and my love for James runs like ants along my arms.

'Then I'll get help. I'll stop, Liv. I'll pay the money back.'

'But...'

James. My life. The life I now desperately want to get back to.

'I'm not asking you to forget him, Liv.' Kit's voice is calm, understanding. 'I'm asking for your help. I don't want to lose you both. I don't want to hide for the next seven years. I don't want to spend my life living a lie.'

I bite down on my lip, looking up at the spark back in his eyes, my first love, the man who could always come out on top, no matter what life threw at him.

'I'm not asking you to choose me. But I *am* asking for your help, a second chance at *my* life.'

My throat is dry: rain and mud; then and now.

I nod.

He claps his hands together. All action, a plan in place.

Maybe I *can* break the chain of events that leads to Kit ruining his life? If I can stop him going, if I can upset the natural order of the events time has in store for us both, then maybe, I can save us all from the pain we've had to live through for so long.

* * *

We talk as I whisk eggs into a bowl, as he chops up onions and peppers. He asks me about my life now, congratulates me on my job, asks about James and his boxing, his face falling when I tell him he stops fighting competitively. He listens while I tell him about Fighting Fit, about how well it's doing. He asks about his parents, and I'm honest. I tell him we don't see them. I tell him how hard it hits Alan. I tell him how Mum is improving. I make more coffee. The sun begins to rise.

Through the window, the wind is kicking up leaves, the rain distorting the view, a soft focus on the morning that I lost everything.

'So, here's the plan.' He grins up, knife slicing through the omelette. 'We don't follow a plan.'

'What?'

'Let's not make a decision.' He leans across the table. 'You just drive. See where the road takes us. Stay awake, as long as you can.'

'OK.'

'If you can get to the next day without sleeping, it will be enough; I know it will.'

'And after?' I ask, sobering him.

'I don't know.'

I reach across the table, taking his hand in mine. 'Kit?' He meets my eyes, scanning the expression on my face. 'If we do this, if we change the future, you have to understand that I can't stay with you.'

'I know. You can't trust me...'

I shake my head. 'It's not about that. I love him, Kit. We've built a life together.'

He takes a deep breath, holds it in his lungs. 'Let's just take it one step at a time?' he asks. 'Please? I know you don't owe me anything, but I'm going to need help. I won't be able to do it alone.'

'OK.' I swallow hard. 'You're right. One step at a time.'

* * *

The sun has come up. It's Good Friday, but this time I'm going with him.

I turn on the kettle again, heaping three spoonfuls of coffee into a flask. 'I'll just make this and then we'll go.'

Kit is leaning against the door frame, his jacket on, the same outfit as the day he left and air catches in my throat. I step across the room, hold his face. 'It's going to be all right; everything is going to be fine.' He leans his head against mine, the wind leaking in around the gaps, the future trying to get in. 'I love you. No matter what happens, no matter what you have done. I will always love you.'

I keep the rest of the sentence locked inside: *but I can't be with you, Kit*. Not any more.

He wraps his arms around me, holding me tight, my hands are hanging on to the back of his jacket, clutching the material tightly.

We part and the sun glimmers through a break in the clouds, a blink of light, a flicker of hope.

'I'll take these down,' he says, picking up the bags. I nod, a watery smile, the kettle clicks and I go back to the counter, my hand reaching for the black of the handle, steam billowing around me as the water hits the inside of the flask.

Kit's feet on the stairs.

The sound of the bags scratching against the wall.

The wind rushing in through the open door at the foot of the stairs.

'I'll put these in the car!' he shouts.

The wind takes hold of the door and the sound rips through me. I drop the kettle onto the counter as the door hits the frame, like a full stop. I feel the impact of it swelling into the flat, darkening the room, ink spilling into my veins.

I spin around.

Run down the stairs.

'Kit, wait!'

My hand reaches for the door and I step through.

37

The sound of the door slamming reverberates through me, my heart colliding with my ribs, nausea hot in my throat as I reach for the wall to steady myself.

I'm back inside room 307, the walls lilting to the side before the horizon line of the windows settle and still. The air is warm around my bare arms, around my calves beneath the ivory of my dress.

I take a moment to breathe, to centre myself.

Everything is the same: the bed still unmade, James's hoody on the bed, my clothes from last night.

I'm back.

Back to the morning where I marry James. A bubble of relief forms in my chest and I let out a small laugh. I didn't lose him; I haven't lost our life together, and more than that, I know that it doesn't matter how our relationship started, because now I *know*, I know without any doubt that I love James. That we belong together. He loved me right from the start. He didn't stay with me because he was picking up Kit's mess, or because I needed him. He's *always* loved me. And I love him, without question or doubt.

I love him for the man he is, for the good in him. I love him because he is proud, and kind, that he is everything that is right in the world.

I can't stop smiling. I need to tell him.

Kit.

His name shoots through me. What's happened to Kit?

My hand scrambles for my clavicle.

The neckless has gone.

Did I change things? Did I save Kit? Is he back?

My eyes skitter and dash around the room again. The door opens, Ava stepping into the room. Her eyes are wary, upset.

'Ava?' She takes my hand, tears in her eyes.

'He's gone, Liv. James. He's gone.' The sound of the river pulses in my ears.

'Gone? What do you mean *gone*?' Then I see the note in her other hand. 'He left this for you. I'm so sorry, Liv.'

I take the letter.

Dear Liv,

I know you're going to hate me for this. I hate me for this, but I knew that if I saw you, I wouldn't have the strength to walk away.

Kit's alive, Liv. And that changes everything. He's staying at Mum and Dad's. Go and find him. He needs you if he's going to have the strength to put things right.

Kit is the love of your life. I've always known that; we've always known that.

I want you to know I love you and that no matter what you decide, I will understand. These past few years have been the happiest of my life but now you get a second chance. I want you to know that I will understand, that all I have ever wanted is for you to be happy.

But I think, right now, we both know that we need space.
I love you,
James

The letter falls from my hands.

I stride past her, run down the stairs. I ignore the rattling conversations coming out from the wedding suite. I run out of the hotel, pins and needles of rain pricking my bare skin, my feet pounding on the gravel; I turn in circles looking for him, running to the car park, Ava on my heels, but our car is gone. I ask for a phone. Ava puts hers in my hands and I dial his number. His phone is off.

'Liv?' I redial and redial. 'Livvy?' she says again, taking me by the shoulders. 'He's gone.' Ava takes the phone from my hands as I sink to my knees, the gravel digging painfully into my knees, the rush of my wedding dress scratching against my skin.

He's left me.

From behind, feet on gravel, Libby and Paige's voices urgently whispering to Ava. I look up, the rain coming down in earnest now. Ava glances towards me, a look of sorrow and reluctance, the rain already darkening her hair. She crouches down in front of me. 'Livvy?' She takes my hand in hers, the bottom of her dress pooling around her knees. 'I'm so sorry, but... but it's your mum.'

'Mum?' I drag my eyes to hers, my reactions slow.

'She's had a fall.'

38

I wake with a start. I'm in our bedroom, in our house, but without James.

Memories of the past four days open up a hole in my chest: Kit at the races, the locket, my wedding dress, Ava's face, my hand clutching the note from James. Then there is Mum. Mum overwhelmed by anxiety and being restrained in the hospital bed, her fingers gripping my arm as they sedated her so she could have more scans.

She'd been trying to come to the wedding, had made it all the way to the kerb to wait for a taxi before the panic attack hit and she collapsed, smashing her head against the pavement. She's out of the woods, thank God. The slight swelling on her brain, which was giving us so much cause for concern over the last few days, has subsided and her panic attacks have calmed now that she's acclimatised to her new surroundings in a side room. She was comfortable and asleep when I finally allowed Ava to take me home from the hospital in the early hours of this morning.

Relief and exhaustion had unravelled me, and I have a hazy

memory of telling Ava what had happened; she'd listened to my fractured sentences as I tried to explain about my week in 2016.

I try to sit up, but my head feels heavy, like it's filled with cement, then I remember the two sleeping pills she had given me so I could fall asleep. Yet, despite my exhaustion, and the pills, sleep has come in staccato bursts, my face burying into James's pillows, my fingers typing fevered messages to him, all of them not delivered; not read.

I reach for my phone, dialling James's number again, but it's still switched off. I bite back tears of hurt and frustration. Nobody has heard from him since the wedding. He'd already left when we got the call about Mum, and yet I keep waiting for him to walk through the door any minute, but the door remains closed and his phone remains turned off.

Kit is the love of your life. I've always known that; we've always known that.

I call the hospital and am told Mum's had a comfortable night and is more settled. The nurse's Brummy accent is thick. 'The consultant wants to send her for another MRI, and we'd like to keep her in for a few more days, just to be sure there is no residual damage, but hopefully she'll be able to come home next week.'

'That's... well, that's great news.'

Ava knocks on the door as I lie in bed, phone still clutched in my hand as I try to settle my thoughts.

'Hi,' she says. 'Thought you could do with a cuppa?' She treads softly into the room, her hair in a messy bun, a pair of my pyjamas hanging off her slight frame. She places the mug beside the bed. 'How are you doing?' she asks gently, lying down next to me.

'Oh you know. My wedding day was a disaster and for the second time in my life, my boyfriend has disappeared.'

'Shit then?'

I let out a small laugh. 'Yeah. Shit. Mum's doing better though... They say she can come home next week, so that's something.'

'Still no word from James?'

Tears fill my eyes. I sit up and cup the tea in my hands, blowing over the rim. 'No. Not a text. Nothing. How could he do this to me?'

She sits up. 'Look, don't get me wrong, right now I'm furious at him, and sneaking off like that was a dickhead move, but... well... I kind of get it.'

'How do you mean?'

'Look, I'm no expert but... Kit is a tough act to follow. If I was in James's shoes? If I was about to watch the woman I love fall back in love with her ex? I'm not sure I'd be strong enough to stick around to see it. We all know what it was like to be on the outside of you and Kit, and I can understand why he wouldn't want a ringside seat to watch the big reunion.'

'But it's James I want to spend the rest of my life with. He must know how much I love him.'

She smiles, her voice gentle. 'He does, but he also knows how much you loved Kit and he also knows that, now Kit is alive, you might not want to marry his brother.'

Kit. At the centre of everything that has been right and wrong with my life.

'Are you ready to see him yet? Kit?'

The past week in 2016 flashes through my mind. I take a deep breath blowing out all of the air from my lungs before nodding. 'Yes.'

I need to know if what I found out is true, if it was all real. And if it was, then I promised Kit I'd help him. Tears threaten again but I blink them back. Maybe Kit knows where James has gone, but then it doesn't matter if he does. James has left me.

* * *

I stare up at Lynn and Alan's house. The exterior is just as immaculate as it was seven years ago.

Where has he been all this time? How did he hide for so long?

I unclip my seat belt and step out onto the kerb, shielding my eyes as I look up. I take a deep breath and walk up the path, my hand reaching for the knocker.

The door swings open, Alan's face breaking wide open, my body immediately pulled against his chest. I can't help but laugh as he releases me; it's as though he's been inflated since I last saw him in this timeline – he's fuller than the man that had so desperately asked me to go for a coffee with him. He looks over my shoulder, with a hopeful expression; there is a brief drop of disappointment at James's absence. Ava had made sure not to mention James's note to the wedding guests. As far as they know, Mum had a fall, the wedding was cancelled, end of story. She hasn't mentioned the note to anyone, and James's absence hasn't been questioned at the club, because Himad and Simon had already agreed to run it while we were on our honeymoon; they must be presuming he's busy with me at the hospital.

Lynn appears, standing next to Alan with her usual air of superiority. 'Olivia,' she states.

'Is he here?' I ask them both. Alan's mouth goes to speak but she intervenes.

She folds her arms. 'I don't know what you—'

'It's OK, Mum.'

My eyes track the voice I know so well. And there he is: Kit. Standing in the lounge doorway.

39

Kit's frame seems softer than before. I've never seen him without his messy hair always artfully falling in the right place, but now it's dark, scalp-short, his skin more weathered, his freckles in the shape of a tick covered by a thick beard. I step over the threshold, the door closing, Lynn's heavy floral perfume hovering behind me. He's wary as I approach, but his eyes meet mine, flickering over every facet of my face. My feet stop walking about a metre away from him like I've been directed to find a mark on a stage. I stand still. Unable to move any closer to him. So different than last week when I saw him standing in our kitchen singing to 'Seven Years', making a bacon sandwich.

He tucks his hand in his pocket, then takes it out again, touching the frame of the doorway.

'Hi, Liv.' His voice is hoarser than it was when he left. It's as though the last seven years have chipped away at him; my own reply remains lodged in my throat. My tongue feels swollen; all the words I need to say sting the inside of my mouth, my throat closing around them.

He glances up, hands not knowing what to do with themselves again. I've never seen Kit nervous like this. Nerves in Kit were always bright, a burning energy that pulsed around him. I realise that I'm feeling something like pity for the man in front of me.

'I'll make some tea,' Lynn adds stiffly, striding past.

'I'll help,' Alan murmurs. Kit releases a small smile of gratitude in their direction that doesn't reach his eyes, but he seems relieved at having something to focus on, other than his ex-girlfriend. The sound of the kettle filling takes over the silence in the hall.

'Do you want to...' He trails off, walking into the lounge. His movements are slower than I'm used to, I notice, as I join him. Kit always did everything at speed. He smells different too. His clothes hold a lighter laundry detergent; his deodorant is more spiced.

'Shall we sit?' he says politely, gesturing to the sofa. I perch at one end, Kit at the other. 'It's good to see you, Liv,' he says, tears pricking, but not falling. 'You don't know how good it is to see you.'

'It's good to see you too.'

Such a simple sentence. *It's good to see you.* In all the scenarios I had envisioned, saying *it's good to see you* to Kit if he ever came home was not something I imagined, but it's the truth. I'm glad to see him. I'm glad he's alive, I'm glad he's home, but all of this is edged with sadness, with regret: for the life we had, the life we lost, the devastation him being back has caused my relationship with James.

Lynn returns with the tea, too much milk, two sugars that I no longer take, but I clasp it in my hands. She hovers by the fireplace.

'Thanks, Mum,' he says with a smile. 'If you could give us a minute?'

She hesitates, then switches on a tight polite smile. 'Of course.'

Kit's hand is still shaking as he lifts his cup to his mouth, wincing as he takes a sip. He places it on the side table, the wood covered in lace, a coaster made of seashells perched on top.

He glances to my hand, my engagement ring catching the light. Does he notice that there is no wedding band above it? His eyes meet mine then look away again. Did he ever imagine that James would leave me if he knew Kit was alive?

'I don't know where to start,' Kit begins. 'I know there is so much I need to tell you, to apologise for, but...' He knots his hands together, looking down at them. 'I don't know how to even begin to...'

'So, start at the beginning,' I say. I want to feel anger at him. I wish I wanted to slap him, to shake him, to scream and tear at his skin, to inflict just a glimmer of the pain that he inflicted on me, but Kit is not the same person I once knew. He looks as though one harsh word would make him crumble.

'I don't know how,' he replies.

'How about I tell you what I think I know and we take it from there?' He looks at me. The green eyes that were so light have turned a different shade, more moss green than sea glass now, as though each year we've been apart has darkened the pigment.

I picture the man folded on the steps of the races, the man who told me how his addiction started, how it had taken over his life, the lies, the deceit.

'You are a gambler?'

'Was,' he interrupts. 'I was a gambler.' There is flash there, a spark of the strength that the man in front of me used to hold.

I hold the fact tightly. It was real.

'I know you were a gambler; I know that you owed money to a loan shark, that you owed money to Rebecca. I know you didn't plan to fake your own death until the day you left, but that you did.'

He nods. Kit doesn't ask me how I know this... Did he tell James?

I reach for Kit's hand, holding it in mine, turning it over just like the morning I found myself back in 2016; the small silver scar from the pasta jar a gossamer-fine line of silver tethering this man in front of me to the man I lost. 'Why did you do it, Kit? We could have helped you.' I meet his eyes.

'I was beyond help, Liv. I was desperate.'

I listen as Kit tells me the same story as he did the night before he left – the night that never existed. I wait for him to tell me about borrowing more money, this faceless man Kane had said he would put him in touch with. 'He got to Mum. Kane. He got to Mum.' He meets my eyes, a whole story explained in one look.

'What?'

I rush back through the past: Lynn's sprained ankle, the fall she'd had the day before he went missing. *Some daft idiot not looking where he was going,* she'd said in explanation. At the time, my mind was consumed with Kit's accident instead.

'He went after Lynn?'

Kit nods. 'The day I hit rock bottom, I came here. I'd lost big at the races and I knew I needed help. I was too ashamed to come to you, so I came here. When I got here, Mum was on crutches. She had no idea who it was who had knocked her over but there was something about the way she described him that made my blood run cold.' Kit looks to the window. 'He was parked across the road from here, waiting for me when I left.' Kit turns to me. 'He said you would be next. Showed me pictures of you going to work, out on a run. I had no other choice, Liv. It was the only way I could keep you safe. I had to take myself out of the picture.'

I stack the events of both nights against each other. In my version, I stopped him coming here. I'd taken him home from the races earlier in the day. He didn't leave the flat until the following morning.

My skin pricks at the thought of Kane hiding in the shadows, watching Kit from outside this house, watching me go about my day-to-day life without my knowledge. I wrap my arms around my torso as if I can protect my body from the past.

'I'm so sorry.' His eyes are etched with regret, with fear. 'I had no idea things would go that far.'

I'm quiet, pushing away the images of myself being followed on my way to work, to the supermarket, on my bike with my earphones in. If I let myself go too far into those memories, the void over my doorstep will return and all the progress I've made will be for nothing. I take a deep breath.

'So...' I exhale long and hard. 'Where did you go?'

He rubs his hands together as if he's trying to bring back some circulation. 'I hid at first. Not far from where I was last spotted. Waited for it to get dark so I wouldn't be seen climbing back up, then moved on. There is a cave. You can't reach it by shore and access to the drop is way off the beaten track.'

The crack between the rocks; abseiling with him next to me, the cave, the pool.

'How long did you stay there?'

'Five days.'

'Five days?' I gasp, trying to imagine him there, in the cold, the dark.

'I figured search and rescue would be done by then, and I'd made sure that I'd been seen further up the coast. I'd packed enough to keep myself warm and fed. I changed my clothes, shaved my head and then, on the fifth day, I waited until dark, climbed back up and followed the coast. I threw my backpack into the sea and caught a late train out. I always went on small journeys, small stations, no ticket barriers, hid in the toilets at the station until I could get on unnoticed. Waited in the loo when the ticket guy came around.'

'Then where?'

'Then, everywhere.' He rubs his beard. 'I bounced from train to train, got off at small stations, waited for the next train or bus, walked for hours. I had no plan, figured it would be better if I just went with the flow.'

The plan is to have no plan; let's go with the flow.

'You just went with the flow?' I can't help the edge of anger in my voice. 'While I was searching for you? While search and rescue were out looking for you? While some psychopath was hiding in the shadows? While me, James and your family were going through hell, you were just going with the flow?'

He can't meet my eyes; he just nods his head.

'I bought a tent with the last of my money and just existed. Lived off cheap cans of food. Time stretched on.' He glances back up. 'I don't know how long I was like that; the days just merged into each other. Every morning I packed up and moved on, place to place, pitching the tent wherever I could, eating what I could find.'

'For seven years?'

He shakes his head. 'No. That was just at the beginning.'

'Didn't you ever think about coming home, or letting us know you were alive?'

He pulls at his earlobe. 'I knew you wouldn't stop searching for me.' He reaches for my hand. His skin feels cold against my own. 'I had to make it convincing.' He squeezes my palm. 'I had to leave enough evidence for you all to believe I was really dead.'

I nod, my throat thick with all the things I want to say.

'So how come you're back now?' I say, pulling my hand free.

'Kane, the guy I borrowed from? He's just been sent down for murder as well as other things. Life sentence.' I let out a long breath as Kit rushes on. 'I... I don't expect anything from you, Liv or James. I don't expect forgiveness; I don't expect anything. I just needed to see you, to see you both, to give you, God, I hate this word, but closure. I wanted you both to be able to move on knowing the truth.'

I sit still, picturing Kit in his tent. How lonely and scared he must have been. 'I'm glad you found each other.' He smiles. 'You and James. Genuinely.' He looks to the door. 'I'm guessing he was too pissed at me to come over?'

'James has left, Kit.' The words trip out from behind my teeth, tears filling my eyes.

'What?' His head jerks up.

'James. He left. Before we got married.'

His eyes widen. He looks wild, lost, his head shaking, his mouth drawn into a tight line.

'No... that's not... I came home as soon as I knew Kane was sentenced. I couldn't come home before that; it wouldn't be safe for you. I wanted you both to finally know the truth. I wanted you to be happy.'

'We were happy.'

'It's my fault?' I don't reply, but it's not his fault, not really. 'I shouldn't have come.' Kit shakes his head, angry with himself. 'I should have waited until after. I just thought... I wanted you to both know I was happy for you. And once the news broke, once I knew Kane was gone for good... I'm sorry, Liv, I should have waited. I'm so, so sorry.'

I'm angry then. It spits and rolls beneath my skin. This is classic Kit, thinking he has all the answers: that optimism in him that means he believes everything will turn out the way he wants it to.

'For which part, Kit? For lying to me? For leaving me? What is it that you're sorry for?'

'All of it. I'm sorry for all of it. I never meant to come between you and James. I just wanted to tell him I was glad you'd found each other. I needed to give you the necklace.'

'Do you think I care about a necklace? I cared about you!'

He nods, knuckles rolling against the inside of his palm.

'I swore I would get it back to you. It took some time to track it back down again. I'd kept my eye out for it online, emailed the shop owner. Finally I found it on eBay of all places.' He gives me a smile that drops when he sees my expression. 'I wanted to give you both my...' His hands gesture around him as though he can catch the right word.

'Blessing?'

'Yes, no... I wanted James to be able to start your marriage without my ghost hanging around in the background. I wanted him to know that I was happy for him, for you both, that you got to have each other.'

'And me? You didn't think you should come to me too? *Me?* I loved you, Kit, I loved you with every part of me. I grieved you, mourned you. Losing you almost destroyed me. Do you know what seeing you has done to James? It made him run away from everything we had.'

'But why would he call it off? James loves you. He's always loved you.' He meets my eye with a sad smile. 'I knew, Liv. Deep down. The way he felt about you.' His words are banging at my skull from the inside, trying to force their way out. 'It was James who swam you back—'

'I know.' I look up at him, scanning his face, the sad defeated smile. 'You're not the person I thought you were, Kit. Why did you let me think it was you?'

'I wanted to be the man that you thought I was.'

'But you weren't. James was.'

He nods. 'I know. But then, when I could see you felt the same attraction to me as I did for you, I tried to pretend I didn't know the way he felt about you. I lied to myself so much I believed it.'

'You should have told me the truth.'

'I know. I've always known that he's the one you should have been with. Not me. Not the man who lied and fucked off for seven years, leaving you thinking he was dead. I'm sorry. I know I should have told you; I should have—'

'Stop saying you're sorry!'

'Sor...' He closes his mouth, takes a deep breath. 'It was the only way I could leave you, knowing how James felt. I knew you'd be safe, loved. I knew James would take care of you, that you wouldn't have to be alone. You were better off without me, no matter how much it hurt to leave you. You were safer without me in the picture.'

'Safer? By leaving me with a loan shark lurking about. He ran you off the road, Kit.'

'How do you know that?'

I shake my head, the thoughts cloudy, confused. Here and there, past and present.

'It doesn't matter how I know. And what about Rebecca?'

He frowns. 'I'm going to repay her. I've been putting money aside, bit by bit, for the last three years. People still need websites building and PayPal is great when you don't have a bank account. It's not all of it, but I hope it'll be of some help. That's why I'm back, to make amends, to repair as much of the damage I've caused before...'

'Before what?'

'Before I turn myself in. Before I go to the police.' His shoulders straighten, like even saying the words physically lifts the weight from his shoulders.

'Turn yourself in?'

'I can't keep living a lie, Liv.'

I hear the sound of metal on metal, a door with bars slamming shut on him.

'Will you be sent to prison?'

'I don't know. I mean, I haven't paid any tax for seven years for starters and, well... there's wasting police time, the thousands spent on search and rescue...' He trails off. 'Mum and Dad have called a solicitor so I'll know more after I've spoken with her.'

He stands, walks over to the window, pulls back the curtain and looks out. 'I've spent so long pretending I don't exist, looking over my shoulder. You have no idea what it's like to not be able to make a mark, to spend every day pretending to be someone you're not. To meet... people who you care about only to have to move on because they are getting too close. I know I'm not dead, but Kit Palmer isn't alive either. I'm a ghost, unable to put down roots, to touch someone and feel like they know me, through and through to my core. To be loved.'

His words settle in the room, tenderness in them.

'You met someone,' I reply. The information he's giving me positions itself. He turns to me, meets my eyes, tears behind them.

'Aria.'

Aria. I want to hate this woman, but all I feel is a deep sense of sadness. For him. For her.

'I tried to keep my distance but she's' – a flicker of a smile, a light behind his eyes – 'persistent. It's the Spanish in her, or so she says.' The light fades; he returns to the sofa.

'Does she know, that you've come back? What you're about to do?'

He pauses. 'She didn't even know my name. She'd fallen in love with a man called Connor. A man who she thought had no parents, no siblings. An honest man who worked on an old laptop in her dad's deli, who made them a website for a new delivery service, who had been eating their sandwiches for the past year. A man who was once in the army, who didn't like to talk about his time on tour, his past.'

'Connor?'

'I had to choose a name that meant something to me, that I would turn my head to. It's James's—'

'Birth father. I know.'

I try to imagine this version of Kit, this Connor, eating sandwiches, the olive-skinned beauty who wouldn't take no for an answer.

'And now?'

'Now she knows the truth. She knows what I did, what I did to you, to everyone.'

'And she wants you to turn yourself in?'

'No. She wants to carry on as we have been. Says it doesn't matter. But how can I? I can't do that to her. There would be no future for us both, no wedding, no family, no mortgage... I can't even have a proper job. She says she doesn't care about any of it.'

'And she knows what you're about to do?'

'Yes.'

I feel a splinter of jealousy then, that he told her the truth, that he's not leaving her wondering if he's alive or dead, but the spite instantly calms. She doesn't deserve this – none of us do.

'You have to believe me, Liv. I never meant to come between you... I just wanted James to have closure, to know that I wanted him to marry you. He deserved the truth.'

'And me? You almost destroyed my life, Kit. I only got through it because—'

'You had James.' He smiles then. It's sincere like everything he had planned had worked out for the best.

'Not any more,' I say. I lift the tea to my mouth but it's too sweet. I cradle it in my hands instead.

'Where did he go?' Kit asks, calmly. 'I'll go and speak to him, put things right.' He stands as if he's just going to hop in a taxi, knock on James's door and fix everything in a five-minute conversation.

'I have no idea. He's not answering his phone.'

'I can help. Help you find him.'

'You've done more than enough!' I snap at him. He tucks his hands in the back of his jeans, head bowed, but then seems to gather himself. 'I know. But let me help. I know places he used to go when we were kids, old friends...'

'James doesn't want to be found, Kit. He wants space and that's what I have to give him.' I push aside the pain and anger and hurt, taking a deep breath and looking at Kit. 'For what it's worth... I'm glad you found some happiness. With Aria.'

'Thank you.'

I think back to the last time I saw him, the broken man, the helplessness, the weight pushing down on him as he told me of his addiction, of the road that led us both to where we are now, the hope that he could change his fate.

'And I'll be here for you, when you decide to go to the police.'

His voice breaks, the words struggling to get out. 'I don't deserve your help; I can do this alone. I've put you through enough.' Tears roll down his face freely.

'Oh, Kit.' I stand, take his face in my hands. 'You don't have to do this alone. You never did.'

'I wish I'd told you.' He leans his forehead against mine.

'So do I.'

I hold him tightly then release him, Lynn appearing like an apparition in the doorway. 'I'll show you out,' she says as if she's lady of the manor and I've never visited before. I turn to look at

Kit over my shoulder as I step into the hall, my hand holding onto the door frame.

'Kit?'

He looks over at me, eyes still watery.

'I never said I love you,' I say, and he frowns. 'The day you left. I didn't say it. I just... I wanted you to know that I *did* love you.'

'I know.' He smiles then, green eyes light and bright, and it feels like a small tear in time where the man I loved in the past is also here in the present. I follow Lynn along the hall, her hand already on the doorknob. I turn to her. I know it's a long shot, but I'm desperate.

'Have you heard from James?' The words rush out of me. She quirks an eyebrow.

'James?' The plucked brows dip, eyes landing on my ring finger. She holds a deep breath, fresh disappointment no doubt held in her chest.

'He left. When he found out Kit was back and I—'

'I can't say I'm surprised,' she interrupts. 'Running away is in his blood. I did try to warn you that nothing good would come out of your relationship.'

Running away is in his blood. The sentence hooks itself to my thoughts, snagging on the periphery.

His father.

Would he have gone to find him?

The small nugget of an idea rolls around, gathering momentum, growing and becoming more solid. I place my hands on Lynn's shoulders. She glances down to her shoulder, face confused.

'Does James know where his birth father lives?' Her body locks, her expression cut-glass sharp.

'No.'

'Yes,' Kit says from behind, the blood draining from his mother's face. 'Yes,' he repeats as he joins us. 'He went to look him up, years ago, but didn't go through with meeting him.' He faces his mother, her skin pale as she lifts her eyes to Kit. 'He just wanted to know where he lived, Mum.'

Lynn doesn't reply. She's stoic, shocked.

'Where?' I ask. 'Where does he live?' Kit's eyes are lighting up. Sea glass back from beneath the depths of loss.

'Scotland,' Alan interrupts coming out of the kitchen, glasses being wiped with a handkerchief. 'Connor lives in Scotland, the Highlands.'

Beside me, I hear Lynn's breath hitch at the mention of his name.

Kit smirks. 'Now, if I was going to run away... and I'm not saying I'm an expert' – he winks – 'but the Highlands is a pretty good place to hide, right? And if I know my brother, he will be having an existential crisis around now and what better way to face your past than tracking down the one man who has been missing from his whole life.'

I bite my bottom lip. 'It's a long shot, right?'

'Yep,' Kit replies.

'I mean, I'd be mad to chase him all the way up to Scotland without knowing he's actually there.'

'You would,' Alan intervenes. 'But that is exactly what you're going to do.'

'Do you have an address?' I turn to Lynn, softening my expression. She looks to Alan, watery eyes being blinked back. There is an unspoken conversation passing between them before she gives a brief, curt nod.

I pull her into my arms, her limbs rigid until she seems to admit defeat, her body relaxing against me.

* * *

'Are you sure you don't want me to come with you?' Kit asks, the peak of his hat pulled down low as he follows me along the path towards my car. Alan is holding a stack of letters with the return address to Rose Farm in his hands.

I shake my head. There's warmth in the spring air. My flight leaves first thing in the morning and I need to see Mum before I go.

'No.' I smile at him. 'I need to do this by myself.' I reach into my bag, looking for my keys.

Alan joins Kit at the kerb as I pull them out. He passes the stack of letters all addressed to James. I look up at him, this gentle man who has been missing from our lives. 'You go and get our boy, Livvy.' He pulls me into a hug, kissing me on the top of my head.

'Please don't do anything rash, OK?' I suggest to Kit. 'Just until I bring him home?'

'I won't.'

'Don't you worry, love. When it's time, we'll all go to the police together,' Alan reassures me.

Kit pulls me fiercely into his chest, arms tight. 'You can do this, Liv.' He pulls back, that smile back in place, green eyes crinkling at the edges. 'Just jump.'

I take one more look at Kit, and hold up my hand in goodbye.

It's time I find the man I should always have been with.

40

SIX DAYS AFTER I LEFT HER

'You did well,' Mac says, rubbing bloodied hay against the lamb's skin. I've just had my first lambing experience. Tim had been dealing with another ewe; the vet had been called out for a breech birth. Mac had told me it was easy, that he's been doing this since he was a 'wee lad'. And I thought to myself, how bad could it be? Well, it's pretty grim, let me tell you. Grim but kind of beautiful. I take another sip of water from the bottle, my hand still shaking. The lamb and mother happily circle each other in the small barn annexe. 'Och, don't feel too bad; it's natural to feel a bit peaky. Lucas puked his guts up the first time he did it. It gets easier. You'll be a pro before you know it.'

'How did you two meet?'

'His car broke down not far from here. He dinnae have a clue how to change a tyre. Had this mangy mongrel in the back of the car.' Mac scruffs Caesar's head. His face looks younger as he talks about him. How Lucas had come back the next day to thank him. How he never went back to Australia. That the cancer was swift.

'He died in my arms. Half the man he was when I met him.'

'I'm sorry.'

'No need. I had three years knowing real love. The kind of love that changes the person you are, that makes the world shine.'

My relationships had never been like that. I had a run of brief hook-ups before Liv came on the scene. The longest I stayed with anyone was six months. Nicola Townsend. I liked her. We had fun. But I thought I had too much of my father in me. Always had the urge to leave. Certain that I wasn't the long-haul kind of man. I'd never met anyone who made the world shine. Until I met Liv.

I bring the water to my lips again, knowing that I need to tell Mac that I won't be here much longer.

Last night, as I tried to sleep, I'd replayed the conversation with Mac over and over. *It was best I stayed away. It was better for you... and for me. I had to let you go, James. It hurt too much to be able to see you and not hold you.*

During my time with Mac, I've never thought for one minute that we're alike. Yet, as I tossed and turned, his words repeating in my head, I realised that we may not be so different after all.

I drink the rest of the water, my hands calming as Mac gathers clean straw and speaks softly to the ewe and her baby. I see it then, the father he must have been, the gentle eyes beneath softer grooves of his skin, before time and the Highlands etched their way across his face.

How different my childhood would have been if he had stayed. Been part of my life. If he hadn't walked away and let me go.

'Why don't you get yourself inside and make us both a brew? I'll be a few more minutes sorting this pair out. There's some cheese and ham in the fridge, lemon loaf in the cupboard. Get some food in you, lad.'

I let my legs carry me back to the farmhouse, Caesar at my heels. I make sandwiches, click on the radio, and light the flame on the hob, placing the kettle on top.

I think of Liv. I picture her folding her wedding dress between paper sheets... that's if it's even back in the box. She might have chopped it up into pieces, cursing my name.

I know that coming here was as much about me finding the answers about myself as it was about Liv. But seriously. What the hell was I thinking?

I need to go back.

I'm not going to make the same mistake as my father. I'm not going to walk away. I'm going to stay. Even if that means not being with her, I still need to be part of her life. Of *their* lives.

Mac returns, heads into the utility room, washing his hands and forearms as though preparing for surgery before joining me at the table. My plate is clear and I'm nursing a mug of tea.

'Penny for them?' he asks.

'I need to go home, Mac.'

Mac reaches for his sandwich and takes a bite. 'Aye. You do.'

I look up into his eyes, the eyes that must have looked at me as a baby in the same way as he looked at the lamb in the shed. With gentleness. Protection. 'So...' He chews. 'Are you finally ready to tell me what happened to bring you to my door?'

I look to the window. Caesar nudges me with his nose, wet and warm against the palm of my hand. I stroke the rough fur between his ears.

'In a nutshell? I've been in love with Liv since I first saw her. Then she met my brother and that was the end of that. They were together for years. He died, or so we thought. But then he came back on the day of our wedding after pretending to be dead for seven years—'

'What kind of love?'

'Sorry?'

'What kind of love? I loved your mother in my own way.'

'The kind of love you had for Lucas. The kind of love that consumes you. Does that answer your question?'

'Aye.' Mac leans back. 'So, he came back?'

I replay that morning, the receptionist passing me an envelope when I came back from my run. Kit's words saying he was sorry. I can hear the sound of my feet against the gravel of the path, the way I had felt as I chased down his figure along the lane as he approached the old car parked on the side of the road. He looked older, like he'd aged twenty years not seven. A thick beard, hair shaved. He'd turned around and stepped into my arms. I didn't even know they were open. He held on to me, head digging into my shoulder. His frame was still firm but he felt smaller, somehow. We'd stood like that for at least five minutes, his body against mine, the same way as it would be when he had nightmares as a child. I held him so tightly, someplace between relief, and love, and anger, and betrayal.

'Why?' Mac asks.

'Why did he come back?'

'No, why did he leave?'

'He's a gambler. Was a gambler. Owed thousands and thousands. He was left with no other choice, he said. Borrowed from some pretty shady people by all accounts. He said that he came back as soon as he could. That he was happy for us, Liv and me, that we'd found each other. That she chose me.'

'So that's a good thing then, no?' He brushes crumbs from the table.

I scratch the back of my head. 'No. Because she didn't choose me, Mac. She had no choice. Kit was dead, and I was there to help her pick up the pieces. But he's not dead; he's alive and that changes everything.'

I shake my head. Try to clear the buzzing in my ears as I replay him giving me the necklace, asking me to give it to Liv.

He'd said he had to go. That he couldn't risk someone seeing us, not yet. That he loved me.

'I went back up to our room to tell Liv, but she'd already gone, the whole groom not seeing the bride before the wedding thing. So I sat there, and I thought to myself that I wasn't going to let him ruin this for me. I love Liv; she loves me. We want to be married; we want kids. We're happy. At least we were.

'I didn't want to tell her. But as I showered, ready to put on my suit, I couldn't look myself in the eye, couldn't do it to her. She deserved to know the truth. So I broke it off.'

Mac snorts and shakes his head. 'You absolute flaming idiot,' he says.

I open my mouth to defend myself, but the words aren't there.

'You're sitting here telling me she's the love of your life.'

'She is the love of my life, but I'm not Kit! You have to understand, I can't compete with him. They were a done deal right from the moment she first saw him and I know her, Mac. I know she would never leave me on the morning of our wedding. It's just not in her. So I did it for her. Made it easier.'

I look up at Mac; my voice is as broken as I feel.

'So you left?'

I nod. 'I gave her the space she needed.'

Mac leans back, arms folded, eyebrows raised.

'I made it easy for her,' I rush on, eager for him to understand. 'I knew if I was there she wouldn't be able to be herself. She wouldn't be able to let herself admit the truth. I think she would still have married me, out of duty, if nothing else. So I left her a note.'

'A *what*?'

'She needed to find the answers herself, Mac. I told her that I loved her, and then I got on a train. If I stuck around, I wouldn't have been able to... stay away. So I came here. The last place on earth she would think of, the last place any of them would think I'd go.'

'That's not why you came here.' He lets out a small laugh, shaking his head, a look of pity on his face.

'Yes, it is.'

'No. It. Isn't. You came here looking for a way out. You came here to find me, to see if that half of you was really as bad as you'd been led to believe. You don't think you're good enough for her. Even after everything he's done, you still think Kit is better than you.' He shakes his head in disbelief.

'No... I...' I get up, pacing the room. 'She needed space,' I repeat. 'She needs to decide without me looking over her shoulder.'

'What a load of arse. You came here for a way out. You thought if you found your father, if you saw this man, this *tyrant*, that you would be able to let yourself of the hook. You'd be able to tell yourself that you're not good enough for her. You're a coward, my boy. You've thrown in the towel before you've even tried to fight.'

'I am fighting! Don't you think I've fought every day since I've been here? Do you know how hard it has been to stay away, to not go running after her? To beg her to choose me?'

'That's not fighting. You know it and now, I suspect, so does she. You've left her on her wedding day to handle all of this by herself.'

'She needed to handle this by herself, don't you see? She needed to do this alone, not with me by her side complicating things.'

'You're a bloody great fool and you're not giving her enough credit. Do you think this lass would marry you if she didn't love you? You can't farm for shit, but you're a good man, James, you hear me? You're as good a man as any and you dinnae need to come all the way out here to find the truth. You'd know it yourself if you just took the time to get your head out of your own arse. You need to stop hiding here and...'

'Jesus Christ, Mac, do you not listen to a word I say? I'm going back. That's what I've been trying to tell you!'

'Oh, well. Good.' Mac claps his hands on his knees, groans and stands up. 'Give me half an hour to pack and we'll be on our way.'

'What, wait, what?'

He hesitates with his hand on the door. 'You don't think I'm going to miss this, do you? This is the most excitement I've had since Lucas went paddleboarding and he fell in.'

'Paddleboarding?'

'Yeee-ss?' Mac asks, as if I have no concept of what a paddleboard is. 'You stand up in a canoe and paddle?' He enacts swinging an oar into a river.

'I know what paddleboarding is. I mean, are you... do you really want to come?'

'Aye. And not only that, I'm going to see your mother and tell her a few home truths that I should have done years ago. Satan's spawn, I ask you. Do I look like the friggin' antichrist to you?'

I look him up and down, tattered brown cardigan fraying at the elbows, bushy brows, kind eyes.

'No, no you don't.'

'That's settled then. Let's go and get your girl.'

41

I fiddle with my bag on my lap as the plane begins its approach along the runway.

I close my eyes and try to find the words I need to say to convince him that he is the one that I want to spend the rest of my life with, and as we take to the air, I finally find them.

The sun is shining as I exit the airport; there is a noticeable drop in the temperature and the wind holds more bite to it. I shift my bag on my shoulder, pull out my sunglasses and walk as fast as I can to the taxi rank, asking for the train station and only just making it to the platform on time.

I stare through the windows as the train clacks along the tracks. It's been over an hour already, the houses and townscapes dwindling the further north I go.

Outside is heavenly: rich grass, mountains and space. Well, he did say he needed it and there is nothing but space here, miles and miles of it. My thoughts roam along the mountains and hills, the vast stretch of sky.

I think about what has happened to me over the past week, that week that seemed so normal to me when I lived it in 2016.

I've asked myself over and over how it happened, why it happened, how I missed the signs of Kit gambling, but the thing is, our *life* is made up of thousands of days where nothing seems to really happen: breakfast, work, dinner; conversations with friends, with family; day trips to the beach. It all passes us by so quickly, just like the houses sliding from view outside the window of this train, just like those everyday 'days' that mould into one. But in each of those everydays are the people around us. And it's in the people we choose to spend our time with that make the everydays special. I wonder how many everydays with James I took for granted.

The train continues, people getting off and on, all experiencing their own everydays.

I try to read my Kindle but the nervous energy pulsing through me means I read the same line four times. I put it back in my bag, lean my head back against the head rest and close my eyes, trying to think of all the things I want to say to him.

What if he says no? What if Kit is wrong? What if *I'm* wrong and he really did only stay with me because he felt some kind of obligation? What if he's nowhere near the bloody Highlands of Scotland?

The train stops. A mum boards with shopping bags filled with all the trappings that mean a return to school after the Easter holidays. The children sit at my table and she squeezes in next to me with an 'I can't wait for the term to start' roll of her eyes. The two girls bicker and snatch each other's snacks.

'Where you headed?' she begins, her accent thick.

'Gladspay?'

'Och, you'll need your thermals once you get there. You visiting family? Friends?'

'Yeah. My fiancé actually.' I smile but feel a dull ache of sadness; I should be saying husband by now.

I open my bag, unfolding the map Alan had found. I had told him I'd be fine with Google Maps, but he'd been sceptical about me getting signal that far out in the wilderness. There is a red circle around Connor's house vivid against the grey images, and I lay it flat on the table. 'I need to get here?'

She lets out a low whistle. 'That's a fair wee trek and taxis are hard to find that end of the track.'

Shit. I can feel the blood drain from my face. 'Ah you'll be fine though, eh? The good news is the weather is set to be dry and you look fit as a fiddle.'

I swallow down the bite of fear. The idea of walking across the Highlands with only a map, and a bag packed while my mind was on other things, is terrifying.

But I can do it. I know I can do it. I *have* to do it.

I say my goodbyes as she leaves, laden with plastic bags and children high on strawberry laces, with sugar around their mouths.

I disembark half an hour later, the air even colder as I stand on the platform and look around the station. It's small and old-fashioned, like something out of *The Railway Children*.

The sun is high in the sky, but the wind rattles through the eaves, kicking up dust and an empty crisp packet.

I follow the only other passenger along the platform, across the bridge, my eyes scanning left and right hopefully, in search of a taxi. I pull out my phone, looking for a local taxi firm to call but I have absolutely no signal, not even a flicker of a bar. Alan was right.

I cross the road, heading towards a small corner shop. A man in overalls is taking down the remains of an Easter display. The bell rings as I step inside. I walk to the counter, grabbing a flap-jack and a bottle of water.

The overall man smiles up and walks behind the counter. He

says something to me. I have absolutely no idea what, his accent is so thick. He takes in my perplexed gaze.

'You'll be wanting a bag?' he repeats, slower this time.

'Oh, no... thanks.' He rings up the till. Cash only. It's like I've stepped back in time. Again.

'I... I was wondering if you could help me? I need to get here?' He leans over, dark hair escaping his ponytail and lets out a low whistle. 'It isnae too hard to find, but you'll want your walking legs on. It's a fair wee trek from here.'

'Is there a taxi I can call?'

'Well, there is old Bill, but he's a bit hit and miss and it'll take him a while to get here.'

I swallow. For the first time, I'm missing 2016 me with her younger legs and cardio fitness. Bloody custard creams and James's cooking. The man talks slowly as he fingers along the route, telling me what to look out for, to help me head in the right direction. There is a rack with some protective gear on it; I grab a pair of thermal gloves and a scarf, digging into my purse for some long-forgotten cash. Then I set off.

The gravel path starts off gradual enough, but there is a pull in my calf muscles as the incline hits. I have to pause often to catch my breath, to check the map.

Wilderness and beauty surround me. I picture James walking this route, his heart heavy with regret.

After the first hour, my heart is beating rapidly, my back sore from the straps of my bag.

I spot a rundown shed. The man in the shop told me to look out for it to signpost I am on the right track. I drain the last of the water, zip up, put my gloves on, wrapping the scarf tightly around my neck despite the sweat running down my spine.

'What am I doing?' I say, looking up. The sun is dropping

quickly in the sky, like it's leaded. This is crazy; he might not even be here.

I push on through the burning in my legs, through the tightness in my throat, thinking of James as I walk. The way he hides behind a cushion when we watch a horror film; how he never kills spiders, just cups them under a glass and sets them free; the look on his face as I open my eyes first thing in the morning, the love there; the sound of his laugh, how it changes his whole face; the feel of his arms around my shoulders; the way he adjusts the pictures on the wall when I hadn't even noticed they were wonky. The hurt in his eyes when he talked about his childhood. The heat between our legs that night in the wine bar, the pulsing attraction that both of us fought.

The trail splits in two. A sound like thunder ricochets through the sky. I cover my eyes against the sun. Three fighter jets whoosh overhead. I grin up. It's like a sign from Kit. I practically hear him singing 'Highway to the Danger Zone'. I check the map again, heading downhill. In the distance, the farmhouse comes into view, another building sitting further up from it.

My face stretches into a smile. I'm almost there.

42

SIX DAYS AFTER I LEFT HER

Christ, this man can't pack for shit. 'Mac, do you really need all of this stuff?' I ask as I shove yet another bag into the boot of the car. 'Is that a camping stove?'

'Aye. What else would it be?'

'Why do we need a camping stove?'

'Think you know everything about these hills after your time here, do you?'

'No I—'

'I've broken down more times than I can say, and let me tell you, you dinnae want to be stranded in the Scottish hills without something to keep you warm.'

'Can't we just get the train?'

'The train?' he asks as though I've just told him to flap his arms twenty times and then he'll take off. 'I don't trust them. Always striking, aren't they? And then where would we be?' He passes me a rolled-up tent.

Fuck's sake. 'Is that everything?' I'm impatient. I've messed up and I need to get back to her before it's too late. At this rate, I won't get back until she's drawing her pension.

'Aye? Why, what else do you think we'll need?'

'I was being sarcastic.'

'Were you?'

'Yes.'

'Well, tell that to your face. *Sarcastic*. You've a lot to learn.'

Clearly. I open the back door, Caesar jumping onto the seat, tongue lolling, settling himself in for a nap.

Mac hands me the keys.

'You want me to drive?'

'No. *You* want to drive. Your hands are twitching like you've got worms and need to scratch your arse.'

Jesus Christ. I'm not sure I can take being stuck in a car with Mac for the next six hours. We both look to the sky, as three fighter jets career over.

'Right then, let's go and get your girl, shall we?'

Finally.

I open the door to the truck, twist the ignition as Mac straps himself in. 'Fruit Pastel?' He shakes the bag at me. I reach inside. 'But not the green ones. They're my favourite.'

This is going to be a long drive. I hold up a purple one for inspection, receiving a nod of satisfaction from Mac. 'Well, are we going to get going or you want to wait here like some damsel in distress?'

I pull down the visor against the low sun, push my foot on the accelerator as a cloud of dust spins out behind us. The regret of leaving Liv sitting heavily on my shoulders. I can only hope she'll be able to forgive me for being such a complete and utter asshat.

43

My knees are aching as I continue my descent, the farmhouse finally coming into view. I stare up at the house as I continue walking. The sun has almost set now, purples and violet light reflecting in the windows. There are no lights on inside, and as I approach the gate, I scan for a car. There are recent tracks, but nothing parked. Maybe it's behind the building. I can feel fear beginning to swell in my chest. What if he's not here? Then what will I do? It'll be dark soon; I'll have to hike back. The thought is edged with fear, but I shake myself. I can do this. If I can survive everything I've been through over the past week, both present and past, I can survive this.

I open the gate and knock on the door. There is no response. No sound other than my laboured breathing and the wind whistling down from the mountains.

Shit.

I cup my hands over the glass. There is a lounge filled with clutter but no sign of anyone here. I follow the walls of the building. Behind the house is a large shed. I push open the heavy door. Shed is the wrong word to describe this place; it's more like an extension of the house. There are pieces of wood, a workbench, but also a small wood-burning stove, a sofa that looks more dog hair than upholstery, tools and a dog basket. I sit down at the workbench. On top is a list. Orders for wood and dimensions, reminders to buy flour and yeast. I open my bag and pull out the stack of letters Alan had given me. All addressed to James. I place an envelope next to the list. The handwriting on the list is scruffier, but it's the same. A small sense of relief budges through me. I have the right place at least.

There is a small fridge vibrating in the corner. I open it. There are a few cans of Coke, some huge pieces of pork pie, and a Tupperware box filled with glucose tablets and insulin and a pack of unopened needles. I close the door, then open it again. I feel like Goldilocks but I take a can of Coke.

I leave my bag in the shed, still drinking from the can, glancing up towards the house at the back. It's a long squat building, the roof sunken in the middle. I pull the gloves back on, drain the last of the Coke and head up towards the house, knocking firmly on the door.

There is no sign of life in there either. My heart sinks.

He's not here. I look through the windows. The inside is tidy, no sign of James, of his clothing hanging on the back of the chair, no shoes kicked off by the fire. Disappointment rings through me, like the clink of a glass before a speech.

I follow the path back down, do another quick sweep of the house, still empty with no signs of life within, then head back to the shed. At least there is food, and warmth. I'll wait. I've waited before; I can do it again. If Connor doesn't return, I'll make my way back into town tomorrow.

The light is fading quickly so I take some of the wood, and by some miracle get it burning. I open the fridge, vow to pay him back, and take a large slice of the pie over to the sofa. I sweep off as many dog hairs as I can and watch the fire sparking into action.

Tiredness takes over me.

What am I doing? This is the longest shot in the history of long shots. What if everything Lynn said about Connor McDonald is true? What if he is dangerous? I eye the tools warily, a thud from outside running goosebumps along my forearms. There is the bark of a dog, another door slamming.

I stand, grab a spanner, then quickly replace it with a hammer. I edge towards the door of the barn. I can hear conversation but the cracking of the logs in the burner, the wind and my heart hammering repeatedly inside my eardrums means it's hard to make out.

This was a mistake. If I scream, no one will be able to hear me.

'Well I cannae be expected to think of everything!' The voice is deep. The dog barks again. 'Caesar! Here!'

'No, but you'd think you'd remember your sodding insulin for fuck's sake.'

James.

I just have chance to register his voice before the lights flick on and I'm knocked off my feet by a giant brown dog.

I'm lying supine on the floor, hammer clattering beside me, my face being washed by a dry tongue that also manages to dribble saliva across my cheeks.

'What the—'

Above me, a man—tall, broad, bushy grey hair peppered with black.

'Liv?' And then there he is. James standing next to him. Dark eyes, wide with surprise, his hair ruffled by the wind, thick grey jumper, the glasses he wears when he's driving.

The man I'm guessing is Connor claps his hands together and

lets out a rip roaring laugh while reaching over and grabbing the dog's collar. I wipe my face with the cuff of my hoody.

'Um, surprise?' I say, not quite able to meet James's eyes for dog hair threading across my eyeball.

'Liv?' James repeats, taking off his glasses for good measure.

'Well don't just stand there like a great bloody arsehole,' Connor says. 'Help the girl up!'

'Right, yes, sorry.'

His hand meets mine, warm, steady. Right. He pulls me up as I try to dislodge the hair from my eye.

'What... what are you doing here?'

'What is she doing here? Honestly, that's the best you can do?' James looks at Connor, with an expression of irritation. I can see the family resemblance there, the same height, stature, same thick hair.

'Sorry.'

I pull the hair from my eyeball and shake my head. 'You don't need to be sorry.'

'Oh, yes he does, leaving you on your wedding day like the bloody great cretin he is.'

'Mac? Do you think you could give us some privacy?' James asks.

His eyebrows bolt towards his hairline then sink with disappointment. 'Right you are, lad. Caesar!' The dog yelps, tail swishing as he follows his master.

'It's nice to meet you,' I say as he heads towards the door. He hesitates by the stack of envelopes with his own writing on, taps the top of them, and smiles over.

'You too, love. I'm just sorry it's taken so long.'

James waits until the door is closed. His eyes are disbelieving, unsure, yet hopeful.

'Why are you here, Liv?'

'Why am *I* here? Why are *you* here?' I say prodding his chest.

I'm shivering. James steps closer towards me, takes off his jumper, leaving a white T-shirt behind. His hair is standing on end as he folds the jumper around my shoulders and leads me to the sofa, wiping it down before sitting next to me.

He turns to me, runs a hand through his hair.

'I... sorry. About the way I left. It was a shitty way to behave.'

'It was shitty.'

He nods. 'I know, I... just. I wanted to let you come to terms with Kit being alive without me being in the way. I want you to have the chance to... choose.'

'Why? Why did you think I needed to make a choice?' I say, my voice soft.

'You know why,' he replies. There are a hundred unspoken conversations in that look. That one big question we have both chosen to ignore during our time together. If Kit hadn't died, would we be together? 'Kit's back,' he says.

'Yes.' I reach for his hand, looking down at his knuckles, scarred from the school fights of his childhood, from the fights he's had as a career. 'Yes he is.' I rub my thumb across the small scars. 'But that doesn't mean I need to make a choice, James.'

His eyes are searching mine; there is disbelief still there, uncertainty.

'I love you, James.'

'I know. But—'

'No. I don't think you do.'

I tilt his chin upwards so that we're staring at each other. 'Kit was my first love. But you?' I push a lock of hair away from his eyes. 'You're my *forever* love.' I cringe. That sounded so much better in my head on the plane after a quickly drunk glass of white wine on an empty stomach. Now it sounds like a bad line from a romance novel and I regret it the minute it leaves my mouth. 'That's a bit crap. I just mean that... you're the one that I want.'

I grimace at that too. Now I sound like Olivia Newton-John.

James closes his eyes, holds his breath in his lungs before releasing it. 'You're sure?' he asks, eyes now open and searching my face.

'Well, I've just travelled through time, halfway across the country, and ended up in an empty barn in the middle of nowhere, so yes, James. I'm sure. I'm one hundred per cent sure.'

'Through time?' His eyebrows dip and rise, that wave I know so well.

'It's a long story,' I say, tears in my eyes, my head shaking that conversation away for now. I try to think of another way to tell him I love him, but the only words I can find are: '*You're* the love of my life.'

He lifts a hand to my cheek, eyes boring into mine. 'I need to tell you something.' My throat tightens. Please. No more secrets. 'That day, on the river...'

I practically sag with relief. 'I know. I know it was you.'

His whole body feels like it's exhaling. His eyes are filled with love as he looks at me. 'I've always loved you, Liv. I don't think I know how to *not* love you.'

'Then don't.'

He leans his head against mine. 'God, you have no idea how much I've missed you.'

'Oh, I think I do.' I run my nose along the length of his.

James pulls me onto his knees, tucking my legs around him. He lifts my hair and kisses my throat. I stroke back his hair, staring into his eyes.

'I love you,' he says.

'I know.'

And I do.

There are moments in your life that you try to capture; to take a snapshot of, keeping the past alive in the present. You can imagine them as Polaroids carefully placed in a scrapbook, surrounded by tickets, by menus, by hastily scribbled notes on the back of napkins. These images tend to be the good days: the Friday nights, the Saturdays, the lazy Sundays – our own inner Instagram posts. Monday and Thursday photos are often discarded, the images fading and the corners curling with time.

But right now?

This is a keeper.

Because I got to fall in love with the man I'm going to marry... twice in one lifetime.

EPILOGUE
SEVEN YEARS AFTER I CAME BACK

The climbing wall is busy this morning. Infant schools are out for Easter and squeals of excitement are made all the louder when mixed with 'Take on Me' playing loudly on the radio. I'm bending down, attaching the harness. Phoebe's eyes are fierce.

'Hurry up, Uncle Kit! I'm going to be the last to the top.' She scowls and I see James beneath the pigtails. 'No you won't, and it's not about being first, it's about—'

'Taking part.' She rolls her eyes as I untwist the straps.

'Uncle Kit?'

'Hmmm?' I ask, wrenching the material out of the fastener.

'What's optomi... op-toe-mist?'

'Optimist?'

She nods, then twists her head towards the wall impatiently.

'Where did you hear that word?'

'Mummy says that's why you went to prison.' I thread the untangled strap back through and run the fastener up, smiling.

'It means someone who always thinks that something good is going to happen even if the truth is that, sometimes, you have to think of the risks too.'

'Are you still an opt... toe. Mist?'

'Well, I suppose so, I like to hope for the very best in life, but sometimes, just being good at something is enough.'

'Grandad Mac says you're an arse but I'm not allowed to say that because it's a rude word even though I can say it when it's just me and him and Grandad Stan.'

I give the harness a little tug. 'Well I *am* a bit of an arse,' I say quietly then put my fingers to my lips. She beams at me, then and my heart melts a little that I lost so much time with her when she was younger, that I wasn't there to hold her when she was a baby. But I'm here now. Kit Palmer, ex-convict, ex tax-dodger, ex-gambler; uncle.

During my seven years on the run, I learnt so much about people. The people who are caring, who offer you a cup of tea on a cold day, a job without questions being asked, or a bed for the night if they can see you're struggling. And, OK, you see the very worst of people, too, right? Looks of superiority when you ask for work, or if your shoes have seen better days, people who give you a sideways glance when you're counting change in the queue for a drink.

There were so many times I turned back, when I picked up the phone just to hear Liv's voice, to ask my brother for help, that I wished with all of my heart that I could turn the clock back and stop myself from ever leaving, from ever placing that first bet. But the shame of what I had done always stopped me.

'Ready?' I ask Phoebe, her hair swinging as she nods, securing her foot on the blue rung, her face a picture of concentration, her lips in a small pout. I stand back as she climbs the wall with ease, a look of joy and triumph as she reaches the top and looks down at me for my approval.

'She's a firecracker, that one.' Nate joins me, looping a rope through his hands.

I scratch the back of my hair. 'She sure is.'

Since being released, I've been astounded by the human capacity to forgive. Liv and James, my parents and even Becky and Nate. After everything I put them all through, they've been by my side.

Phoebe is sitting at the top of the wall now, chatting to one of her friends, her head leaning forward conspiratorially, hand covering her mouth as she says something that makes her friend's eyes widen before she dissolves into laughter. I'd hazard a guess that the word arse has just been fired.

I let Phoebe have another half an hour until I tell her we need to go home.

Her small hand is in mine and she skips along the path from the climbing centre to her house. It's about a twenty-minute walk back but it takes half an hour as 'we are not allowed to step on the cracks'. I hop skip and jump my way home, the sun warm on my body, my face on display to anyone who walks by. I say hello to any dog walkers and joggers. It's like a new addiction, this feeling of being free.

The sun is warm on my back, her small hand clammy.

And, OK, I know this isn't like a big red-letter day, but I don't take even one minute for granted.

We knock on the door, Phoebe balancing on one leg, having made it five seconds without putting her foot down when Liv opens the door.

'Hello, you two, have fun?'

'We did. I got to the top really, really fast and Uncle Kit told me he's an arse. Can I have a chocolate bar?' She rushes past, stopping next to her mother's gigantic stomach, giving it a kiss, then runs along the hallway.

'Careful, your dad's just polished it.' In answer she changes her run into a slide, and careers into the kitchen. James picks her up and lifts her onto his shoulders.

'Hello, peanut, have fun?'

'The best.'

'Knackered you out?' James asks me.

'Not yet.'

'Thanks for taking her.' Liv smiles.

'You look good,' I say and it's the truth. Motherhood suits her, and there is still the same fire in her that I fell in love with in the way she treats Phoebe, encouraging her to try new things, letting her have just enough freedom.

'You're still full of shit. I look like a whale.'

'Did the monster behave for you?' James asks walking towards us.

'Daddy!' She leans over his face.

'Steady,' he replies lifting her down and plonking her on the floor.

'She was fine – quite the climber.'

'Yeah well, Liv's been taking her since she was three.'

'You all set for tonight?' he asks, arms around Liv's shoulders. She leans into him.

'Yep. You still coming?'

'We wouldn't miss it for the world.' She smiles at me. 'Mum is coming over to look after Phoebes. At least she will be if the weather holds.' She glances behind me to where the sun is still beating down. 'The forecast is good but Ava is on standby... just in case, so don't worry, we'll be there.'

'Unless...' James nods to Liv's stomach.

'We'll be there.' She bats him away. 'I'm not due for another four weeks,' Liv replies but in all honesty, I can't see how she can possibly continue to grow for another month.

'I'd best get going,' I say stepping back.

Phoebe is holding her mum's legs, hands cupped around her mouth, whispering something to her unborn brother.

'What do you say to your uncle?' James prompts.

'Thank you.' She steps forwards and hugs me. 'I like you. Even if you're an arse.'

'Phoebe!' Liv's face reddens but I laugh.

'She's astute.'

'Too astute,' she replies, eyes watching her daughter hurrying up the stairs.

'No such thing.' I step back. 'See you later.'

They close the door behind me and I tilt my face to the sky with a smile.

* * *

The community centre is busy, I take another sip of water as more members flood in. James and Liv are here; Dad is fetching a better chair for Mum. I wasn't sure she'd come, but it looks like Dad talked her around. Her relationship with James is improving. Once Phoebe came along, after I was sent down, something in her softened... or maybe she simply wasn't happy letting Mac take all the grandparent glory.

Losing that last time at the races was the lowest I have ever felt in my life. I felt like dirt before I knocked on my parents' door, but I honestly didn't know what to else to do. My parents have always had my back. They would help me get out of the mess I was in, but when Mum opened the door and I saw her on crutches, when she told me how it happened, I knew I had to get out. When I left, I was ready to tell Liv everything, until I saw Kane. I was convinced that Liv would be next if I didn't find the money.

I glance back over at Liv and James.

Watching them together gives me hope.

I hope that one day I will have what they have. There is no jealousy. The man I was when I was with Liv is very different to the man I am now.

Liv told me that she had the strangest experience the morning of her wedding. As time passes, she says she wonders if it happened at all, that she spent a week with me before I left everyone I loved behind. James believes her. He says he doesn't understand it, doesn't know how it could happen but he believes in Liv, and if she thinks it happened then it happened. And OK, obviously I joked that I wish I'd gone back, at least I'd have known which horse to bet on! But in all seriousness, I sometimes wish I *could* have gone back, had the chance to put it all right, but then again, everything happens for a reason.

I take another sip of water, standing off stage, behind the heavy blue curtains. My sponsor, Helena, walks to the microphone and thanks everyone for coming.

'Some of you will know Kit.' She tucks her blonde hair behind her ear. 'But for some of you, this may be the very beginning of your journey. Kit has been in recovery for fourteen years, and today marks the anniversary of the day that changed his life. So without further ado, I'm going to pass you over. Kit Palmer, everyone.'

There is clapping as I walk on stage. It feels kind of ridiculous that I should be getting a round of applause, and yet the sound makes me smile as I look onto my friends, my family, and the addicts who can't see a way out.

I wait for calm to settle and lean forwards towards the microphone.

'I first placed a bet, the year I broke my leg,' I begin. I'm not nervous. I've told this story before, but I do feel humbled, that these people think they can learn from my mistakes.

'A free bet. I was bored, fed up of being stuck inside, and I thought what harm can it do? What. Harm. Can. One. Free. Bet. Do?'

There is a rumble, a mixture of saddened laughter and mmms of understanding.

'For the majority of people, there would be no harm done, but for someone arrogant...' I quirk a smile. 'Arrogant enough to believe they can beat the odds. It can destroy your life, and the lives of those around you.

'I told myself I was in control. I wasn't losing enough to affect my day-to-day life. I had a hard line, or so I told myself.

'But that hard line began to wobble. I started faking my gambling accounts, getting more free bets; I started claiming expenses from my business account that weren't the business lunches I claimed them to be. You'd be surprised how easy it is to pick up a bill left on a table in an expensive restaurant. A group of five people with a bill of three hundred, four hundred. I wasn't doing anything wrong; there was no harm done. Nobody would miss those receipts.

'I'd take the exact amount on the receipts out in cash. And go to whichever betting office was closest.

'I still had this hard line though. It wasn't as though I was *losing* money. I was keeping my business afloat; I was doing well. At least on the outside.'

Another murmur from the crowd. 'And the optimist in me, would promise me all kinds of things. I knew I was in trouble but I was hopeful. Optimism told me that I could get myself out.

'But I couldn't.

'Instead, I borrowed another chunk, then another, then another. My debt got sold to a new loan shark. And this man meant business. So... then I borrowed from an old friend.'

Becca is holding Nate's hand. She gives me a little 'go on' nod.

'She was grieving, had lost her mum. I convinced to her to invest in my company. "Look!" I said to her. "Look at how much money I can make you, look at my accounts, aren't they great?" And they were, from the outside, everything looked fine. I had that hard line, you see.

'I was going to pay back the loan shark with some of that money, then I was going to stop. But the optimism was back. If I put all of that money on more bets, I'd be in the clear. I could save myself.

'But I lost it all in the space of two hours.'

I take a pause. People shift in their seats; there is a muted cough from a man in the front row.

'Loan sharks are called sharks for a reason. They circle around you, keeping their heads below water. They watch your movements, and then...' I glance at Mum. 'They start taking bites. Because the thing is, loan sharks are predators and they are never satisfied, they will come for another bite and another and when there is nothing left of you, they will move on to those around you.'

The room stills. Alan drops an arm around Mum's shoulders, her head still held high despite the truth being told to a room full of strangers.

'I had no way out. I couldn't pay them back. I contemplated ending it all, ending my life and then it came to me. I *could* end my life... at least the one Kit Palmer had been living.

'So,' I continue, placing the microphone back in the holder, 'I lied to my girlfriend. I packed my bags knowing what I was about to do. I let her believe I was fine, better than fine, actually. I was *full* of life. But I knew she'd be better off without me. They'd all be better off if I was dead.

'Some of you may remember the search for me, seeing the coastguards looking for my body. Some of you may have seen my family, standing waiting for my body to be retrieved. Some of you may be thinking there is no way out. But there is.

'Ask for help. Live in the now. Not the past where all of your mistakes are, not the future where you see yourself winning that big bet, but now.

'The present is such a gift. Living is such a gift. Don't let it slip through your fingers. You've all been braver than I have ever been, because you're all here.

'This is your first step to a better life. To a life worth living. A life worth keeping.'

The audience claps. People are standing, shaking my hand as I walk down the steps into the room. Dad pulls me into an embrace, wiping tears from his eyes.

And then I see her.

She's smiling, her head tilted, brown eyes challenging. Dark hair over her shoulder.

I walk over to her, noticing the smug smile on Liv's face as she sees my expression. I stand in front of her, not knowing what to say.

She puts out her hand. 'Hi, I'm Aria and you are?'

I take her hand in mine, feel the way it fits perfectly in my own. 'Kit,' I say. 'Kit Palmer.'

'Well,' she replies, chewing the inside of her cheek before breaking out into the smile that I love so much. 'It's good to finally meet you, Kit Palmer.'

ACKNOWLEDGEMENTS

The first glimmer of the idea for this book came when I was at my brother-in-law's wedding. I have such a dreadful sense of direction and found myself wandering the corridor of the hotel, looking at all the identical doors, trying to find our room. When I finally made my way back down to the reception, I told my family about this and Uncle Dave said: that sounds like a good idea for a book – so my first thanks go to Uncle Dave, it turns out you were right – it was!

Behind every novel I write, is a team of people who are part of the process. Some know they have given me advice along the way, and been involved in keeping me sane, but often, the most important people who help me write are completely unaware. So I'd like to thank the people who might not know how fundamentally important they are to me: my readers. Without you, there really wouldn't be another Emma Cooper book – sharing my stories and characters with you really is the greatest pleasure. Without your encouragement, reviews, and messages, it would be so hard to get my bum in the seat day after day so thank you.

As always, the hugest of thanks go to my superstar agent, Amanda. You are the hardest working woman I know. You are always there when I need you with endless ideas and suggestions to make sure my books are the best they can be. I will be forever grateful that you took a chance on a working-class girl who sounds a bit like Noddy Holder.

To my editor Rachel Faulkner-Willcocks. Your insights and

passion for this novel have given it new wings and am so thrilled that I get to work with you and that I have you in my corner – you're blooming brilliant!

Wider thanks go to the whole Boldwood team who have given me such a warm welcome. I'm hugely excited to be part of such a dynamic and inventive group – you're all superstars.

Thanks also go to Candida Bradford and Helena Newton for their enthusiasm and amazing editorial skills. Further thanks to Cherie Chapman for my beautiful cover. I fell in love with it the minute I saw it!

Some of you may know that my 'day job' is working for Jericho Writers. Being a tutor on the UNWC course is such a joy, and so huge thanks go to the whole Jericho team and my fellow tutors, with a special shout out to Kat Ashton, Verity Hicks, Jonny Milne, and Imogen Love, who are always there working tirelessly in the background.

Working on the UNWC means I get to meet talented and emerging writers, which is such a pleasure. I really do feel incredibly privileged to be part of your publishing journey so a huge shout out to all of my mentees both past and present.

A must give a special mention to my incredibly talented former students, Sarah Jane King, Cory Sinnott and Kathryn Cooper. Thank you for keeping in touch and for cheering me on... I can't wait to share the bookshelves with you.

A huge hug goes out to Emily Brancher and Ruth McGill. Thank you for keeping me company during our writing sessions over the past year and for sharing my love of all things Nicolas Cage. An additional thanks also goes to Barbara Brady who took the time to fetch me from Euston and guide me around London (see earlier reference to my awful sense of direction!) you are an absolute gem and a wonderful writer.

To my writing tribe who are always there to celebrate the

good, and who lend an ear on the days where I feel like everything I've written is a pile of pants: Caroline Hulse, Josie Silver, Kim Nash, Natali Simmonds, Amy Beashel, Anna Vaught and Holly Seddon. Thanks for being there and for understanding the highs and lows of this bonkers job! You're all ace.

To the wonderful blogging community and book clubs who champion me and other writers – thank you for the time and endless support and for being the driving force behind the publishing world. Special shout out to Linda Hill, Anne Cater, Rachel Gilbey, The Fiction Café, The Savvy Writers' snug, Em @EmDigsBooks, Claire @Secretworldofabook, Jenna @book_club_momma, Kathryn and William at Tea Leaves and Reads and more recently, Telford Book Club – with a special mention to Kay Evans and Carrieann Clayton – thanks for the coffee and chats and for all the energy and thought that goes into spreading the book love.

Now, on to friends and family closer to home.

As always, to my bestie, Nicola Smith – thank you for being you. You've been there at my lowest, darkest times and make the really good bits even better!. You are the very best of humans and I would be lost without you in my life.

Raising a large glass of wine to Emma Jackson, Claire Ashley, Amanda Hedison and Teresa Merry. Thank you for always being there and listening to me bang on about my ideas and for your endless support – you all rock.

To my wonderful extended Evans family – I love you all. I'm so proud to be part of this bonkers, wild and loving family. As always, I need to give a special shout out to my wonderful mother-in-law, Jac – you are the glue that holds us all together and we love you more than we could ever say.

Thank you are two words that aren't enough to express how

grateful I am for my amazing mum who is everything a mum should be. I love you to the moon and back.

To Chris, the very best wine topper-upper a girl could ask for!

Huge love and thanks to my dad for everything (but especially his mince pies!) and to Terry for her constant support and love.

On to my brood: Ethan, Ally, Max and Delilah, who make me forever proud, and thankful. You are my best creations, and you're ALL my favourites!

Last but never, ever, least... my Russ. This year marks thirty years with you – thank you for making me smile every single day, for making me a better person, for everything. You are my world and the very best romantic lead that I've never written.

ABOUT THE AUTHOR

Emma Cooper is the author of highly acclaimed book club fiction novels and is known for mixing humour with darker emotional themes. Her debut, *The Songs of Us*, was short-listed for the RNA contemporary novel of the year award. Her work has since been translated into seven different languages.

Sign up to Emma Cooper's mailing list for news, competitions and updates on future books.

Visit Emma's website: https://emmacooperauthor.wordpress.com/

Follow Emma on social media:

       facebook.com/EmmaCooperAuthor
       x.com/ItsEmmacooper
       instagram.com/itsemmacooper
       tiktok.com/@emmacooperauthor

Boldwood

Boldwood Books is an award-winning fiction publishing company seeking out the best stories from around the world.

Find out more at www.boldwoodbooks.com

Join our reader community for brilliant books, competitions and offers!

Follow us
@BoldwoodBooks
@TheBoldBookClub

Sign up to our weekly deals newsletter

https://bit.ly/BoldwoodBNewsletter

Printed in Great Britain
by Amazon

57861809R00178